Provenance: A Novel

Donna Drew Sawyer

Creative Cache, LLC

2015

30775 7565

R

Printed in the United States of America
Published in the United States by Creative Cache, LLC.
www.creativecache.biz

Cover design: Francesco Di Biase and Federica Quadrelli
Interior design: Jera Publishing
Author Photo by: Dwight Carter

Provenance: A Novel is a work of fiction. All incidents and dialogue and all characters, with the exception of some historical and public figures, are products of the author's imagination and not to be construed as real. Where real-life historical or public figures appear, the situations, incidents and dialogue attributed to those persons are not intended to depict actual events and are used in a fictitious manner. Any other names, characters, businesses, places, events and incidents are fictional and any resemblance to actual persons, living or dead, or actual events or locals is purely coincidental.

First Edition
ISBN: 978-0-9916143-2-5

Library of Congress Control Number: 2015948208

To Granville, for your love and support,
and for believing I was a writer long before I did

PROVENANCE, a noun

Origin: From the French provenir, to originate, to come from.

Definition: Where something originated or was nurtured in its early existence.

Art enables us to find ourselves
and lose ourselves at the same time.

~Thomas Merton

Prologue

Park Place, Virginia—Fall 1909

"HANK, RUN!" WAS THE LAST thing he heard Junior say. Deputies struggled to hold and handcuff his two brothers while the sheriff tried to restrain Hank. The old man was no match for the 18-year-old; Hank fought his way free and ran. He could hear the sheriff's labored breathing behind him, sweat was stinging and clouding his eyes; he needed to reach the safety of Park Place, the black side of town.

"We're Richard Whitaker's boys, you know us!" Hank shouted over his shoulder, not slowing to see if his words made a difference.

Angry, red-faced and short-of-breath the sheriff sputtered, "Then you know! No niggers 'llowed in town after sundown. You look white but you ain't! For sure, you the Whitaker boy that needs a lesson, and I'm the one to teach—"

Hank turned just in time to see the sheriff grab his chest, drop to his knees and fall face forward onto the unforgiving pavement. Hank stopped, not sure what to do until he heard,

"Sheriff, did you git that other nigger?" Hank took off, leaving the sheriff bleeding and gasping for air. He did what Junior told him to do—he ran.

———⏤➤●◀⏤———

The toe of a man's boot awakened him.

"What you doin' sleeping out here, youngin'?" Hank opened his eyes and squinted into the sun blinding his view of the man's face. Was he one of the sheriff's men from last night, the one who told him he could fix it so he and his brothers would never see the light of another day?

Hank was where he'd collapsed the night before – legs aching, out of breath, confused, scared, and tired. Damn tired of being treated like a criminal for just wanting to see the end of the Negro League game at Hampton Normal and Agricultural. If they'd just caught the early ferry, he and his brothers would be safe at home in their own beds. He'd needed only a few minutes of rest—but now it was morning and his back was still against the broad oak that hid him last night. Hank's hand slowly searched the cool damp earth behind him for a rock, a stick, anything to defend himself. The man reached toward him, blocking the sun shining in Hank's eyes. The outstretched arm was that of an elderly white man, not the vigilantes from last night. He extended an open hand instead of a clenched fist.

"Let me give you a hand up. We shouldn't be 'round here, that's Park Place over yonder. I'll take ya back to our part of town then you git on home from there," the old man said as he started his truck. To this stranger, Hank's fair skin, hazel eyes and sandy-colored straight hair made him a white man. People in Llewellyn knew he looked like his mother, who looked like her Scotch-Irish father, not her African mother.

"You don't wanna be gettin' so drunk you end up in these parts. I know some of you youngins like those little colored girls. Don't believe in race mixin' myself, but you youngins' gotta satisfy those desires, I understand it. Don't recommend you keep up that behavior—somethin' go wrong and you'd be caught up in it, like last night. Sheriff and some of his deputies chased a bunch of niggers out of Llewellyn. Everybody knows this here's a sundown town. One of 'em put the sheriff in the hospital. Heard say he's bad—ain't gonna make it."

What the hell? I didn't touch him, Hank thought.

"Whole of Llewellyn's jumpy this morning, they lookin' for that boy. Glad I'm headin' home and outta these parts, that boy's gonna swing."

"What happened to the others? You said there were other... niggers?" The word stuck in Hank's throat, he was desperate for information about his brothers so he spoke the old man's language.

"Yeah, a couple of 'em was already in custody when the other one got away. Heard those two got a beatin' for good measure and they sent 'em back over to nigger-town. They'll get the one that got away, always do."

3

Hank swallowed hard. Looking out of the passenger side window, he watched the landscape change from familiar to strange as the truck headed away from Park Place and all Hank knew, and all who knew him. He had no choice now but to keep going.

"Where you from, youngin'?" the man asked.

"Richmond," Hank said, naming the first city that came to mind.

"Well hell, that's where I'm headed. Need a ride?"

Part One

Surrealism:

An art movement between 1924 and 1945, associated with the Paris-based artists who often explored images from dreams, using realistic painting techniques that juxtaposed unexpected objects, creating an alternate reality.

Part One

Surrealism:

An art movement between 1924 and 1945, associated with the Paris-based artists who often explored images from dreams, using realistic painting techniques that juxtaposed unexpected objects, creating an alternate reality.

Part One

Surrealism:

An art movement between 1924 and 1945, associated with the Paris-based artists who often explored images from dreams, using realistic painting techniques that juxtaposed unexpected objects, creating an alternate reality.

⁓ 1 ⁓

Richmond, Virginia—Early Summer 1912

(I)

AGGIE BENNETT ESCAPED TO THE front porch to avoid the stifling formality of an evening in the parlor with her mother and father. She moved the wooden porch swing back and forth to the rhythm of the cicada chorus, ever grateful for the shadowy solace of the outdoor room and the distance it offered from her mother's withering gaze. She had disappointed her mother once again by failing to attract one of Richmond's eligible bachelors to the Bennett's porch on this prime summer evening. But Maggie had the gentleman caller she wanted in her sights. She watched the not so subtle young man as he pretended to stroll by her house, his hands nervously rolling his cap into a cylinder that would render it unfit for wearing. He was tall and lean; his long legs stretched out to cover the distance between her house and the intersection in half the time it would have taken her. Walking together, she would have had to run to keep up with him. He walked up one side of the wide boulevard and then crossed the grassy median to stroll past her house again.

This would be the third time he'd passed this evening. He would stop and speak this time, she decided. Maggie got up and walked to the porch steps, "How many times are you going to go by here?" she called out to him. "You lost or something?"

She startled him so that he thought his voice would come out as a squeak. He took a deep breath and managed to lower it.

"Uh, no, Miss, I'm just enjoyin' the cool night air."

"As many times as you been up and down this here block, I suspect you worked up a sweat rather than cooled one down," she said. "Want some sweet tea?"

"I don't want to trouble you, miss."

"No trouble, wouldn't have asked if it were."

"Well, if it ain't no trouble."

Coming home late from his office one evening, he had seen her sitting alone on her porch after first noticing her down at Beal's General Store. Though he knew it was best to keep to himself, there was something about this girl that made him want to ignore all the reasons that he should. Now, after finishing work each day, he often took the route past her house for his evening strolls, always longing for a reason to stop. She looked different up close, nearly a foot shorter than his six feet, delicate and needing to be taken care of. Her voice however, was strong, clear and purposeful, not at all what he expected.

"Come on up and sit," Maggie said, motioning toward the wicker chair across from the porch swing. "All the ice is melted but I can have Frances chip more if you want."

"No, no, this is just fine for me. Sweet and wet is all I need."

"I'm Miss Margaret Bennett. But everyone, except my mother, calls me Maggie. I've seen you around town," Maggie said, placing the glass of tea she poured for him on the table between them. "Seen you with the men cleaning up—"

"I'm not a janitor," Hank blurted out. "I owns my business."

"A janitor business?"

"Property Services," he said.

"Do you have a name, Mr. Property Services?"

"I'm Hank—Henry—Mr. Henry Whitaker of Whitaker's Property Services. I'm the boss, I owns my business. I got a dozen men workin' for me. We clean up, make repairs, paint— whatever needs takin' care of. I got accounts with City Hall, the library, I'm biddin' on the new hotel downtown and I got a retail establishment, Beal's General on Main." *Where I first saw you,* he thought.

"That's quite the resume, Mr. Henry Whitaker of Whitaker Property Services." Maggie took a sip of her sweet tea but kept her gaze on Hank. "I go down to Beal's sometimes to buy a few things. I think I've seen you down there." *Where I went looking for you,* she thought but didn't say. Maggie had noticed him a couple of months before and several times since. Mr. Beale never allowed Hank and his cleaning crew in the front of the store until all the customers were gone so Maggie began to show up just before closing time. She'd take a seat at a table in the sewing section pretending to page through the pattern books while watching Hank direct his men as they started their work in the back of the store. Even though Maggie knew Mr. Beale was anxious for her to leave and Mrs. Beale was probably waiting dinner on him, she needed a little more time to surreptitiously study Hank.

She liked the way he took charge, wearing a white dress shirt with the sleeves rolled up just so, pants crisply creased, shoes shined, his sandy hair neatly slicked back. Even late in the day he looked clean-shaven. *He looks like he has a wife who takes good care of him*, Maggie thought. But she saw no ring on his finger and that made her hopeful.

Maggie liked what she saw from a distance, and even more what she saw up close tonight. He seemed taller and his eyes were beautiful. In the shadows of the porch lights she couldn't see the exact color but they were light-colored, serious and a little sad—like he had lost something or someone. He had high cheekbones and a mouth perfect for kissing—a thin upper lip atop a full bottom lip. She would kiss that mouth one day, she determined.

"I didn't know you worked all those places," Maggie said, or *I probably would have started going there too.*

"I don't, they's clients. That's what you call them when I work for me and they hire out their property work."

"Sounds very business-like."

"Oh it is, it is," Hank agreed. He picked up the sweet tea Maggie had placed in front of him, hoping she would keep the conversation going. Hank watched her move the porch swing back and forth, waiting for him to say something. He looked down and away from her intense stare, taking sips of his tea, wanting it to last so he would have an excuse to stay; it would be an insult, he decided, not to finish the entire glass. Here he was on the porch of the woman he had longed to talk to for months, and he wasn't capable of a simple conversation. Hank had no trouble talking to his clients, but he struggled to talk to Miss Maggie Burnett.

"Just sayin' hello to a white woman can end a black man's life," his father had drilled into the Whitaker boys from the moment they were old enough to understand. It was a lesson they learned early and one that their father repeated often. But here in Richmond everyone believed he *was* a white man so black women feared him and he was afraid when white women found him desirable. The dilemma sent the twenty-one year-old Hank to places where identity didn't matter, there were no questions and he could satisfy his physical needs for a price.

But Hank longed for more warmth than a sexual transaction could offer; he wanted the deep emotional connection his parents had – a connection so strong that only death had ever separated them. Because of a careless adventure one night three years ago, the possibility of a life like theirs in his homeplace of Park Place was no longer an option. Hank looked at Maggie, she excited him like no woman, black or white, ever had. He couldn't explain it but he could definitely feel it.

Before the silence of Hank's thoughts and Maggie's gaze reached an awkward stage, the screen door swung open and an elegant, shapely woman stepped onto the porch. She paused for

11

a few moments under the porch light, as if walking onto a stage. She wore a stylish dress, complemented by several strands of opera length pearls; her attire more appropriate for dinner out than an evening at home. When Hank looked at her face, he saw a mature version of the young woman on the porch swing across from him, both truly beautiful women.

"Margaret, who are you talking to out here?" she said. When she saw Hank her face went from anticipation to disappointment.

"Oh Momma, this is Mr. . . ."

"Hank Whitaker," he said, jumping to his feet, nearly spilling the contents of his glass. Maggie saw her mother start to finger the pearls around her neck; the inquisition was about to begin.

"And who are your people, Mr. Whitaker?" Charlotte Bennett asked, as she looked him over - head to toe and back again.

"I'm alone in this world, ma'am. No family," Hank paused for a second, "here in Richmond."

"I see," Charlotte said with a palpable chill. *Strike one.* She looked at his open-collared shirt, rolled up shirt sleeves, no tie or jacket, a worn cap shoved in his pocket. *Strike two.*

"Mr. Whitaker owns his own business, Momma. He has accounts, clients, with businesses all over town."

"What kind of business, Mr. Whitaker?" Charlotte said with a tinge of hopefulness.

"Property management services, ma'am," Hank said proudly.

A janitor, thought Charlotte. *Strike three. Mr. Whitaker has struck out.*

"Margaret, it's getting late," she said as she turned her back to Hank. He took her cue.

"Thank you again, Miss Maggie, ma'am," he said, directing his gaze first to Maggie, then to Charlotte and back to Maggie, where it stayed until he drained his glass. He wiped his mouth with the back of his hand and handed his glass to Maggie in a deliberate motion that ensured their fingertips would touch. They both felt the electricity. Charlotte felt it too and loudly cleared her throat to put an authoritative damper on the connection.

Hank walked down the wide porch steps to the street and turned to take one last longing look at Maggie. "Well, goodnight, ladies," he said, wishing he had more time to make an impression. Maggie leaned over the porch railing to watch him walk away,

"Goodnight, Mr. Hank Whitaker of Whitaker Property Services," she called after him.

Hank was still within earshot when Charlotte opened the screen door, motioned her daughter inside and said loudly, "Come on in, Margaret. He's not our kind."

Hank removed his cap from his back pocket, unfurled it and pulled it low over his brow so that the rumpled visor pointed in the direction he knew he was going—forward, always and only forward.

(II)

Maggie knew what her mother was thinking before she spoke the words, "Not our kind." How many times had she heard that about would-be suitors?

Charlotte had bigger plans for her daughter than a man who earned his living cleaning up after other people could offer. "One step above a nigger," was how Charlotte described him while brushing Maggie's hair the nightly hundred strokes that made it shine like patent leather.

"But he's not a nigger," Maggie protested. "He's going places, Momma, I can tell."

"Well, you're not going with him," Charlotte decreed. "I want more of a life for you than that boy could ever dream. We want a college man, Margaret, someone to move us up to a bigger house on Centennial; the son of one of your father's business acquaintances, a graduate of the University of Richmond or Washington and Lee, a southern gentleman."

"They're not really gentlemen, Momma. You know how they are; they think every girl in Richmond, and her Momma, wants them and they take advantage of it. They won't see me, all I'll ever be is a reflection of one of them. I want a man who sees me, Momma, who wants me. Not my family or our money. I don't want to be like you and Daddy."

Charlotte's hand stopped in midair, "Like me and Daddy?"

Maggie knew she had said too much, but it was said, so she might as well go on. "I want more. I want to be beloved. Do you understand, Momma? I don't care about the other stuff; the house, the clothes and money are nice, but I could be happy without—"

"Without what?" Charlotte demanded, "You have no idea what you can do without. You don't even know the difference between want and need. You've never had to, and if I have anything to say about it, you never will. You certainly don't know anything about me and Daddy, what we have and what we don't have. And quite frankly, Margaret Ann Bennett, what's between your father and me is our business and none of yours. You don't know anything about what we've gotten — no, what *I've* gotten for you in this life. Beloved, my ass!" she said throwing the hairbrush across the room and slamming the door as she stormed out of the room.

Maggie had gotten beneath her mother's pristine veneer; her Mother said "ass." Charlotte never used coarse language — decorum was an integral part of her carefully crafted image. Maggie was nine years old the last time she remembered her mother using profanity. She overheard Charlotte and her father's sister, Elsa, out in the yard one afternoon; her mother was using language she had never heard come out of a southern lady's mouth. Maggie went downstairs to investigate and arrived at the back door just in time to see Charlotte grab Elsa's arm and pull her within inches of her contorted face. Charlotte, loud enough for Maggie and everyone in the house to hear, called Elsa a bitch. While Elsa desperately tried to extricate herself from Charlotte's grip, Maggie heard her mother say she would "beat the shit out of Elsa if—" something Maggie could not make out. Charlotte pulled Elsa even closer and whispered in her ear, her spit landing on Elsa's face and in her hair. When Charlotte finally released her, Aunt Elsa's eyes were wild, her face was even paler than its normal pallid shade and there was a crimson imprint of her mother's fingers on her aunt's arm. Elsa did not even notice Maggie standing by the door as she nearly killed herself falling up the back porch steps to get away from her sister-in-law. When Maggie looked back at her mother, she had fallen to her knees, her head down, her back to the house. Her shoulders heaved—was she crying? Maggie was not quite sure what to do. Should she go to her mother or should she stay a safe distance from the shrew she had seen her mother turn into? Before Maggie could decide, Charlotte was on her feet, moving fast; she strode toward the rose arbor. Pulling pruning shears from her apron pocket, she began to deadhead the climbing roses like she was decapitating more than spent flowers.

Maggie shivered recalling that memory. She could count on one hand, and still have fingers left, the number of times Elsa had visited their home since then—and only when Charlotte was away on one of her excursions to New York, London or Paris.

Maggie still did not know what provoked Charlotte that day. She knew her mother had secrets; a person who controlled her own life and all the lives that touched hers as tightly as Charlotte did, must have secrets. Maggie was determined that her mother's secrets, whatever they were, would not control her. Maggie had always gotten what she wanted in life, she was certain she always would. If she wanted Hank Whitaker, then she would have Hank Whitaker and anything else she chose.

(III)

Charlotte stormed into the bedroom she reluctantly shared with her husband, Walton Wainwright Bennett, III. He sat on the side of their bed in his shorts and tee shirt waiting hopefully for his wife to return from her nightly visit to their daughter's room.

"Walton, either put on some clothes or put your pajamas on and go to bed," Charlotte snapped on her way into the bathroom, slamming the door behind her.

There will be no sex tonight, Walton thought as he stared at the closed bathroom door. He could hear her running the water for her bath. He imagined Charlotte removing her clothes. *She is naked in there*, Walton lusted, his penis and his mind in sync. He alone knew—at least he hoped—that the woman he married *appeared* soft only when covered by the stylish clothing she insisted on from the department stores on New York's famous Ladies Mile and the expensive shops she'd discovered in Paris. When stripped of all accoutrements, Charlotte naked, was a bold, aggressive, powerful sexual predator. Walton once believed he aroused that passion in her. Looking down at his protruding belly that completely obscured his view of his small feet, he knew Charlotte's passion, like his physique, was a thing of the past. He considered walking in on her, naked, fully engorged; maybe she would reconsider. It had been months since she had let him have her; but he knew better.

Walton reached around his belly and rubbed his penis, "Down boy," he said. Pleasuring himself was his only option tonight. Covering himself, he ran across the hall to his study, closed and locked the door. While he masturbated, he imagined himself still the man for whom the young girls of Richmond had competed. He could have had his pick – his credentials were the ones Charlotte insisted on for their daughter's suitors – but he had chosen Charlotte. Or had he?

Walton remembered the first time he met Charlotte Ann Cox, the new stock girl at his mother's dress shop. Wearing the simple blue cotton shirtwaist dress with a white collar that his mother made all of the girls in the shop wear so that they never out shined their customers, Charlotte managed to outshine everyone anyway. With her long dark hair, piercing hazel eyes and olive skin, she was exotic, or was it erotic? Her sensuality was palpable. He had stopped by the shop to look at the store's ledgers, something he did once a month for his mother. But after Walton met Charlotte, he visited three times in one week and then every day thereafter.

One day, he walked in on Charlotte in the back room of the store. She was changing out of her uniform. She wore only a thin slip that clung to her curves in just the right places. She stood facing him, making no attempt to cover herself. Through the sheer fabric he could see her as if she were naked – he, and she, knew he had to have her.

That was 20 years ago and this is now, Walton thought after his inadequate climax. He lit a cigarette and studied his reflection in the glass-front bookcases that lined his study, considering how little was left of the man he had once been. *I spend more time in this leather chair masturbating behind a locked door that I do making love to the I woman sleep next to every night.* After a few more minutes of disappointed reflection, Walton stabbed out his cigarette, walked to the door and peeked into the hall to make sure neither Maggie, nor the maid, Frances, were around. He removed his soiled underwear, wiped his flaccid genitals, and then threw the garment into the laundry chute in the hall. Back in their bedroom, he did as his wife had told him; he put on a pair of pajamas, climbed into bed and fell asleep.

(IV)

What the hell is he doing out there? Charlotte thought as she languished in her bath until she was certain that her husband was asleep. The luxurious warm blanket of bubbles had long ago dissolved into cloudy tepid water. She could no longer hear him lumbering about in the bedroom but she could smell cigarette smoke. How many times had she chastised him about smoking in her house?

"That's the smell of money," he always replied and she knew he was right. As long as Virginia's cash crop was tobacco and Richmond was where tobacco was bought, sold and paid for – her husband's bank and her family would remain prosperous.

Charlotte stepped out of the tub and admired herself as she patted the thick towel along the curves of her body. Even after the single pregnancy she'd allowed, she held her figure. She was thirty-five but could still turn heads, perhaps not as hard and fast as she once had, but she didn't need to anymore. In one generation she had seduced, calculated and cajoled her way from a rural sharecropper shack where tobacco was picked, to a fine city home where she saw how that labor turned into gold; that new perspective courtesy of Mr. Walton Wainwright Bennett III. She knew the day she met him that he was the man she had been looking for. His daddy was president of one of the largest banks in Richmond and Walton III was his handpicked successor. Walton was raised to believe he was the catch of the new century, a lie based on his family's money and stature in Richmond, not on the man himself. Walton at 26 was as unattractive as he was today; squat, balding, plain-faced and perpetually rumpled. Even the substantial Bennett family money had not been enough to make him attractive to most of the young women of Richmond. Charlotte overheard them in his mother's shop tittering over how pathetic Mrs. Bennett's son was—but never within his mother's earshot. Walton Wainwright Bennett III was exactly what the 16 year-old Charlotte wanted in a husband; a man who would be grateful for her attention and for whose affection she would not have to compete. Walton had the ultimate criteria—money and standing in the community; Charlotte could have cared less about the man himself.

He had been so easy to seduce and steadfastly impossible to dissuade when his family objected to their marriage. Now after 20 years of having him sweat and smother her with his needy passion the few times a year she allowed him spousal favors, Charlotte still felt it was not too big a price to pay for what his position afforded her in life. She didn't love him;

she wasn't sure she could love any man. He was more like a pet—obedient and loyal and he rarely got in her way. Despite his abundance of inadequacies, Walton had given Charlotte her treasure, her Margaret, and he loved their daughter as much as she did. Charlotte made a calculated risk when she let Walton impregnate her before they were married but her gamble with Mother Nature paid off. Margaret, now 18, was pretty and certainly smart enough to attract a husband from one of Richmond's finer families. *Margaret is headstrong*, Charlotte thought, *but she is no match for me.* Margaret was the southern beauty who would marry them to an even higher social level. It was all Charlotte cared about, all she worked toward and the only thing that mattered.

⤜ 2 ⤛

(I)

"OH, IT'S YOU AGAIN," CHARLOTTE said when she responded to the knock on the screen door. "Evenin' Mrs. Bennett, ma'am. Miss Maggie asked me to join her on the porch this evening," Hank said. Before Charlotte could tell him that her daughter was not available, Maggie, dressed in a delicate summer dress and smelling of her mother's mimosa bath oil, breezed down the front staircase and past her mother. Without a word to Charlotte, she swept through the screen door, grabbed Hank's arm and settled on the porch swing farthest from the door that, in Maggie's wake, slammed in her mother's face.

Hank Whitaker was a fixture on the Bennett's front porch nearly every evening during the summer of 1912. Charlotte made a point of treating Hank like the mongrel she considered him to be, never inviting him inside the house let alone to dinner. She ordered her husband to chaperone their daughter and Hank while Charlotte sat in the parlor stewing over Hank's presence. Walton quickly grew tired of the awkwardness of watching his daughter and Hank watch him. Despite her pleas, he now sat with Charlotte in the parlor most evenings.

"There is something about that Hank Whitaker that makes me uneasy," Charlotte told Walton who was happily engrossed in his copy of the Wall Street Journal. "I just can't put my finger on what it is."

"I don't know why you don't like the boy," Walton said from behind his paper, "He's always polite and respectful to us and to Maggie. Sitting out there on the porch with him all those evenings, we got to talking and he's got a pretty good head on his shoulders. That business he owns is doing nicely. I asked around and he's got a dozen men workin' for him; and I heard he's got most of Capitol Square as clients, even Mrs. Atkinson's new hotel downtown."

"He's not a boy," Charlotte said, "He's a full grown man and a threat to your daughter's future. He's nothing but a glorified janitor."

"May be," Walton said "but he's a prosperous one from what I hear."

———⟫●⟪———

While Charlotte and Walton bickered in the parlor, Hank and Maggie took advantage of the time to fall in love. Their first few evenings together they had talked and laughed with each other about some of the peculiar eccentricities of Richmond.

"Why do people say, 'It's nice to see you' instead of 'it's nice to meet you'?" Hank asked sitting as close to Maggie on the porch swing as he dared.

"Oh, that way if they've forgotten that they'd met you before you won't be able to tell. If we're anything in Richmond, we're ruthlessly polite."

"And what about, 'Do I know your people?' That was the first thing your mother asked me," Hank recalled.

"That's the first thing she asks everyone," Maggie said, "Everyone here is obsessed with your family's history and heritage. Nothing is more important than the family you come from. I think it's silly, if anyone shouldn't care who you are or where you're from it should be my mother. She lost all of her family when she was very young. Her parents died in a fire when she was a little girl. She was sent to live with a great aunt or something. I think the old woman mistreated her."

"I'm sorry," Hank said understanding Charlotte a little better.

"Don't be," Maggie said, "she has everything she could ever want now and she's still not happy. Some people just aren't, don't you think?" When he didn't answer, Maggie moved closer to Hank and turned his face to hers, "There's a sadness about you too, not mean like my mother, just sad. I saw it in your eyes that first night out here on the porch. What are you sad about, Hank Whitaker? I want you to be happy. I want to make you happy," she whispered then kissed him. She pulled back to look at his face, his eyes were open to watch their first kiss.

24

He laced his long fingers into her hair and pulled her to him, kissing her fervently and deeply like a man quenching a long thirst. "You make happy, Maggie," Hank said smiling, his lips still on hers. "You make my sadness go away." From that moment on, they belonged to each other.

(II)

Just before Labor Day, while Charlotte was at one of her Woman's League meetings, Walton, tired of sitting alone in the parlor, wandered out on to the porch to join Maggie and Hank.

"Hey, Daddy," Maggie said affectionately.

"Thought I'd join you young people. It's cooler out here than in that stuffy parlor. Felt like the walls were closing in on me." Walton turned his attention to Hank,

"So Maggie tells me you're from south of here – a farm boy she says."

"I came to Richmond after my parents died. With just me and a couple of field hands there was no way I could scratch a living out of the land they left me. This country boy thought he'd make a go of it here in the city," Hank said, now practiced at lying about his past.

"I shouldn't tell you this but since you've taken an interest in my little Maggie, I looked into your holdings at the bank. You've started to become one of the bank's better customers young man," Walton said as he walked to the edge of the porch and spit over the railing into the gardenias, then settled into a wicker chair across from the young couple. Hank tried not to wince. He could not imagine what kind of hell his late mother would have raised if his father or brothers had spewed anything off the front porch into her flower beds.

"So you're workin' for that Atkinson woman now, the one that owns the Richmond Hotel."

"Yes sir. The biggest hotel in town and my best client," Hank said proudly.

Walton rubbed his belly thoughtfully then said,

"Women shouldn't be runnin' a business like that. You know she let coloreds work for her."

"I don't see how that's a problem, sir. When I made my way to Richmond from the farm, her construction site was the first work I could get. I worked 'long side colored men doing the excavation for the hotel. They's good workers, Mr. Bennett. Wouldn't mind havin' that kind of industriousness on my crews," Hank said.

"Wouldn't have 'em Hank, that kind of race mixin' can put you out of business here in Richmond, I guarantee. Races have no business mixing, down on the farm may be necessary but in the city, that's nothin' but trouble – for you and for them. Wouldn't have them around," Walton repeated, "not even if they was shinin' the shit off my shoes," he added.

Hank wasn't inured to the things white men said about Negroes, he had just learned not to react to them. *If you knew the race mixin' I'm doin' right here on your porch*, Hank thought as he put his arm on the back of the swing behind Maggie's shoulders.

"Keep making the right moves, Hank, and you let me know if there's anything I can do for you, ya hear? City ways ain't country ways so if ya don't know, just ask. If ya gonna be sparkin' with my Maggie I want to be sure you've got resources," he said winking at Maggie who snuggled in closer against Hank.

Walton yawned and stretched, took a sip from the glass of bourbon he'd been nursing all evening.

"You and Maggie keep my offer to help from Mrs. Bennett's ears, ya hear now?"

"Yes, Daddy," Maggie said, smiling up at Hank.

"Thank you, sir, for your encouragement," Hank said looking at Maggie. If they were to move their relationship past the front porch they would need Walton to deal with Charlotte Bennett.

The fans on the porch's aurora blue ceiling strained against the humid warmth of the early September night, offering not even a hint of a breeze. Walton leaned over the porch railing and knocked the remnants of his pipe tobacco into the gardenias, then pulled a crumpled white handkerchief from his pocket and mopped the perspiration dripping from his forehead,

"Seem to have a touch of indigestion," he said to no one in particular then leaned back in his rocker, rubbing his chest. Walton closed his eyes unable to resist the soporific effect of the night air. Maggie and Hank eyed each other waiting for Walton's first snore. Maggie stifled a laugh, as she watched her father nod, nearly wake, nod again and finally, settle into a steady snooze. Still snuggled against Hank, she waited a few minutes then slid off the porch swing and beckoned Hank to follow her.

They retreated to the shadows of the side porch shielded from the street and Walton's view, though it was improbable that he would awaken anytime soon. At first, they went there for a quiet place to talk, then to kiss. As the summer got hotter so did their hunger for each other.

That night Maggie had purposely worn an off-the-shoulder dress. As she backed up against the clapboards and into the side porch's shadows, she pulled the shoulders of her dress down to reveal her breasts to Hank. She pulled him against her, pressing herself into him.

Hank pulled back to look at the luminous glory of Maggie's body.

"Oh my God," he said, surprised by Maggie's boldness and by the sight he'd so longed to see. He kissed her, his mouth then traveled the length of her neck to her shoulder and then to the fullness of her breasts where he buried his face. Maggie held her breath, cradled his head, stroking his soft hair. She exhaled as she pulled his hips toward her so she could feel him hard against her. The thought of making love to Hank *one day* could no longer satisfy her. She would be nineteen in a few months and she wanted to be married to the man she chose, not someone her mother decided was more appropriate.

Charlotte had started inviting young men she deemed worthy over for dinner, desperate to provide Maggie with a more suitable alternative than "the janitor," as she referred to Hank. Her mother was too pushy and Hank was too much of a gentleman; Maggie decided to take the matter into her own hands.

"Hank," she breathed into his ear, "I need you. Stay with me, make love to me tonight."

Hank pulled back to look at Maggie. Over the weeks their passion had been increasingly aggressive. He had not yet figured out how they would deal with what was becoming more difficult to deal with, but what she was asking was impossible.

"I'll take you round back, to the rose arbor. You wait for me there. Momma will be back within the hour. As soon as Momma and Daddy go to bed I'll come back to be with you. Wait for me under the arbor." Maggie did not wait for him to respond to her plan. She pulled her dress back into place, took the reluctant Hank's hand and led him deep into the back garden of the house, into the shelter of the arbor thick with a fragrant curtain of rose and honeysuckle. Before Hank could protest Maggie kissed him and was gone, dashing across the garden and up onto the porch just in time to hear Walton stir as his wife walked up the stairs to the front porch.

"Margaret! Where are you? Walton, wake up, you're supposed to be keeping an eye on things!" Charlotte said. Maggie slipped silently in the back door of the house, ran through the kitchen and up the back stairs. Losing her dress as she reached her room, she grabbed her robe, pulled it on and called down from the balcony over the front porch as she heard her mother continue to berate her father.

"Momma. I'm up here. Hank left a while ago. I didn't want to wake Daddy, he was sleeping so soundly."

"Walton, let's go," Charlotte snapped, dragging her husband through the front door and slamming it behind them. Maggie went to the hall and watched her parents ascend the stairs—her mother leading, her father in tow. "Boy's got a good head for money," he was saying to Charlotte, his voice lethargic.

"That's a waste seeing as he doesn't have any," Charlotte said.

"You'd be surprised Charlotte, he's on his way," Walton assured her. "You mark my words. Maggie could do a lot worse than Hank Whitaker, I tell you, a lot worse."

"Don't you go putting ideas in *my* daughter's head Walton Bennett, I've got other plans and not a single one includes that Hank Whitaker."

"What about my plans Momma?" Maggie asked emboldened by her father's support and the knowledge that Hank waited for her just a few yards away. Charlotte stopped in the hallway and looked at her daughter,

"You don't have any plans except the ones I make for you. You will have the life I've planned for you and when you eventually see through that Hank Whitaker, as shallow as he is, then you will thank me young lady."

"Daddy likes him!" Maggie blurted out. Charlotte looked at her daughter as if she had lost her mind.

"Do you think for one second that I care one whit about you or your father's opinion on this matter?" Charlotte asked as if Walton were not standing next to her. Maggie looked to her father; he made no effort to defend himself or his daughter. Charlotte walked to the master bedroom at the opposite end of the long hall from Maggie's room. "Go to bed Maggie," she ordered, "It's late. I'll brush your hair in the morning. Time for bed, Walton," she said holding the door to the master suite open for him to follow.

There would be no further discussion, Charlotte had spoken. Walton did as he was told, daring to stop for a moment to kiss his only child good night.

Maggie remained in the hall until she saw the light go out in their bedroom.

How does he stand it? She wondered. *Daddy can't even breathe without Momma's permission. She's smothered him—he has no will, no opinion and no wants—except what she wants. It's too late for you, Daddy,* Maggie thought knowing her future was waiting for her on the other side of the Palladian window that overlooked the garden. *But it is not too late for me; Momma will never suffocate me.*

(III)

Hank could not see the house through the thick vines and the Bennetts could not see him – only Maggie knew he was here. The full moon cast shadows through the trellis above him falling across the earth under his feet making it look like he was in a cage. What if Maggie didn't come back? Here he was, a black man hiding on a white man's property waiting to have the man's daughter. He was an intruder in a white man's world— he could be hanged for less than this, he almost had been. Why did he ever think he could pass? He'd heard about other blacks passing as white but he'd never met anyone like him and if he had, would he have known it? Why did he pretend to be the very thing that tried to annihilate him? Why did he fall in love with Maggie, someone who would hate him if she really knew who he was? Why hadn't he ever had this kind of feeling for a Negro woman – someone like his mother? Hank couldn't breathe, he wanted to run but he wasn't sure his legs would carry him back to the street let alone to his life as a black man. Sweating profusely, Hank crouched in the darkest shadow of the small structure. His mind went back to the night he ran; all he wanted then, and now, was to be was back with his family in Park Place, not hiding from another white man. But he couldn't run again, *I have no place to go*, he thought remembering the old man's prediction, "That boy's gonna swing." It was just one hundred miles between Richmond and his homeplace but in the last three years he had put a world between himself and Park Place. He could never return, his family would be accused of hiding him and that would be fatal for all of them. He was trapped; his only salvation was Maggie.

"Hank," Maggie whispered, "Hank, are you here?" He waited for a minute, to be certain she was alone,

"Over here," he whispered as he stood up. In a second, she was on him, kissing him, groping him. She wore only a robe, which she had opened to put his hands on her body.

Hank grabbed Maggie's wrists and held her off, "I can't do this. I can't do this, here." His heart was pounding so loud it was hard to hear her speak or himself think. "I want you Maggie, I want you so bad but I, I…"

"You can have me, Hank. I'm all yours."

"Not like this, not in the dirt, like animals."

"I want you, I need you," Maggie said, not understanding Hank's hesitation after all the nights they had left each other longing. She needed tonight to be different.

"Not like this," Hank said. Maggie pulled back from him. "What's wrong?"

"You're better than this," Hank said. Maggie began to whimper, humiliated by Hank's rejection.

Hank had not known he was going to leave Park Place the night he ran. He did not know he would change who and what he was until he had done it. Tonight he did not know he was going to ask Maggie to be his wife. He had thought about it often enough and always dismissed the idea because he could not marry just Maggie, he had to marry her mother, her father, Richmond, her race. He would have to turn his back on everything and everyone in his past; he would have to become the white man he now pretended to be, forever.

Maggie began to cry harder, Hank grabbed her and pulled her to him. Suddenly, none of that reasoning mattered. He would make his life with the woman he loved, damn the rest.

"Ssh, ssh," he said, stroking her hair to soothe her, no longer afraid of what they both wanted. "We are better than this," Hank said softly. "I love you, be my wife in the proper way. Be my wife," Hank said. "Do you want to?"

"I want to. I want to but," Maggie said stifling her sobs, "what about Momma?" Charlotte would never allow them to marry and Walton was powerless.

"I'm not asking your Momma," Hank said, "I'm asking you, Maggie. Be my wife. Marry me and I will love you proper for the rest of my life."

(IV)

The next morning Charlotte, in her dressing gown, sat at the table on the screen porch waiting for Frances to serve breakfast. She hoped Walton would sleep in a little longer so she could avoid the lurid remarks he made and the self-satisfied grin he wore the entire day after they had sex. After his comment about Hank Whitaker being a suitable suitor for Margaret, Charlotte needed to cement Walton's loyalty and commitment to her and only her. Charlotte used sex to catch Walton Bennett and she used it to keep him in line. If he had been considering solidarity with Margaret on the subject of Mr. Hank Whitaker, she was certain the sexual performance she gave last night would dispel any insurrection.

Charlotte smiled at her prowess when she recalled how she had exhausted Walton. When he came, he let out a guttural moan, rolled off her and there he lay for the night. He had not even stirred when she got up to wash him off of her. She was easily in the bath an hour and when she returned to the bed, he hadn't moved.

Frances brought in Charlotte's breakfast, a two-egg omelet, and two slices of white toast with the crusts removed, freshly squeezed orange juice and a pot of her beloved rose hips tea.

"Frances, when you are finished here, run up and wake Miss Margaret," Charlotte said as she removed the white cloth napkin from the table and opened it in her lap. "It is high time she got herself down here for breakfast. I think we'll have lunch today at the Richmond Hotel— see who is visiting our fair city this week."

"Yes Ma'am. I will do so directly," Frances said as she scurried back into the house. *She's a good enough housekeeper,* Charlotte thought, *but not much of a cook.* As usual, her omelet was cooked to the texture of shoe leather. Charlotte would have preferred a colored girl in the kitchen but she just couldn't have colored help in her house.

Charlotte heard someone run down the steps from the second floor,

"How many times have I told that blessed girl, ladies do not run through the house," she said throwing her napkin into her plate as she got up to reprimand her daughter. Instead of Margaret, she met Frances in the hall. The young woman looked like she had seen a ghost. She thrust a folded sheet of Margaret's personal stationery into Charlotte's hand and fled to the kitchen.

"What in the world?" Charlotte said as she opened the sheet and read the one sentence note Maggie had left for her parents. Charlotte fell against the doorframe; the room spun, she slumped to the floor.

"Walton!" Charlotte screamed at a volume that should have been able to wake her sleeping husband except that Walton Wainwright Bennett III—who the night before had kissed his beloved daughter goodnight and then made love to his wife—conveniently died before Charlotte learned their daughter had eloped with Hank Whitaker.

≈ 3 ≈

Spring 1913

(I)

I'VE AVOIDED YET ANOTHER DAY *of detection*, Hank thought
as he looked out of his office window onto the majestic
view of Capital Square and wondered what he had gotten himself into. The only place Hank could give his constant
worries just consideration was away from Maggie and out of
Charlotte's suspicious sight. He was in the center of the seat of
the Confederacy and in just four years Hank had gone from a
black boy, to a white man, to business owner, to husband and
head of household. He had not yet grown into any of those
roles and now, he was about to add father to the list. *What if
the baby's black?* Hank thought. One small baby, no matter how
beloved, could dismantle his whole life by being born. *What
if the baby looks more like his father's side of family than his mother's?* He was almost sure he and Maggie would make a baby

that would not reveal his heritage but he could not be certain. Countless times he wanted to tell Maggie who he was, but the fear of losing her had stopped him. Now he had even more to lose – his wife, his child, his thriving business; it was too late, he would be who he was now, a white man, forever.

"You look troubled," James Stephens, Hank's bookkeeper said as he locked the safe for the day.

"Not troubled," Hank said, "just tired."

"You too young to be tired," the older man said. "Man like you, married into a good family, got a good business, a few coins in your pocket, getting ready for fatherhood? Life has smoothed out like silk for you boy, just like silk."

Hank considered his words. "Just not the way I'd planned," Hank said without turning from the window. "You're right though," he turned to face James, "just like silk. It's just that bein' a husband, soon a father, the business— it's a lot to take on."

"Any less would not be enough for you, Hank. You'd be lookin' for more to do. I've never seen a man grow a business so fast, like you're racin' against something unseen," James said as he took off his green visor, pulled the sleeve garters from his arms and buttoned his vest.

"Well, I'm headed home, the wife will be puttin' dinner on about now and I don't want to miss a spoonful."

"Lucky man," Hank said, thinking about Frances' excuse for a meal awaiting him at home. The newlyweds were currently living with Charlotte— who despised the fact of Hank and Maggie's marriage, but hated living alone more. She made sure the young couple felt responsible for Walton's death and used

Maggie's guilt to force Hank to agree to stay with her for a few months that had turned into a year. The couple had finally bought their own home, just down the street from Charlotte, and were planning their move. However, that would not solve the problem of a good home cooked meal today.

"Wife can't cook?" James asked.

"I live with three women," Hank said. "Two don't care where the kitchen is and third one has no idea what you're supposed to do in there."

"Get yourself a woman to cook for you, Hank, someone who knows where the kitchen is and what to do in it," James said laughing. "You know, I may know of someone."

"I would be eternally grateful if you could arrange for us to meet her. And the sooner, the better," Hank said.

"I'll see what I can do," James said.

As he walked home, James Stephens wondered what a man like Hank Whitaker had to worry about. James knew the woman he would recommend to Hank, Del Holder, could solve his housekeeper problem. He had known Del for years, her sister Charlene cleaned for his wife and their mother had cleaned for his mother. Del's husband had recently died and she needed the work. Was the fact that his maid can't cook really the worst of Hank's worries, James wondered? Hank was a good businessman, a go-getter but sometimes he would get dark moods that worried James. *There's some trouble under those still waters*, James thought, *I can sense it; don't know what it is but I pray he can keep it under control.*

(II)

Delora Holder took the streetcar from her home in the all-black neighborhood of Jackson Ward, arriving well before the scheduled noon interview at Hank and Maggie Whitaker's house. *One thing you can count on,* she thought as she stepped off the streetcar, *they'll always be a direct route from my part of town to the West End where the white folks live so that the help can get to work on time.* Del pulled the little piece of paper from her purse on which James Stephens had written the Whitaker's address. The homes in her part of town were small and sturdy brick row houses; here in the West End the homes were large, spacious, single family houses on big lots, newly built for white folks with tobacco and every other kind of money. While it was safe for whites to visit her neighborhood, a black woman strolling the streets this time of day was suspect, and a black man would get his behind run out, arrested or worse. You had better be on your way to work, at work or on your way home— at this point Del wasn't any of these so she walked quickly to find the address then went around to the back entrance and knocked. As Del waited, she surveyed the dusty porch and neglected yard. *Ain't nobody lovin' this house,* she thought; *if it looks like this outside, what's the inside gonna look like?*

It had been a good ten minutes since she'd arrived and she had knocked several times to no answer. Del stepped off the porch and craned her neck to check the address again. She was at the right house but she started to sense that maybe she was in the wrong place. Del kept an orderly house and was punctual. She wasn't sure working for a sloppy unreliable white man would suite her. At 55 years of age she knew that her standards were not about to change. *Maybe this ain't such a good idea*, she thought, and started down the back porch steps just as the back door opened.

"Mrs. Holder?" Hank said, descending the steps to meet her. "So sorry to be late. I had to pick up Maggie, my wife, from her mother's house, that's where we're livin' right now. Did you have any trouble finding us? We haven't moved in yet, I guess I already told you that. If we find the right person to help us we'd like to go ahead and move in here. Mr. Stephens, whose opinion I value, tells me that he knows your family and that you're an excellent cook and housekeeper and that you have experience raising children. We're about to have our first in a few months…" Del raised her hand to stop Hank's rambling.

"'Scuse me Mr. Whitaker, but is this here my interview?" Del asked. "'Cause it seems like you ain't askin' me enough questions let alone givin' me a chance to get a word in edgewise." The color began to rise in Hank's cheeks.

"I've never hired household help, or a woman, before. Not sure how this works."

"Pretty much the same way it works when you hire anyone else," Del said. "You ask about my experiences, tell me 'bout the job, what you're wantin' to pay, then you ask me if I think I can do the job. But before I can answer, I needs to look around, meet the missus and make a good assessment. So Mr. Whitaker, shall we get started?" Del said as she took her late husband's pocket watch out of her purse, opened it and looked at the time. "'Cause as it stands now, we seem to be behind schedule."

Hank smiled listening to Del. If he really was a white man he might have been offended but Del reminded him so much of his late mother, Augusta Whitaker. She too had little or no tolerance for being late, lazy, sloppy or dirty. She died a year before the incident that brought him to Richmond. He missed her. Through this brief interaction with Del, he felt the kinship of the people he had known for the first eighteen years of his life; this was as close as he'd been to his life before Richmond.

"Well then Mrs. Holder, I guess we had better get started," Hank said as he bounded up the back porch steps. He turned to see the tall, wiry, mahogany-colored woman with the wide-brimmed straw perched precariously on her head, surveying the back garden as if it were her own.

"Flowerbeds could use some tendin'. You're gonna need to hire a man to take care of all of that. Between you and the missus and the baby, cookin', cleanin' and what not, there is not enough of Del to take care of the yard too. And the laundry, we'll need a girl to help with the laundry at your house."

"Yes, ma'am, Mrs. Holder," Hank said with a broad smile on his face. Del walked up the porch steps. Hank held the door for her and, as she stepped into the house, she said, "You all don't need to be callin' me Ma'am. Mrs. Holder t'ain't necessary neither. I'm Del, folks just call me Del."

(III)

Maggie and Hank were never sure whether they had hired Del or Del had hired herself—but now, in her, they had a housekeeper, cook and experienced nursemaid. Del had taken care of finding them someone to do the laundry and take care of the yard. There was no reason for them to remain Charlotte's unwanted guests. It had been over a year since Walton's death and Charlotte, along with her personal maid Frances and her house staff, could manage without them.

"You should never have let Hank bring that woman into your house," Charlotte admonished Maggie after she met Del. "I would never let a colored woman run my house. They have different ways of doing things and they are a temptation to your husband." The last part of Charlotte's statement made Maggie laugh so hard she cried.

"Del?" she asked Charlotte. "Del is old enough to be Hank's mother! You're being ridiculous Momma."

Charlotte was undeterred. "Then you make sure you manage her, Margaret. You make sure that she does only what she was hired to do and that she doesn't put your private business in the street."

"Momma, please. Hank and I can trust Del, she came very highly recommended. She's worked for white families before, there is nothing to worry about." Del had already proven herself. In less than a month she had Hank and Maggie's household running smoothly and Maggie did not have to lift a finger.

"You won't be seeing much of me over there till the baby arrives," Charlotte declared, washing her hands of the whole situation. "But you mark my words Margaret, one day you'll regret hiring that woman."

(IV)

Charlotte and Frances left on an extended trip to Europe as soon as Maggie and Hank moved into their own home. It was her way of letting them know she did not appreciate their impertinent independence. She was a widow, her only daughter should have at least asked her to move in with them. She knew it was Hank who refused to consider the idea. Now she was further convinced that he was hiding something.

"I'll be back before the baby is born," Charlotte promised, hoping that her absence would teach Maggie a lesson. "I'll bring back some layette items from Paris. We will have the most fashionable little one in Richmond."

⸺⬥⸺

"Will you miss the home you grew up in?" Hank asked Maggie their first night in their new house. He was thinking about the last time he left the house he grew up in. He and his brothers left to go to a Negro league baseball game across the bay on the campus of the Hampton Normal and Agricultural. When the game went into extra innings, they should have left in time to catch the ferry that would get them home before dark. Llewellyn was one of Virginia's many sundown towns; on the outskirts of town signs warned, "Niggers Leave Llewellyn by Sundown, or Else..." The only way the Whitaker brothers could get home that night was to chance a run from the docks, through Llewellyn, to the safety of the black community of Park Place on the other side of town. The sheriff knew there would be stragglers from the game and he was waiting when they arrived. Now Hank would never see home again.

"We'll be right around the corner, Hank. I can go to Momma's anytime I want," Maggie said, bringing Hank back to Richmond from Park Place. "This is home now. Our child will be born in this house and I don't think we will ever leave here." Hank took his wife in his arms. Between them was Maggie's expanding belly; their child might be the one person that would force Hank to leave home again.

⮜ 4 ⮞

Richmond, Virginia—June 1913

(I)

MAGGIE WENT INTO LABOR A month earlier than her due date. "It is not an exact science. Babies come when they come. We're ready, Mr. Hank, don't you worry," Del assured him. With Dr. Bridges in attendance and Del assisting, Maggie cried like a baby through the delivery. She pleaded for her mother but Charlotte, thinking she had a month before the baby was born, had not yet returned from Europe.

Hank paced outside the bedroom door waiting for news, for the baby's wail, for anything to let him know what was happening. Del came out a couple of times early on to let him know that women's work was still being done. When he heard nothing for what seemed like hours, Hank became even more anxious. Finally, he heard the baby cry, then silence. Was Maggie all right, was the baby healthy? Was the baby—colored?

Hank panicked. He banged on the bedroom door.

"Is everything alright in there?" he shouted. It took several minutes but Del finally opened the door and in her arms was a perfect, pink baby boy.

"Look what perfection God and the two of you done made," Del said, rocking Hank's newborn son. "You wanna hold him, Daddy?"

Hank's eyes welled up as he looked at his son,

"I'm afraid I'll break him."

"More likely he'll break you," Del said. "Boys be a handful, I should know, raised five brothers. Go on, Mr. Hank, take your son to see his Momma."

"I can see Maggie?" Hank asked, taking the baby in his arms.

Dr. Bridges met him at the door, "Just for a minute, the little mother had a rough time of it but she'll be fine. The next one will be easier on her. You two decide on a name for the birth certificate and then you let her rest, she's plumb worn out."

Hank took careful steps into the bedroom holding his son. He sat in the chair Del had placed next to Maggie's bed. "Look what we did," Hank whispered, when she opened her eyes. "He's beautiful, Maggie, just like his mother. What are we gonna name our son? What's his name, Maggie?"

Maggie opened her eyes and looked at Hank holding their child. This was the moment she'd waited months for yet she felt none of the joy she imagined at the birth of their child.

"I'm so tired, Hank," she said, "I just want to sleep."

"The doctor needs his name," Hank said, disappointed by her lack of enthusiasm.

"You name him Hank. You pick the name, that'll be alright with me."

"How does Lance Henry Whitaker sound?" Hank said looking at the baby. He looked back at Maggie but she had already closed her eyes to sleep. Del moved in and took the baby from Hank.

"She's gonna need to nurse him, so you go on and deal with the doctor. Lance Henry and I will stay here with the little mother. Go on now, we right as rain here."

Hank named his son Lance for his favorite brother, but told Maggie he chose the name because Lance sounded regal. He remembered his oldest brother telling him how he hated being a man called Junior so he gave the baby Henry, Hank's given name, as his middle name to save his son from the same fate. With his family intact, his secret safe and Del in charge, that night Hank slept like his newborn son.

(II)

Two weeks after Lance was born, Hank met Charlotte's train from New York with the news that Maggie had given birth. Her guilt that she had been away for the delivery turned to joy that a male child was born into the family. Her joy became rage when she learned the baby did not have the Bennett family name.

"The Bennett name has been synonymous with Richmond since there was a Richmond. How dare you dishonor our family's tradition?" Charlotte berated Hank.

"Naming my son is in no way a slight to Mr. Bennett's family," Hank said. "The boy will do just fine with his given name, Charlotte. Won't be any doubt who his family is. His name won't make us love him anymore or any less."

"But the Bennett name means something in this town. We are changing it," Charlotte decreed, "to Bennett. I suppose he can keep Henry if you like. Bennett Henry Whitaker; that will be his name."

Hank gripped the steering wheel of the new Packard he bought to celebrate his son's birth, trying hard not to run it off the road and Charlotte with it. His response to her was through gritted teeth, "My son's name is Lance Henry Whitaker, Charlotte. His name will remain Lance Henry Whitaker until the day he dies and there is nothing you can or will do about it."

Charlotte was used to Hank being solicitous so his ire shocked her into silence—temporarily. Neither of them spoke during the remainder of the ride to the house. Charlotte's maid, Frances, cowered in the back seat of the car hoping the smoldering silence would not erupt into flames. From the time Hank appeared in Charlotte's life it had been obvious to Frances and everyone else that these two people had the same potential as a match and a gallon drum of gasoline.

Hank parked the car and walked around to open the passenger door for Charlotte. She refused his hand when he tried to help her out of the car. Looking past him she said, "Hank, take Frances and my bags to my house. Carry my bags up to my bedroom so that Frances can start unpacking."

She took a few steps toward the house then turned back to address Hank again.

"And we shall see about the baby's name."

(III)

Maggie was lying on the chaise lounge in her bedroom. As soon as she saw Charlotte, she burst into tears.

"Momma where were you? I needed you. Del and Dr. Bridges were here but it wasn't the same. I needed you!" Charlotte swept in and cradled her daughter like she was the infant, not the mother of one.

"Where's Hank?" Maggie whispered.

"He took Frances and the bags to my house."

"Good, I need to tell you something. Something I can only tell you, Momma."

Charlotte, concerned, pulled back and looked at her daughter's tear stained face. "What is it my little girl? Did Hank do something? Is there something wrong with the baby?"

Maggie buried her face in her mother's neck, "No, no, Hank's been wonderful and the baby, he's healthy. He's beautiful, but Momma," Maggie murmured, "the birth, the delivery, it was horrible."

Charlotte laughed with relief, "Oh that. I remember. Soon you'll forget it all, I promise."

"I won't," Maggie said. "I love my baby. But now that I have given Hank a son, I don't need any more children. I don't *ever* want to do that again. Momma, tell me how to keep from ever getting pregnant again."

Just then, Del knocked on the door. "Miss Maggie, little Lance here heard he had a visitor."

"Give me my grandson," Charlotte demanded. Del had long ago steeled herself against the rude behavior of people like Charlotte Bennett. Without a word, she brought the baby to Charlotte and placed him in her arms. Charlotte opened the blanket and looked at his ten pink toes, his rounded belly, his tiny hands, hazel eyes and mop of sandy hair. Maggie was right; he was an exquisite baby by any measure.

"You are a wonder," she whispered. "The child of my child." The three women gazed at Lance, who broke the silence with a wail for his mother's breast. Charlotte placed her grandson in her daughter's arms and helped Maggie position him so he could suckle.

"This is so *bovine*," she said, looking to her mother for a solution. "He wakes me up all hours of the night, I can't get any rest and," she said, shifting the baby as he tried to stay connected to her breast, "it hurts."

"He's a good feeder," Del said proudly. "Thriving like a big boy." Maggie's distaste for this primary role of motherhood was obvious and both Charlotte and Del feared the baby would sense it.

Charlotte turned to Del and without asking Maggie's permission said, "We are going to need a wet nurse."

(IV)

"Woman don't want to do nothin' that the Mama's 'spose to do," Del said as she helped her sister Charlene hang out the wash on her Sunday off. "If she could have hired someone to birth him I suspect she would have. She loves that baby boy, no doubt, but Lordy, she don't want none of the dirty work. 'That's what I have you and Mammy for,' she tells me soundin' as sweet as syrup. That's what she calls Claudia, the wet nurse. *Mammy*, like we livin' in plantation time."

"You know how some of these white women can be," Charlene said. "And some of these high yella Negro women too. Think theys too good for women's work."

"Don't you be talking 'bout your sisters in skin like that Charlene. Most folks here in Jackson Ward just livin' and lovin' the life they worked hard for," Del said.

"I suppose, though some of these women 'round here are light, bright and damn near white enough to pass easy. But to their credit, they don't," Charlene said. "Could go up north, live like whites but then they'd have to leave their kin, everything they know. I wouldn't never leave home. Besides, I like bein' colored."

Del peered at her sister over the white sheet she was hanging on the clothesline. She jiggled it and mouthed "K-K-K" to remind her that being colored in the south could be downright dangerous. Charlene picked a clothespin out of the basket and threw it at Del.

"You right. Charlene, crazy Klansmen aside, we make a pretty good life for ourselves," Del said, "but you know full well whites got it better on most fronts."

Charlene shrugged, picked up another piece of laundry and continued with her work.

"I think all that privilege disconnects you from what's important in life," Del continued. "Mrs. Bennett, Miss Maggie's mother, always talkin' 'bout obligation to folks she hardly knows and that probably don't care one whit 'bout her. She's getting' Miss Maggie all caught up in this League and social club business and that takes her time away from that precious little boy and her husband. I'd be fearful of taking a day off if it wasn't for Mr. Hank. Now he's a Daddy who loves his baby boy. After Claudia fed him one time last week, Mr. Hank, comin' in after a hard day's work, wants to hold his son and takes to burpin' him like he know what he doin'. Tells Claudia to go on down and rest a spell knowing she'll be up all night 'cause that little one feeds every couple hours or so. I go up to the nursery to spell him when she tells me Mr. Hank is up there all alone. By the time I get there, he done changed the baby's diaper all by his lonesome."

"Say what? A man like him wipin' a baby's bottom?"

"And Charlene, he did a good job too. Cleaned that boy up as good as you or I would."

"Oh my Lord. I hope that woman knows what she's got over there. A provider, a gentleman and he can manage a youngin'. Can he cook?" Charlene asked, and both women laughed.

"I don't know about that but he sure can eat! Somewhere in his history there was a colored woman cookin' cause Mr. Hank loves him some of Del's down home cookin'. I believe he could eat a pot of greens with neck bones and pan of candied sweets by his lonesome. Miss Maggie and Mrs. Bennett don't go in for that cookin' but Mr. Hank, 'thank you Del and pass the corn pudding!' I'm glad I'm the only one in that house can rattle pots and pans otherwise I suspect he could give me a run for my job," Del laughed.

⇜ 5 ⇝

Richmond, Virginia—Summer 1918

"MOMMA!" FIVE-YEAR-OLD LANCE SHOUTED as he ran down the hall to Maggie's study with Del in chase. Bursting into the room he rushed to his mother, nearly scattering the Women's League invitations she and Charlotte were addressing for the civic group's annual gala.

"Del won't give me no cookies!"

"*Any* cookies," Charlotte said without looking up from her work.

"Not 'till you finish your dinner," Del said, arriving at the door on Lance's heels. "Del told you, finish your plate and then we'll have a cookie, not the other way 'round."

"Lance, you know the rules. Del is correct – dinner then dessert," Maggie said, putting her hand on Lance's shoulders to keep him at arm's length. The last thing she needed was to have him put his sticky fingers on or scatter the carefully arranged stacks of hand-addressed invitations she was working on.

"But you can change the rules, Grandmamma said so. She said Del doesn't make the rules. You make the rules and Del follows them." Lance looked to his mother and then Charlotte for confirmation. Maggie arched an eyebrow and looked across the table at her mother who continued with her work. With a finger, Maggie lifted her son's chin to look into his eyes.

"That was talk for grownup ears not little boy ears. You go with Del now, and you do what she tells you – that's Momma's rule. When Momma is done with her work I'll come see you. Right now you go and eat your dinner."

"You're always busy with your work," Lance pouted.

"Momma has very important work to do for the League. They really need my help and you have Del to help you."

"The 'Leek' is your little boy, and I'm Del's?"

Maggie was a little taken aback by Lance's assumption. "No Lance— " Maggie started.

"Come to Grandmamma," Charlotte said, taking charge. She took the boy's tiny hands in one of hers as she removed the lace hankie she kept tucked in her sleeve. Wetting it with her tongue, she gently rubbed the boy's cheek and wiped his hands, sticky with the remnants of his dinner, while giving Del a disapproving look.

"You are our only little boy, there is no one but you." Charlotte said putting her arms around the squirming boy. Lance was growing fast—he had his father's sandy coloring and was slim and perpetually in motion which made him seem like he was all legs and elbows. "It's just that your Momma is a very important lady here in Richmond; she has so many people to help, very important people. You have to be a big boy and share her. Even Grandmamma has to help your Momma, see?" she said, pointing to the invitations she was addressing. "You'll see your Momma when she's done," Charlotte said, kissing Lance's cheek, then turning the boy around and gently pushing him toward Del who was waiting at the door.

"No I won't. You and Momma have the 'Leek,' " Lance said as he ran to Del and raised his arms.

She lifted him into her warm embrace and Lance whispered in her ear just loud enough for his mother to hear, "You can be my momma, Del. But I'ma keep my Daddy."

"Sorry for the disturbance, ladies. We're goin' back to the kitchen to finish the young man's dinner," Del said, disappearing down the hall with Lance's face buried in the crook of her neck.

Maggie started to get up to follow them, but Charlotte held her in her seat.

"You should have told him he could have a cookie or whatever he wanted. Let him assert himself with the help or they will never respect him," Charlotte said, not caring if Del was still within earshot.

"Since when do five-year-olds need respect?" Maggie asked. "All they need are breakfast, lunch and dinner on a regular schedule and to be bathed and put to bed at the appointed hour. However, what I need from you, Mrs. Bennett, is to let me run by house in my way."

"Listen to me, Margaret. Negroes take orders from whites—Lance must learn that. He should know as early as possible that he can fulfill a request from a Negro but that it is just that, a request. He does not take orders."

"He is five years old, Momma, and Del is doing a fine job with him."

"And with you," Charlotte said. "She runs this house and everyone and everything in it. She's got Hank wrapped around her little finger. All she has to do is feed him some of that colored sharecropper food and the man is happy. All the household help reports to Del. That is not the way it is supposed to be, Margaret."

"Everything Del does, she does for me. Negroes are grateful for the opportunity to work for us, why would we be afraid—"

"I'm not afraid," Charlotte said, cutting Maggie off. "I'm just wary, that's all."

"Of what?" Maggie asked, "Why are you so suspicious of Del? Did something happen between the two of you?"

"Nothing happened, I just don't make it a habit of being in the company of colored people," Charlotte said, returning to her work. "Let's finish here, we need to get these in the mail today. We don't want the right people to fill their social schedules before they commit to the gala."

The two women worked in silence for a few more minutes then Charlotte abruptly got up from the table and went to the window. Standing with her back to her daughter, she smoothed her hair then her hand drifted to the strands of opera length pearls that always adorned her graceful neck.

"You don't know what it is like to be disrespected," she said. "It does not matter who does it— white, Negro, man, woman—it cuts the same, deep wound, and it's impossible to heal." Maggie was not interested in a lecture on respect from her mother. No one in Richmond would dare disrespect her; she was Margaret Bennett Whitaker, the only child of the late financier Walton Wainwright Bennett III. Her mother had groomed her since birth to take her place in Richmond society. She'd fought her at first, but as Maggie matured and her husband's business grew to be more and more successful, Maggie realized the advantages of being in the right social circle— one of which was never worrying about being respected.

"Keep your guard up at all times, Margaret," Charlotte said as she turned around to face her daughter who had already stopped listing to the wisdom her mother was trying to share.

"Margaret!" Charlotte snapped as she walked over and slapped her hand on the table upsetting the stacks of invitations. "If you hear nothing else, hear this. Never expect anyone to have your best interests at heart. You'd best learn that lesson now or it will break you later. Trust no one, Margaret— not your husband, not your son, not even me."

≈ 6 ≈

Richmond, Virginia—Spring 1928

(I)

LANCE WAS ALREADY WAITING WHEN his father came down the back stairs into the kitchen.

"We have to leave now, Daddy. Momma will be down here before you know it and then we'll never get out of here."

"Oh no, come hell or high water, we're goin' fishin'. Your mother's got those League ladies here today and you know how I feel about being anywhere near the—what did you used to call them? The Leek."

"That's your wife you're talking about. They're not as bad as you make them out to be, Daddy," Lance said, thinking of the young girls his age to whom he'd been introduced by their mothers in the League.

"No, they're worse, your Momma's the one exception."

"What about Grandmamma?" Lance asked.

"As I said, your Momma's the one exception," Hank said, making them both laugh. He pulled the picnic basket Del had packed for them across the table. "Let's see what all's in here," he said as he opened the basket and called out the menu for their day trip to the James River, "fried chicken, ham sandwiches, deviled eggs, a jar of tomatoes and cukes, a bag of brown sugar pecans and some of Del's chocolate iced golden layer cake."

"Damn! Gonna be some good eatin' today!" Lance said, as Del came into the kitchen.

"Watch your language, young man," Del said. She was dressed in the formal uniform she wore when Miss Maggie was expecting guests. The long sleeve black dress and white lace bib apron made her look more subservient than her preferred short-sleeved grey cotton dress and flowery apron with the deep pockets. She might have looked different, but she was still Del.

"Yes 'em," Lance said obediently.

Del noticed Hank digging through the picnic basket.

"Mr. Hank, please! Don't you go poking around in there for it gone and you two don't have no lunch."

"Just a taste, Del. We need something to get us going this morning."

"You think I didn't know that?" Del asked as she closed the basket and moved it next to the back door. She walked over to the oven and took out a metal lunch pail with warm sausage biscuits wrapped in a gingham cloth. "I think these'll get you 'all started off right. Now the two of you scat or you'll be helpin' with the fixins for all those fine ladies about to descend on your house."

"We're gone!" Hank said, grabbing the biscuits and the picnic basket. Lance took a thermos of hot coffee and a burlap bag containing several bottles of Coca-Cola from the kitchen's long wooden table.

"Be sure to put the bag in the stream to chill the sodas as soon as you get settled," Del said affectionately rubbing his back. Lance had stopped letting her hug and kiss him years ago, but she still loved feeling the warmth of him.

"Bye, Del," they said in unison as they headed down the back porch steps to the garage.

"Don't forget to anchor the bag good to the riverbank and don't you 'all bring me home nothin' scrawny. A fried fish dinner depends on you!" Dell called after them. *Father and son*, she thought as she watched them from behind — one the spittin' image of the other. This year Lance had his growth spurt and now looked just like his Daddy—tall and sandy-haired handsome— but there was no doubt that he had his mama in him too. Lance liked the finer life like Miss Maggie did; Del felt him pulling away from her the way the youngins' do when they come to understand there's a difference between coloreds and whites. She knew with Lance grown, things would change for her in this house. She'd have to set her mind to what was next, but for now, there were still a few things she could teach the boy—though some things were the purview of his Daddy, and fortunately, Mr. Hank was always there for his boy.

Lance was turning fifteen this year and was already being recruited for dances and cotillions. The mamas of the young ladies in the West End had already identified Lance Henry Whitaker as a prospect for their daughters. While cleaning the parlor a few months back she'd heard a bit of a conversation Mr. Hank and Lance were havin' out on the porch.

"You wanna treat women with respect, son. I know you got urges but we're not animals, we can control them. You don't want to have relations with a woman you don't plan to marry."

Del moved her dusting to another room to give them some privacy. *Hope he's got enough of his Daddy in him to keep his wits and other parts about him*, Del thought. *If Miss Maggie and Miss Charlotte had their way he'd be courtin', matched and married in no time. Thank God for Mr. Hank. He'll help the boy manage all them airs and such his mama and grandmamma put on.*

"Speakin' of puttin' on, I'd best get lunch for the ladies ready," Del said as she thought about the menu she'd prepared for the Women's League Lunch—the same as what she sent with Mr. Hank and Lance on their fishin' trip—except served up on Miss Maggie's fine china. The League ladies might point their pinkies in the air for tea but whenever they came to Miss Maggie's for their meetings they always requested Del's fried chicken.

"They be peelin' off them white gloves and eatin' with their fingers— not a one of 'em too uppity when faced with a plate of Del's fried chicken," she chuckled and got to work.

(II)

"Lance! Looks like you landed a big one!" Hank said, jumping up to watch his son wrangle a big mouth bass to shore. They watched the fish flail on the bank of the river.

"Reminds me of you, Daddy."

"How's that?"

"You're a big fish in Richmond," the boy said proudly.

"Oh, I thought you meant hooked and flailing, that's more what I feel like these days."

"Why would you feel like that?"

"Just sometimes life gets ahead of you, that's all."

"I don't understand," Lance said.

"I never had a plan, Lance. Life just, kinda, happened to me. Like this fish, you get hooked and next thing you know you're flailing around someplace you never expected to be."

"Are you taking about life or business?"

"I guess both. I hadn't known your Momma but a few months. We loved each other so we ran off and got married. Charlotte wasn't too happy about that."

"So I've heard."

"Same thing with the business. I just saw the opportunity and started Colonial Enterprises. It was just a property services business before then—but me and Mr. Stephens saw the opportunity and bought some tobacco warehouses. Next thing I know, we're making more money then I knew was possible. That was almost twenty years ago, before I met your Momma, before you was born. I never imagined that little janitor business I started,

Whitaker Property Services, would grow into what Colonial Enterprises is today. We went from cleanin' and fixing other people's property to buying and managing industrial buildings and warehouses down on Tobacco Row. No plan, I'd just see an opportunity and take it." Hank rubbed his forehead as if he couldn't believe how well things had worked out.

"You were lucky," Lance said, studying his father.

"I guess, so far, but things are changing. I feel like the business is less about the work and more about what folks want from me, the man. I'm not like your Momma, I don't take to the public life. Not comfortable with people tryin' to get next to me now that I have something they think they want. Was a time the people smiling in my face wouldn't have let me shine the shit off their shoes," Hank said, remembering what his future father-in-law once told him.

"You should be proud of what you've accomplished. You came from nothin'—"

"Don't say that, Lance. I came from good people."

"I didn't mean it like that. Just that you never talk about your family. I know everything about the Bennetts but all I know about you is that you're the only child of only children and that your parents died before I was born."

Hank looked down at the dying fish who had all but given up his struggle except for a few desperate thrashes of his tail. He was just like this fish – he was completely hooked and out of his natural environment. After all these years he was still thrashing around like a fish out of water.

"Not much more to tell. Where I grew up, everyone, everything's gone," Hank said, hoping he was wrong and that his brothers were thriving. It had been nearly two decades since he ran. He often wondered what would have happened if the sheriff hadn't died. Mr. Connors, the man who had given him the ride out of Park Place, confirmed the sheriff's death when he ran into the old man a few weeks after arriving in Richmond. Connors had been back in Llewellyn on business and a new sheriff had just been sworn in. Hank knew then he could never go back.

Hank's fishing line was still in the river. He felt a tug on the pole.

"Looks like you hooked something too, Daddy!" Lance said.

"Here son," Hank said handing him the pole. "You reel him in." Lance turned his attention back to the river while Hank picked up the big fish from the ground and put him in the pail of river water with the rest of their catch. When he looked up he saw that the fish on Lance's line had gotten away. The boy turned to his father, shrugged, baited the hook again and then waded back into the river.

Maybe Lance will get away too, Hank thought hoping his son would escape the consequences of the racial dilemma he had created for both of them. *Maybe he'll never have to know his Daddy's secrets.*

(III)

"I'm not interested in working at the bank this summer. I'm going to work with Daddy." Lance said, sitting on the porch with his mother and grandmother.

"You and your father have discussed this?" Maggie was surprised that Hank had not mentioned anything to her.

"No," Lance said, "but if that's what I'm going to do after college I might as well start getting some experience. Daddy said it's best to have a plan and that's my plan – to run Colonial Enterprises one day."

"So you want to be a janitor like your father. You're already dressing for the position," Charlotte interjected. She had already made him aware of her displeasure with his bare feet, open collar and rolled up shirt sleeves.

"Stop calling my father that," Lance barked at Charlotte.

"Who do you think you're talking to, Lance Henry Whitaker? You're not talking to Del," Charlotte said.

"I don't have to talk to Del like that. She loves and respects my father," Lance protested.

"Oh, please. Del loves your father's money."

"And so do you," Lance shot back, knowing that his father had just given Charlotte a car and driving lessons—making her one of the few women on the West End who drove an automobile.

Charlotte stood up from her rocker and started toward Lance who was sitting on the other side of the screen porch. "You are not too old to—"

Maggie grabbed her mother's arm and pulled her back into her seat.

"Momma, this is not about you or Del. It is about Lance's future. Lance, stop antagonizing your grandmother," Maggie said trying to get their discussion back on track. "Your grandmother has her heart set on you following my father's professional path. You come from a long line of bankers, Lance. It's a respectable profession for an educated young man."

"Momma, I agreed I'd go to college, as you asked, but I am an entrepreneur like my father."

"A what?" Charlotte asked.

"An entrepreneur. It's French. It means you own and manage your own business. That's what I am going to do—with my father."

"You're going to do what with your father?" Hank said as he stepped onto the porch with his newspaper.

"I want to be like you, an entrepreneur. I'm not going to be a banker. What about making Colonial Enterprises a father and son operation? Can't you see us working together? I can start learning the business this summer," Lance said.

Hank smiled, looked at Maggie and then over at Charlotte.

"So you're interested in janitorial work?" he said, winking at Lance.

"Yes I am, sir," his son said.

"What do you think, Maggie? Think I should find a place for this young man?"

"Momma arranged for him to clerk at the bank this summer."

"How do you feel about that, Lance?" Hank asked knowing Charlotte had acted without consulting anyone.

"I have my heart set on being a janitor, Mr. Whitaker, sir. This summer is just as good a time as any to start realizing my dream," Lance said, trying to keep a straight face.

"I can always use a good young man on my work crews. We can start you off like I did—sweeping up, mopping, fixin' what needs fixin' down at the warehouses," Hank continued the ruse.

Charlotte was aghast, "You want your son around those filthy men down on Tobacco Row?" she sputtered. The area was as gritty as the businesses that functioned out of them. Colonial Enterprises holdings were not pretty but they were very profitable.

"Well, Charlotte, you're right. Those bankers down there are thick as thieves sniffing and swarming all over Tobacco Row. Are those the filthy men you're talking about? Your husband was a banker and Mr. Bennett always used to say that the scent of tobacco was the smell of money."

"You are teaching your son to be impertinent. I don't appreciate it and I don't find it at all humorous. Margaret, say something. Your son's future is at stake."

Until now, Maggie had been able to keep from laughing at the fun her husband and son were having at her mother's expense, but Charlotte's overwrought plea was just too much.

"Momma. What would be the harm in your grandson doing as well as his father?"

"He would do better if he followed *your* father's professional path, Margaret." Charlotte turned on Hank. "You are no one from nowhere. If you hadn't had the insane good fortune of marrying my daughter, you never would have made anything of yourself. If you want your son to work for a living, then drag him into your pedestrian environment. If you want more for him you'll encourage him to be a banker, a respected profession that exudes culture and class."

Inured to Charlotte's insults, Hank asked, "So, bankers don't work for a living?"

"I'm going home," Charlotte sputtered as she rose from her rocker and stomped off the screen porch. Slamming the door she headed for her car. She had driven the two short blocks from her house to her daughter's that evening.

"Do you want me to drive you home? I can walk back." Lance called after her.

"No, you stay there and work out the terms of your indentured servitude," Charlotte said.

While she arranged her dress, put on her driving hat and gloves, Lance said, loud enough for her to hear, "So, Daddy, what's the going rate for an ambitious young janitor these days?"

⌒ 7 ⌒

Richmond, Virginia—1930

(I)

"**H**ANK, WHY WON'T YOU GO? I'm president of the League. I have to be there and I can't go without my husband," Maggie said, leafing through the latest edition of *Vogue* magazine. "I'm picking out my dress right now and I'll be ordering you a tuxedo as well."

Hank looked up from the business section of the *Times-Dispatch* and took a swallow from the tall glass of bourbon that had become a fixture on the night table each evening. "Maggie, I already told you. I don't want anything to do with that society crowd and their fancy galas. I just want to go to work, come home and be with you and Lance. That's all I need—just us."

"Hank Whitaker, every year since Momma sponsored me for the League, I've made one excuse after the other for you not

71

being able to attend our events. There are only so many colds or conflicting business appointments a man can have before it is obvious to everyone that you refuse to escort your wife and mother-in-law to any of our events. This year Hank, you have to go and don't you dare tell me no. All you have to do is stand around, have a few brief conversations, eat dinner and then we'll go home. If you're not there, everyone will wonder why. What do I tell them?"

"Tell them I'm sick," Hank said, downing another mouthful of bourbon.

"No, not again, I will not lie for you this time," Maggie said. She looked over at Hank, he had put down the newspaper and was moving a hand fitfully back and forth across his mouth; his other hand was tightly clenched around the near empty glass of bourbon. His eyes were distant. He looked desperate, like a man being asked to commit some heinous crime. This was more than not wanting to go to a League Gala.

"What is it Hank?" Maggie asked, softening. "Talk to me. What's the matter?" She got up, walked around to Hank's side of the bed and knelt next to him.

"I don't fit in," Hank said, barely above a whisper. "There are things I can do. I can make a good living for you and our son, I do just fine when it comes to workin' with clients, negotiating and supervising—as long as it's work and it has some purpose. But getting all dressed up to sit around pretending to be better than everyone else—pretending to be someone I'm not, I can't do that."

"Hank, look at me," Maggie said, taking his hand in hers. "These people aren't any better than you are. Just because you came from a humble background doesn't mean you don't deserve to take your place with the other wealthy businessmen in Richmond. Whether you want to acknowledge it or not, Mr. Whitaker, you've made quite a success of yourself." Maggie's praise made Hank smile.

"I'm so proud of you, Hank Whitaker, I want to show you off," Maggie said and kissed him. "I want to walk into that ballroom on the arm of my handsome husband. I know you hate this kind of thing. Whenever the ladies come over you disappear. I know you struggle during our dinner parties—but you always survive. I promise we'll only stay as long as we have to and then I'll bring you home and I will reward you for being so gracious to your wife," Maggie said, playfully rubbing Hank's thigh.

Hank looked at his wife. He loved her and their son, but the life he'd constructed seemed to be collapsing in on him more and more each day. He remembered his mother telling him that sooner or later all the lies you tell catch up with you. Maybe if he had told Maggie who he was in the beginning he would not have twenty years of lies eating away at his soul. For all that time, to keep from being exposed, he'd kept his head down and avoided the false camaraderie of Richmond's social organizations and business clubs. Maggie, following in her mother's footsteps, became increasingly involved in Richmond society and her involvement put constant pressure on him, and his son, to be involved as well. This was the part of passing that Hank found the most difficult to negotiate.

"Hank please, we have obligations," Maggie pleaded, "Will you go for me, just this once."

(II)

"Aren't you proud of your wife, Hank? My Margaret, president of the Women's League—presiding over the 1930 Spring Gala, one of Richmond's biggest social events," Charlotte gushed from the back seat of the car.

"I am always proud of Maggie," Hank said.

"I'm just glad you aren't pretending to be sick or traveling on business. I don't know what I would have told the ladies if you hadn't escorted me this year," Maggie said.

"I'm here, Maggie," Hank said as he steeled himself for the event.

"It's going to be the most beautiful gala ever, Hank, you'll see. Everyone will be talking about this for years to come," Maggie continued.

Richmond's early spring felt more like late summer as Hank drove Maggie and Charlotte downtown for the dreaded event. The air was warm, thick with scent of magnolia and honeysuckle; the syrupy sweetness was suffocating. As the women chatted excitedly in the car, Hank felt sweat form a warning on his upper lip. The collar of his new tuxedo shirt and white tie seemed to be wrenching tighter and tighter around his neck in competition with the ridiculous waistcoat that was pressing all of the air out of his diaphragm and his dinner jacket was close to smothering him.

"I don't know why we have to put on all these clothes," Hank complained.

"Stop fidgeting like a four-year-old," Maggie said, as she reached over and rubbed Hank's arm. "You look very distinguished tonight. The little touch of grey in your hair is very attractive," she brushed her finger through his hair. "I dare say you'll be the most attractive man there. I promise you'll have a good time. All you have to do is be yourself and have a few conversations with the men you do business with. They'll all be there. We'll eat dinner and then we can go home."

"I do business with these people; I'm not interested in being their friends. I don't fit in," Hank said barely audible.

"Hank," Maggie said, putting her hand on his, "we talked about this," she leaned over and kissed his cheek. "I know how you feel about tonight and I appreciate you escorting Momma and me. Isn't that right Momma?" Maggie said, turning to look at Charlotte in the back seat of the car.

"We all have obligations," was all Charlotte would offer.

"And burdens," Hank responded to Charlotte's sarcasm. Fortunately, they were pulling up to the hotel and Charlotte did not have time to take another verbal jab at her son-in-law.

"I'll park and meet you inside," Hank said as he dropped Maggie and Charlotte off, refusing the bellman's offer to park the car. Hank drove to the far end of the parking lot. After pulling into a spot he took his handkerchief from his breast pocket and mopped the sweat from his face and neck. He looked toward the line of cars pulling up to the hotel, pulled a flask from his jacket pocket and took a couple of sips, hoping to take the edge off of his anxiety. He knew he needed to cut back his drinking. James mentioned that a couple of customers had made remarks about smelling alcohol on his breath. However, this was not the time to start rehabilitation. He needed bourbon to get through tonight. Hank started to return the flask to his breast pocket but instead he drained its contents, fighting the urge to get back in the car and drive away. Only the thought of Maggie waiting for him propelled him toward the bright lights of the hotel. He had to do this, yet another of the endless hurdles he had to negotiate to maintain his impossible transformation from colored to white.

(III)

Maggie was waiting for Hank outside of the ballroom. In the dress she had ordered from Paris, she looked like the exquisite, southern woman of means she had become. She was no longer the spirited girl he fell in love with. She had settled into being the traditional southern society woman her mother always wanted her to be. He shared her with the League, Charlotte and Lance, in that order. He still loved her but they were on different paths—his more private and hers more public.

Lance was stretched between his parents' worlds. Working with his father summers and in the afternoons in this year before he left for college, Lance began to yield to his father's influence and the way Del had raised him. Lance had more of

Hank's upbringing than he thought was possible. *My family would be proud of my son*, Hank thought and it pained him that they would never know he had a son.

"There you are," Maggie said, kissing Hank on the cheek. "There's my handsome husband."

"Don't leave me tonight," Hank whispered in Maggie's ear.

Maggie looked at Hank, she could smell the bourbon on his breath but she laughed off her concern saying, "Don't worry; I'll keep the women at bay."

They made their entrance and the event was exactly the spectacle Hank knew it would be. He was plunged into a large room filled with southern gentry, a sea of whiteness. Hank instinctively pulled his wife closer. Approaching middle age, they were still a most attractive couple. Hank tall and fair and, despite his success, his eyes still held that tinge of sadness Maggie had seen in them so many years ago. Maggie was still the petite raven haired beauty. Hank looked down at his wife of nearly twenty years remembering the young girl sitting on her porch, the one he thought needed taking care of. In reality, he was the one who needed her and that was still true. Hank could still feel the warmth of the whiskey in the pit of his stomach. It did not help the panic that he felt rising from the same place. He tightened his arm around Maggie.

"Hank, you're about to crush my dress. Relax, please," she whispered, escaping his grip. As the guests waited for dinner, servers passed glasses of iced tea and soda water from silver trays, a difficult concession to prohibition. While Maggie chatted with her friends, Hank watched the black and brown men in their ridiculous waistcoats, frilly shirts and white gloves, move silently through the crowd of white men and women who only acknowledged their presence when they wanted something. Hank noticed how aged some of the servers were. They looked as if they could barely move yet they hoisted heavy silver trays filled with drinks, dispensing them throughout the crowd, then replenishing the trays to begin the ritual again. Others, younger than his seventeen year-old son, wove between the partygoers with canapés and more drinks, their eyes always cast downward.

I see you, I know you, Hank wanted to say but none of them would make eye contact with him. Negroes never looked a white man or woman directly in the eye. They would only speak when spoken to and then it was usually a mumbled *yes sir, no sir* or *yes'em, no my lady*. To these Negro men, Hank was the enemy – someone to be served and loathed in silence. *I'm your brother*, Hank wanted to say, *or at least I used to be*.

"Hank Whitaker," he heard his name and looked around to see John Morris, the man who had taken over as bank president when Maggie's father died. "One of my best customers," Morris said, clapping Hank on the back. "Let me borrow you from your lovely wife for a few minutes. I promise Maggie, I will have him back to you in time for dinner."

Morris signaled for Hank to follow him into a room off the main hall. "We shall retire briefly to the library," Morris said chuckling as he opened the door to a room filled with men, bourbon and brotherhood. "Only place a man can get a real drink at this shindig, God damn prohibition," Morris said with a hardy laugh.

"What is your pleasure, sir?" one of the waiters, a young black man, asked Hank.

"Bourbon," Hank said, relieved that he had the option of something other than weak tea. He watched the young man as he went to the sideboard and poured the drink. By his diction and demeanor, Hank could tell that he was probably a student at Virginia Union, the Negro college in Richmond. He returned with Hank's drink on a silver tray.

"How old are you?" Hank asked as he accepted the glass.

"Sir?" the young man asked surprised to be addressed by a white person with anything other than an order or complaint.

"How old are you? Seventeen, eighteen?" Hank asked, making the boy even more uncomfortable.

"Eighteen," the young man said and then attempted to leave to fill another order, but Hank reached out and touched his arm.

"I have a son close to your age. Are you in school?"

"Yes sir, over at Virginia Union."

"That's what I thought," Hank said as Morris walked up.

"What do you think you're doin' standin' around talking to the guests? We pay you to get drinks not to socialize."

Hank put his hand on Morris' arm. "I was asking the young man to get me another drink," Hank said, retuning his already empty glass to the silver tray. "This time, make it a double will you, son?" The young man quickly disappeared in the direction of the bar. "Careful how you talk to niggers," Morris said. "Don't want them to forget their place."

"He's about the same age as my son," Hank said.

"But he ain't your son," Morris said, "We need to make sure these niggers know their place. We were just talkin' about that earlier. When they get to that nigger's age we got to keep the pressure on, keep 'em away from our women."

"He's not a threat to anyone here," Hank said, thinking of some of the frightfully unattractive women he'd seen this evening.

"And we're makin' sure of that," Morris said, motioning to a group of men near the bar to join them. "We were discussin' our next step with the Racial Integrity Act. I know you'll want to be a part of the effort here in Richmond. If we hadn't gotten that Act passed by the legislature they'd be marrying our women and there'd be race mixing to point where we wouldn't be able to protect our whiteness. I want you to join our chapter of the Anglo-Saxon Clubs of America. We're a progressive group; don't go in for cross burnin' and lynching like the KKK. We're committed to racial purity based on scientific social policy."

Hank accepted another drink and tried to tune out Morris' racist ramblings. He could handle the insecurity of being who he was with a few people, but at a large social gathering he felt as if his true identity would somehow become apparent, revealing the Negro in their midst and there would be no way for him to escape.

It was even harder to hold his tongue when he had to listen to racist remarks and threats. He hated the pretentious formality of Richmond social events. Negroes, at least the ones he grew up with, didn't have cotillions and galas. They had folks over for supper; they had parties to celebrate real things like marriages, birthdays and holidays. They always came as themselves, not dressed up like they weren't who they were every day.

Hank looked over at the young waiter again and saw himself at that age. When he looked back at Morris, he saw the face of the sheriff that had forced him to leave Park Place. He saw the man's mouth moving and the other men in the group nodding in eager agreement, Hank shook his head to get the image of the dying sheriff out of his mind. He caught the last part of Morris's racist rant,

"…pass legislation keeping anyone of any color, except pure white, from marrying our women."

Fueled by several glasses of bourbon, Hank could feel the words, *you're too late*, forming in his throat. Before they reached his mouth, the door to the library swung open and Morris's wife and several other women interrupted the gathering to the sound of a bell clanging and a booming baritone announcing, "Dinner is served."

Mrs. Morris grabbed her husband by the arm and dragged him away saying,

"We need to get to the table first in case I need to rearrange the seating cards."

Morris called after Hank, "We'll talk more after dinner."

Not if I can help it, Hank thought.

"Saved by the bell," Maggie laughed as she found Hank, slipped her arm through his and guided them toward the dining room. "The Morrises," she said shaking her head. "He's pompous and she's insufferable—they are perfect for each other. That's half the fun of these events," Maggie whispered. "You get to see who belongs to whom and you wonder what on earth he is doing with her or she is doing with him."

"What do you think they say about us?" Hank asked Maggie.

"I think they say what a handsome couple Margaret and Henry Whitaker make," she said.

Hank looked at his wife and said, "You look beautiful tonight Maggie, that's what they would say." *If they knew me,* Hank thought, *really knew me, they would be speechless.*

(IV)

Maggie climbed the steps ahead of Hank to seat them on the dais.

"I don't want to sit up here Maggie, up here with everyone looking at us," Hank said. He had already had enough bourbon and bull for one evening.

"Don't be silly Hank, I'm the League president; this is my event."

"Why don't you let your mother sit up here with you; these folks here don't want to see me."

"Hank stop it," Maggie snapped, tired of trying to put Hank at ease. "I've had enough of your foolishness." From the potent combination of alcohol, the stifling heat in the room and the anger Morris's racist comments generated, Hank was in danger of losing control. He pulled the chair out for his wife but instead of sitting down next to her, he walked unsteadily down to the main dining room floor where Charlotte was seated with several of her friends. As he arrived at the table he tripped, nearly landing in her lap.

"Charlotte, I'm not feeling well. Would you sit up there with Maggie tonight?" Charlotte looked at Hank warily. "I will arrange for you two to get home," he continued, slightly slurring his words.

"You're drunk, Hank Whitaker," Charlotte whispered as he escorted her to Maggie's side on the dais.

"Hank, sit down!" Maggie whispered to her husband.

"I can't, I'm sorry, I just can't." Hank said, then turned and walked toward the exit without looking back to see the horror on the faces of his wife and mother-in-law.

(V)

Hank burst through the front door of the house. He was still very drunk and had nearly driven the car off the road several times trying to get home to see his son. He stumbled up the stairs to Lance's bedroom.

"Lance, Lance," Hank said, shaking his sleeping son. The boy was in that deep nearly impenetrable sleep that only someone with no worries can attain.

"Wake up son. I need to talk to you," Hank said, looking at the almost eighteen-year-old spitting image of himself. Instead of his son, Hank kept seeing the young waiter at the dinner tonight. The only reason Lance had all the potential the world had to offer was because his father had deceived everyone he loved.

"Can't it wait until tomorrow? God, what time is it anyway?" Lance said, struggling to wake up.

"I need to talk to you boy," Hank said, sitting down heavily on the bed.

"What is it?" Lance asked as he shrugged his father's hand from shoulder. He could smell the liquor on his father's breath and in the wedge of light coming into the room from the hallway, he saw that his father was dripping with sweat and barely able to sit upright.

"You're drunk. Where's Momma? You're supposed to be at her gala. Did something happen?"

Hank didn't answer his son's questions; he just dropped his head into his hands.

"Daddy! Did you hear me? What's going on? Where's Momma? What happened to you?"

"Your Momma's fine, I'm the one in trouble. She'll never forgive me, I'll never forgive myself. I thought I could get through anything but after more than twenty years I can't stomach any more of this shit!" Hank spat out the last word in disgust.

"What are you talking about Daddy? Twenty years of what?" Lance asked. He had noticed changes in his father over the last couple of years. He seemed to be aging quickly; it wasn't the grey that salted his sandy hair, it was the weariness that enveloped his face and a malaise that seemed to be taking his father away from him. Hank would close himself off in his office at work or his study at home, furiously writing in a leather journal that he kept with him or hidden away. He noticed his father's frequent surreptitious swigs from the silver flask he kept in his breast pocket and the glass of bourbon that he filled and refilled every evening at home. Hank would often sit alone on the back porch at night staring out into the darkness and, at least a couple of times a week, Hank was too drunk to get himself to bed so Lance would put him in one of the guest rooms so as not to wake his mother. His father was disintegrating before his eyes, and he did not know what was driving him from proud to pathetic.

"What is the matter with you, Daddy?" Lance asked again, climbing out of the bed and coming around to face is father.

Hank looked up at his son with bloodshot eyes,

"I thought I could get used to it," Hank said quietly. "After hearing it all my life I tried not to let it bother me anymore, but tonight when Morris said—" Hank stopped for a moment as his anger built. "I watched those black men moving around that room like they were invisible, Morris talking about them like they weren't human, saying things about purity and keepin' them in their place like he was God and they were nothing. I was raised by colored people Lance, and I never understood why white people treated them like they wasn't God's children too. But I think I've finally figured it out; behind the white man's hatred for Negroes, for Indians, for everyone, is nothin' but fear. The only way they can feel powerful is to weaken everyone else. The only way they feel smart is to convince themselves that everyone else is ignorant. The only way to stay rich, is to squeeze another man until he has nothing at all."

Hearing the commotion Hank made getting into the house and stumbling up the stairs, Del came from her room near the kitchen to see the front door ajar and Hank's tuxedo jacket laying at the foot of the stairs. Not wanting to overstep her boundaries and intrude on Mr. Hank and Miss Maggie's personal affairs, Del picked up the jacket and waited at the foot of the stairs until she heard young Lance asking, "What happened to you? Where's Momma?" Her foot was on the step when there was a knock on the front door. Del opened it to find Charlotte's maid, Frances, wearing a shawl over her nightgown.

"What you doin' out in the night dressed like that, Frances?" Del asked. In her monotone voice, Frances repeated exactly what she had been told to say.

"Miss Charlotte said she wants Mr. Lance to know that Miss Margaret is at Miss Charlotte's house and that he should come by there in the morning to fetch his Momma. Miss Charlotte also said not to tell Mr. Hank a goddamn thing." When she finished she pushed her wire rim glasses up on the broad nose that took up most of her round plain face and stood like an obedient child waiting for Del to give her another task.

"Frances, you go on home now," Del said, wishing the woman had at least an ounce of discretion to go along with the half ounce of brains God seemed to have given her. "Del has things in hand over here. Mr. Lance be 'round there in the morning. You tell Miss Maggie not to worry." Frances waddled back out into the night, the wind whipping the long braid down her back and her cotton nightgown around her barrel-shaped torso.

Storm comin' Del thought as she closed the door, referring to more than the weather.

"Mr. Hank, is that you?" Del said taking the steps two at a time to find Hank sitting on Lance's bed and Lance kneeling in front of his father, trying to shake him out of his stupor.

"Oh, Del, Del," Hank moaned, but did not look up. His head was still buried in his hands.

"What the hell is the matter with him," Lance asked Del. "Do you know where my mother is?"

"Don't you worry none," Del said to both of them. "Frances come over to tell us Miss Maggie's down at Miss Charlotte's house. They doin' a little gossipin' about the evening they had. Your Daddy had a little too much of the spirits, Lance, but he be all right. We gonna go down to the kitchen and get some black coffee. You go on back to bed, everything be all right."

As it had been Lance's entire life, Del was there to fix things—a skinned knee, salve for the body, food for the soul, words of encouragement and a firm hand for guidance when it was needed. Lance and everyone one else in the Whitaker house counted on Del for those things. Del helped Hank to his feet – she was in her early seventies yet she was still strong, unlined and trim. No one thought of her as old, just wise.

Like a child hanging onto a parent, Hank grasped Del's hand and she walked him out of Lance's room and sat him in a chair in the hallway. She reappeared in the doorway of Lance's bedroom.

"You go on to sleep now, boy. Your Daddy gonna be just fine. You know how mens get when they get together. He be right as rain in the morning. Come on now, climb on in the bed. Want Del to tuck you in like I'd do when you was little?"

"You take care of Daddy," Lance said, not wanting to take on the burden of his father's problems. "He needs you more than I do right now." Del closed the bedroom door but Lance could hear her coaxing Hank to his feet. He heard the two of them shuffle down the hall to the back stairs, descend into the kitchen and close the door. In the darkness, Lance prayed Del was right, that his father would be just fine in the morning but in his gut he knew there was more to his father's troubles than a night of too much to drink.

(VI)

"Del, I'm in some kinda trouble and I'm in so deep I can't see my way out," Hank said as he sat at the big wooden table in the kitchen and watched Del pour hot coffee into a mug from the enamel pot she kept on the stove.

Del knew Mr. Hank needed someone to talk to tonight—in a way she wished she wasn't the one here to listen. She didn't want to know anything that would change how she felt about this beautiful man. If he had the strength to tell whatever it was, she had to be strong enough to hear it.

"Del's here to listen, Mr. Hank" she said. "Sometimes that's all a body needs, someone to listen." Del watched Hank closely as he sat quietly and sipped the coffee she had poured for him, his eyes in a faraway place.

After a few minutes, Hank put down the cup and leaned his elbows on the table. He looked up at Del standing on the other side of the room near the stove.

"Will you sit down here with me?" Hank asked, patting the chair next to him. Even though the kitchen was Del's domain, this was Hank Whitaker's house and she knew to stay in her place. Though she wanted to take him in her arms and tell him things gonna be okay, she could not sit down at the table with her employer.

"Mr. Hank, you know I can't do that," Del said.

"Yes you can," Hank said. "We're the same, Del, you and me, we're the same."

"Mr. Hank, I know we all God's children but on this here earth we ain't the same. I understand that and I'm at peace with that—you have to be too."

"Del, I'm askin' you to please sit here next to me," Hank said. "I so need the warmth of humanity near me for what I have to do." Hank's eyes were pleading and now Del was afraid. She walked slowly to the table and perched on one of the straight wooden chairs, a couple of seats between her and Hank. Hank reached over, took Del's hand and gently pulled her into the chair next to his. The rain that threatened earlier battered the tin roof of the kitchen porch and even with the windows open and the door to the screen porch letting in the cool damp air, the kitchen, filled with Hank's sorrow and pain, was as close as an August afternoon. Both Hank and Del felt it. Tonight had the same fatal tension as the night Del's husband died and before that, her mama and her daddy.

Hank's hand on Del's felt heavy, cold and soft from years of having others do the hard work for him; hers was small and rough from a lifetime spent doing hard work for others. Hank took a finger and gently traced the raised veins on the back of Del's hand. She felt a tear hit her hand and looked to see tears streaming from Hank's eyes.

"You have hands just like my mother's," he said, "My momma was smart enough to teach school but she scrubbed floors because that was the only work she could get from white folks. She was better read, more refined, generous and humble than all the white folks in Richmond put together." Though he looked in Del's direction, Hank's eyes were not looking at her when he spoke—he was back in Park Place.

"She educated us, me and my brothers, we didn't have fancy schools like Lance goes to here in Richmond. Shabby wreck of a school but they taught us the best they could. My Daddy was wise, smart as a whip, could quote from Shakespeare and the Bible." Hank laughed at that memory then turned serious again. "He could figure a row of numbers in his head and calculate the maximum crop yield without a single lick of school-taught arithmetic. He didn't need to know how much money a man had to decide if he was someone worth knowing. My parents understood character, do you know what I mean Del? My Momma and Daddy were strong, smart, honest and proud; and they raised me and my two brothers to be that way too. Our little community was a family; people used common sense, generosity and humility instead of taking on these pretend social airs like the white folks here in Richmond."

Del understood without hearing the exact words, Mr. Hank was passing. All this time and she had never suspected. He was a Negro passing as white. She knew Miss Maggie and Lance didn't know. The thought of Miss Charlotte finding out made her draw in a breath. She looked at Mr. Hank's shoulders slumped under the weight of a ton of deception. Her worries about the others would keep, tonight Mr. Hank needed her.

"You go on ahead and talk to Del, Mr. Hank. You safe here in Del's kitchen. Just like it's been for all these years, ain't nothin' gonna get served from this here table unless you want it to."

(VII)

Hank talked for hours. By the time pale crimson streaks of sunrise lit the kitchen, Hank had told Del things he had never told another living soul—the story of his life in Park Place, his escape to Richmond, meeting and marrying Maggie. How sometimes he would drive through Negro neighborhoods just to see colored families, young and old together. How when he first got to Richmond he used to hope he would come across someone from Park Place so he could get word to his family. After he married Maggie he prayed for just the opposite but he still wondered about his brothers all these years. Whether they married and had children like he did. All of his past, present and fears for the future rushed out of him like a torrent and then trickled to a stream.

"Mr. Hank," Del said when he was spent, "Was there somethin' that made this burden heavier than it had been for all this time?"

"My boy," Hank said. "Lance turns eighteen this year. He's about to start his own life." Hank paused for a few seconds thinking of the young man at the gala. "It's been gnawing at me good Del; the shame and guilt for I what did to my family. The pride I feel when I think back on who they were and how they raised me, the values I got, the way they loved me, Del, the same way I love my son, the way other families love their sons. I didn't touch that man but everyone thinks I did and whether he died or not they were comin' for me. I had to leave my family to stay alive. I left my brothers and I ran. I kept running 'cause I was so damn tired of only havin' as much as a white man said I could. In Park Place, that's the way it would always be. I wanted more—I didn't even know what that really meant until I got here—far enough away to realize I could stop runnin' forever. I know I'm gonna pay for my lies one day and before that judgment comes I want my son to know who his Daddy really is. I want him to carry the pride of the people he came from. Right now he's just got me and his mother and—" Hank swallowed hard, "Charlotte. We're all the kin he has." I thank God for you, Del, because you taught him some of the things my family would have taught him."

Hank did not say, "Del, you're like family," though he'd felt a kinship toward her all these years. He'd heard enough white families claim the Negroes they employed were "family" while they worked them like they owned them—even passed them from one generation to the next like they were property. Hank respected Del too much to patronize her that way. "I know you have your own family, Del. But havin' you here, helping to raise Lance was like blessing him with my heritage. Havin' him know something of what I came from. You did that, Del. You did that for both me and my boy."

"I'm grateful to be that comfort, Mr. Hank. Nothin' you told me tonight is gonna change how I feel about what's between us, but you needs to think on what you want to tell of who you are and where you're from to your wife and son. What would come of them if folks here in Richmond knew who you really was? I needs you to think on that. Young Lance don't know how to be anything other than what he thinks he is and that's white. Don't matter what you look like, only matters what folks believe. We all make judgments about who you be and how you be based on things that don't hardly matter—the color of skin, the kink of hair, whether you big or little, old or young, rich or poor, who your kin is. We all know that with the Lord, nothin' matters more'n the kindness of heart. But with man—well now, that's different."

"I'm so tired of trying to be someone else," Hank said. "I created this burden and now it's mine and too heavy to carry."

"Helps when someone else has a piece of it," Del said. "Even though neither of us can tell of it, I might could help with it now and then, Mr. Hank," Del reached over and smoothed the hair on Hank's bowed head. She knew it was out of place for who they were to each other, but she also knew it was appropriate for this grieving man. Hank put his hand on Del's and held it for a while. When he looked up at her, she said, "You a good father to Lance and a fine husband to Miss Maggie; and you a saint when Miss Charlotte tries you. You made a fine life for them and for yourself. You got to make sure this here secret don't take all that from you without givin' somethin' back. I think the boy's got to know, when he's wantin' to marry, make a family," Del continued. "You gon' hafta tell him. Might have made it easier on you if Miss Maggie had known and could have helped you all these years, then you two together could tell the boy. I ain't judgin', Mr. Hank. Folks do things for different reasons and ain't none of us fit to judge the other. But there's gonna be misery in the tellin' of your true story, so you gotta be good and sure about how you tell it and when. I'm just speakin' the hard truth here. But one thing I do know, Miss Maggie and Lance love you, Mr. Hank."

Hank got up from the table and stood in the doorway looking at the sunrise, his back to Del, he sighed and shook his head. He knew Del was right, he should have told Maggie that night in the rose arbor when he asked her to run away with him. He remembered the night Lance was born and the panic of not knowing whether the baby would reveal his secret and shatter the façade of his comfortable life as a man he was never supposed to be.

The rain had stopped and Hank looked out at the spotless serenity of the day's first light. He could not fathom how or when he could tell the two people he loved the most that he had lied to them all these years.

"I'm so tired Del; my mind, body and soul are so tired. I know I have to fix this but when and how, I don't know…" Hank's voice trailed off. He was quiet for several minutes then he turned and looked at Del sitting at the kitchen table; he reached out and gently rested his hand her shoulder.

"Thank you for—" he said, but there was no need to finish the sentence. He knew he did not have to ask her to keep his secret. Del patted his hand and nodded her head in response to the pact they had just made.

"Guess I'd better get cleaned up and go collect my wife. Time to meet Maggie's wrath and Charlotte's judgment." Hank said as he walked to the door that opened to the back stairs.

"Mr. Hank," Del said as Hank put his foot on the first step. "White, colored or whatever; I think you's a mighty fine man. One of the best I've ever known."

8

Richmond, Virginia—March 1931

(I)

HANK GRABBED HIS WIFE'S SHOULDER and pulled her to him.

"Do you love me, Maggie?"

"I love you more than you could know," she only had tonight to tell him.

"Should have trusted you," he gasped. "Should have told you. I waited 'cause I never wanted you to regret choosing me."

"I never have," Maggie assured him, while her mind tried to process this nightmare. It happened in an instant. Hank started across the street, then turned back to say something to James Stephens. The car hit him head on. James rushed him to the hospital, but by the time Maggie and Charlotte arrived the doctors told them Hank's internal injuries were too extensive—there was nothing they could do to save him.

Hank was conscious and in pain but he begged the doctors not to sedate him.

"Get the boy, Maggie. I got some truth to tell 'for the Lord steps in."

"I'm not leaving you, Hank. I'm staying right here. James went to find Lance. He'll be here soon, don't you worry."

"Go Maggie, please! Get our son—we don't have much time. Please!"

Maggie rushed past her mother sitting outside Hank's hospital room.

———⊷●⊶———

As soon as her daughter disappeared down the hospital corridor Charlotte went into Hank's hospital room to confront her dying son-in-law.

"Hank, did you make a will? What happens to your business when you die? Did you leave it all to Margaret? Is there enough money to take care of us?"

Hank opened his eyes to see Charlotte hovering over his bed. *My last sunset*, Hank thought as he looked past Charlotte, noticing the rich amber hues of early evening and how they softened the antiseptic white of the room. Hank knew nothing would soften Charlotte's calculating concerns, not the beauty of this sunset or that he would not live to see another sunrise. As always, Charlotte demanded that he attend to *her* needs. He was so tired of this woman; she would not be the last person he saw before dying.

"Can there be enough for you, Charlotte?" he asked. "Never thought so, no matter what I did, I could never measure up to your standards. Now, don't have to. Get out, Charlotte, I don't want you here. I just want my family."

Before Charlotte could open her mouth to sear him with a vicious retort, Lance and Maggie rushed in. Charlotte backed away from Hank's bed and out of his view.

"I'm here, Daddy," Lance said as he approached his father's bedside. He winced when he saw how mangled and swollen Hank was. His mother had tried to prepare him. Lance wanted to believe his father would survive; now he knew he wouldn't.

"Help me sit up, son; I need to look in your eyes."

"Hank, no," Maggie said. "The doctor wants you to lie still. We can see you just fine, just lie still."

Hank took a few shallow breaths. "Maggie, come closer. I need to see you." She stroked his hand but his pain was so intense he could not feel her hand on his.

"I thought I would be with you longer, 'til you was a full grown man. I know you're not a boy, Lance, but you're just eighteen. I remember when I was eighteen; I just wanted you to have a few more years, couldn't bring myself to tell you, but I have to now. The Lord's gonna take me, I can feel his hand on me, and I'm not goin' 'til you know..." Hank spoke barely above a whisper. Maggie and Lance leaned in to hear him, excluding Charlotte from their conversation.

"Hank, sweetheart, Lance knows you love him. Rest sweetheart, don't struggle. We know, we know." Maggie said as a tear streamed down her cheek.

"Nobody knows," Hank said and let out a moan that pained all three of them. It took him a few moments to gather the strength to continue.

"I came to Richmond runnin' scared; they said I killed a man. I didn't, I couldn't, but they'd have hung me anyway. I had to leave, left my brothers, all the family I had, I was a danger to them," Hank sobbed.

Maggie looked at her son. Hank was a fugitive? He had family. He'd told her that his parents were dead; that he was the only child of only children. Twenty years of marriage and he had kept these secrets from her?

"I don't understand," Maggie said, but Hank kept his eyes on his son.

"Will you find them for me, Lance? We were all each other had and I left them. Richard Jr. — the oldest—and Lance, I named you for, my middle brother. Find your uncles, tell 'em I'm sorry for all the pain I caused. It will be safe now, with me gone. I want you to share what we got, tell them I'm sorry. Will you do that for me, son?"

"I'll do whatever you want, Daddy," Lance said.

"Promise me, Lance that you'll take care of your Momma. Promise you'll do that," Hank pleaded. "Take care of your Momma and find my family. You promise me, son."

"I promise, Daddy. Momma will be fine and I'll find your brothers. Don't worry, I'll find them," Lance stroked his father's head; Hank closed his eyes.

After a few moments, he looked at his wife. "I asked God to make it so he'd be born lookin' like his momma, so he wouldn't have to struggle like I had to, before I came here. Everybody thought…," Hank's voice trailed off and he closed his eyes again.

"Thought what, Daddy?" Lance asked, looking for life in his father's face. "Don't you die on me Daddy, don't you leave me!"

When Hank opened his eyes, he looked at Lance, his eyes were fierce, his voice stronger. "I don't hate what I am. I hate how I was treated *because* of what I am. Shouldn't be that way, Lance. I kept my secret 'cause what folks didn't know made my life smooth out like silk. That's what James told me once—he was right. I wanted that smooth as silk life and to get it, I needed to be white. That was the only way to make you my wife, Maggie, and to give our son the same good life. I just didn't realize it would cost so damn much." Hanks tears overflowed again.

"Hank," Maggie said, "What are you saying? That you're really a…" Maggie looked to her mother to help process Hank's incomprehensible words. Charlotte had both hands over her mouth trying to suppress the wail that was forcing its way up her throat; but it escaped as a scream that seemed to reverberate throughout the entire hospital. Charlotte's outburst brought the nurses running to Hank's room, arriving in time to witness the final minutes of Hank Whitaker's life.

Oblivious to Charlotte's outburst and the audience it drew, Hank continued.

"We share the same blood. What's in me is in you. Be proud to be a Negro, be a better man than I was, son. There's beauty on both sides of your family. Don't forsake one for the other. Otherwise you don't belong to no one, and you'll pay the same lonely price I did." Hank coughed, sending his body into spasms, but he was determined to keep talking. "I wrote it all down for you," Hank gasped. "Find my people, your people, they're the best there is. Find them; share some of what we have. They have what you need: family, people to love you, to show you the right way. Do that for me, Lance. Promise me you'll find my family, your family. Will you do that?" Hank pleaded.

"Daddy, what are you saying? I don't understand what you're saying," Lance questioned.

"Why would you say this, Hank? It's not true," Maggie said.

"Shouldn't have been ashamed of being colored, didn't have the courage, too afraid to lose everything, especially you, Maggie, but you love me, and oh my God, I love you," Hank said, grasping for his son and his wife. "I had to tell you who I really am. I couldn't die with this lie; you *had* to know. Maggie, Lance, I love you so much," Hank's last words came out as a gasp.

Maggie shuddered. She stared at the man she thought she knew everything about.

"Hank, why would you say that you're, you're. . . "

"A nigger!" screamed Charlotte dropping to her knees, beating the floor with her fists, "Oh my God, oh my God," she wailed, rocking back and forth.

Hank's hand on Maggie's felt like ash, dark and weightless. She pulled her hand away, wiping it on her dress, as if soiled.

"Why would you say this, Daddy?" Lance asked. "Why would you say this?" he asked again grabbing his father's shoulder and shaking him.

Hank looked past his son as he watched a replay of his life. He saw his family home in Park Place, his mother and father, his brothers, the people who had nurtured him whole. He replayed the night he ran, the sheriff falling to the ground, his life forever changed. He remembered when he met Margaret Bennett, and when she defied her mother and married him anyway. When they had a son, Lance Henry Whitaker, the physical incarnation of his father, and now heir to his deception. He saw James Stephens, his partner and his friend. And Del, more a mother than his housekeeper and until this moment, the only person to hear his confession. She had kept his secret just as she promised. Hank had finally revealed himself to the people he loved; the loneliness that he'd felt for more than twenty years finally left him. Unburdened, Hank slipped away, leaving his wife and son with the truth and an uncertain future.

(II)

Lance and Maggie sat in the hospital room after they took Hank's body away.

"How could your father betray us?" Maggie asked trying to understand what had just happened to her perfect life, "I never knew, never suspected. Why did he have to leave us with this?"

"I don't know, Momma," Lance said, too numb to deal with his mother's shock and grief as well as his own.

"Where's my Momma?" Maggie asked.

"She left before they took Daddy away," Lance said. They sat in silence for a few more minutes then Lance jumped up and headed for the door. "I gotta get outta here. I'll ask Mr. Stephens to take you home." Before Maggie could protest, Lance was gone.

Wringing her hands, tears streaming down her face, Maggie looked like a distraught widow, but felt like an abandoned child.

"Momma was right. Momma was right," she whispered to herself. She remembered the way Hank had loved her, the way he made love to her and today revealed that she had been with a Negro. She felt the confusion of loving Hank and being conditioned to hate what he was. She felt sick; bolting to the bathroom she vomited in the sink. She ran cold water on a towel and wiped her face. There in shadows, she stared at her image in the mirror, "*What do I do now?*" she whispered, as if her reflection could answer questions she could not. Then she heard voices coming from the hospital room.

"Why do we have to strip the bed, if they're going to get rid of the mattress too? No one in this hospital would use it now that a nigger done died on it."

"Did you hear her Momma? If she hadn't been screaming and carrying on nobody woulda heard his confession, ya know. Do you think his wife knew? She had to know. There're differences, aren't there?"

"How would I know? You think I ever seen a nigger naked?"

"All those years, livin' like a white man and nobody knew. They's some treacherous people, I tell you. Just like my Daddy said, all they want is to get with a white woman."

"It ain't legal for a nigger to marry white in Virginia. What's the wife and her nigger-son gonna do now?"

"Think they'll go to jail?"

"Probably worse. You know what they do to lyin' cheatin' niggers 'round here. That boy gonna hafta pay for what his daddy did."

"That'd be right, keep somethin' like that from happenin' again now wouldn't it?

"Never know who you talkin' to, do you? What do you do after gettin' news like that?"

Maggie, unnoticed in the dark bathroom, could not answer that question for herself or her son. She looked at herself in the mirror again. She could see the woman she once was disappearing before her eyes. How would she explain this to her friends? What about Lance? Would he have to pay for what Hank did? Would the rules for Negroes now apply to him too? She was a white woman with a colored son, in the heart of the segregated south. She was sure the shame she felt was the only thing people would see from now on. When she heard the door close as the two nurses left the hospital room, Maggie buried her face in her hands and moaned,

"Momma you were right. Help me Momma, help me please."

(III)

Charlotte did not get any information from Hank about his will so as soon as she arrived at their house she rifled through all the drawers in Margaret and Hank's bedroom, then his study, but found nothing. If they were going to salvage anything, she would have to move fast. By tomorrow, Hank's deathbed confession would be rumor. Within three days, the efficiency of gossip in Richmond society would ensure that Hank Whitaker's passing was all people talked about. Charlotte was not about to wait for talk to turn to action – there were severe consequences for colored folks who tried to pass for white. She'd seen trees bearing the bodies of black men for doing a lot less than Hank had. *They will not take their vengeance out on Maggie and Lance, no matter what Hank did*, Charlotte vowed.

"Shit, shit, shit," she muttered as she poured herself another glass of sherry. "I knew he was hiding something. I should have been able to see what Hank was." She knew the nurses heard everything when she saw them huddled together whispering. When they saw her, they fell silent and looked away.

I should have offered to pay them something to keep their mouths shut. They just would have taken my money and talked anyway, Charlotte thought as she looked at the piece of paper crumpled in her hand. She'd gotten the number of an undertaker from a colored nurse in the hospital's segregated ward.

"Go to the hospital and get him tonight," she instructed the undertaker after giving him the pertinent details. "Bury him in Evergreen," she said referring to the Negro cemetery in Richmond's East End. She didn't tell him Hank Whitaker was her daughter's husband, she told them she was paying for the burial because his family couldn't afford it. "We're not having a service. I'll come around tomorrow to pay whatever it costs." With that, she had taken care of the inconvenient remains of Hank Whitaker. Now she needed to take care of her family.

Charlotte heard a car pull up in front of the house. She drained her glass of sherry then frantically wiped the tears from her face, raked her fingers through her hair, and smoothed her dress as she went to the front door. When she opened it there was Margaret, looking dazed, smelling of vomit and sorrow. Charlotte did not recognize the man with her.

"My baby!" Charlotte said, attempting to embrace Maggie, who pushed her away.

"Where did you go? Why did you leave me?" Maggie said, turning her back to her mother.

"Thank you for bringing me home, James," she said to her escort.

"James?" Charlotte asked.

"James Stephens. He works for Hank. He was with Hank when - he took Hank to the hospital."

"I'm Margaret's mother, Charlotte Bennett."

"Ma'am?" James said, bowing slightly and removing his hat.

"I don't know what I would have done without you, James," Maggie said.

"Do you need me to see to Hank tonight?" he asked.

"I've taken care of everything," Charlotte said, putting her arm around Maggie and guiding her into the house. "Nothing left for anyone to worry with. You go on upstairs, Margaret. I just want to have a few words with Mr. Stephens."

Once Maggie was out of earshot, Charlotte turned on James.

"I need to know if Hank said anything to you about a will or the disposition of the business," Charlotte said, as if her son-in-law had died weeks, not hours, ago.

"Ma'am, this is not the time for that. I just lost my partner and my friend. I need to go," he said as he started to his car.

Charlotte caught his sleeve, "Partner? Did you say partner?"

"Ma'am, I am not going to discuss business with you now." James pulled away and continued to his car. "There will be time for that later," he said, choking up as he got into his car and pulled out of the drive. Charlotte watched James' car disappear down the street then stalked back into the house slamming the front door in frustration. *I am not going to wait for you to contact me, Mr. Stephens. I'll be at Hank's office first thing tomorrow.*

Maggie had only made it as far as the first step of the staircase, where she sat, draped against the balustrades.

"Where's Lance?" she asked. "Is my son here? He said he couldn't stay at the hospital, he had to leave."

"Don't worry, sweetheart, I'm sure Lance is fine. Let's get us both cleaned up," Charlotte said, as they walked up the stairs, Maggie leaning heavily against her mother.

"Frances," Charlotte barked. "Draw Miss Margaret a bath."

(IV)

Lance went directly to Del, the one person he always went to when there was trouble. When Charlotte moved in with Hank and Maggie last year, Del left the Whitaker household after nineteen years. She had raised Lance as far as she could and she was not about to start taking orders from Miss Maggie's momma. At seventy-five, her mahogany-colored face showed few wrinkles though her hands were gnarled and rough, and her knees creaked and ached from sixty-three years of cooking, cleaning and caring for white folks. What time she had left in life she planned to tend to herself.

Her plan was to live with her sister Charlene and her husband but Hank had surprised her with a house in Jackson Ward, the middle class Negro community in Richmond's East End. Del protested, but Hank was adamant.

"All these years you've made our home comfortable, now I want you to be comfortable in your own home," he'd told her. "It would mean everything to me, if you would let me do this."

Del finally accepted and her home was now as comfortable and welcoming as she was. It was her haven and it became the same for Hank. At least a couple of times a week he would stop by on his way home from his office for her cooking, and conversation he could only have with the one person who knew everything about him.

Occasionally, Lance would join them. Del would cook, and father and son would do the dishes while the three of them reminisced. That had been the plan for tonight. She had fixed one of Hank and Lance's favorite meals: chicken smothered in rich brown gravy, hot buttered rice, collards and mustard greens seasoned with onion and salt pork and cooked until just tender. Earlier in the day, from the peaches she had put up last fall, she'd made a peach cobbler for dessert and was about to put the cracklin' corn bread in the oven when she heard Lance's urgent knock.

"Would you give an old woman a chance to get to the door?" Del said, laughing as she opened the front door.

"You all must have a mighty appetite tonight. Where's your Daddy?" She asked looking past Lance; then she noticed the expression on his face. Del grabbed his arm and pulled him inside, "What is it, what happened?"

"Daddy's dead."

Del's hands flew to her mouth, tears filled her eyes. "Oh my Lord," she whispered.

"Hit by a car."

"No, no, no," she moaned.

"What do I do now, Del? What do I do now?" Lance asked, tears also filling his eyes.

"Oh my boy, my boy," Del said as he crumpled into her arms. She could not heal this wound; she had no sage wisdom that would soften this pain. All they could do was hold each other and cry out the hurt and loss that had come too suddenly to comprehend. Lance had lost a father, and Del, who had no children of her own, felt as if she had lost a son.

"Ain't the natural order of things, Mr. Hank is supposed to be here," Del said, as she led Lance into her small, tidy kitchen with its red gingham tablecloth and white lace curtains. The aroma of the dinner she had so carefully prepared for the people she loved filled the room. Their sorrow and the gaping hole that Hank's death left in their lives made the cheerful room seem dark and somber. Knowing that she would never see Hank Whitaker again filled Del with such sorrow that she felt like she could not breathe. She opened the back door to let the blossom scented breeze blow in from the garden then retrieved the pot of coffee that she always kept warm on the stove. Pouring a cup for herself and one for Lance, they sat at the table that was supposed to have hosted a dinner of good talk and great food and sipped the strong, hot coffee in silence.

Del looked at the man-boy sitting across the table from her. *Lookin' just like his daddy*, she thought. She wanted to tell Lance about the long talks and black coffee she and his father had shared on her back porch. Most of the time they talked about Lance's future—Hank's hopes and dreams for his only son. She remembered the night Mr. Hank told her he was passing. Did he ever tell Lance?

"His whole life was a lie," Lance said, breaking the silence. He looked down as tears again welled up in his eyes. *He told him*, Del thought, as she reached over and put her hand over the place on the table where Lance's tears fell, as if catching them would also capture his sadness. As Lance told Del about his father's confession, she avoided his eyes and said nothing.

"You knew?" Lance asked. He knew Del as well as she knew him. "He told you and not his own flesh and blood?"

"He wanted so bad to tell you, Lance, he just didn't know how to…" Del said.

"Bullshit!" Lance shot back.

"Watch your mouth when you're taking to a lady," James Stephens said, surprising both of them as he came through the open back door.

"What are you doing here?" Lance asked. James wanted to be the one to tell Del what happened. James had introduced Del to the Whitaker family before Lance was even born. James had known Del all of his life—she should hear about Hank from him.

"I came to tell Del about your Daddy," James said, his voice thick with sadness.

"Did he tell you too?" Lance asked.

"Tell me what?" James asked.

"That he was a nigger." It took James a single step to go from the doorway to where Lance sat in the middle of the room. He grabbed the boy by the shoulders, raised him to standing and pulled him to within inches of his face.

"Don't you ever," James said struggling to remain calm, "call any man, woman or child, a nigger," he spat out the last word. "Do you see Del sitting there? You show some respect."

"Did you know Daddy was passing?" Lance challenged James. He could see from James's expression that he had no idea. James let go and the boy dropped back into his chair. James rubbed his forehead and shook his head.

"I didn't know anything about this," James said, sounding dazed. "All I know is that your father is a good man, did the best he could by you and your mother. He did the best by all of us. My God," James whispered as he leaned against the table for support—first Hank's death, now this revelation – it was all too much.

Hank had helped James understand that no one should prosper from discrimination. He had been adamant about adding colored men to their work crews.

"Every man deserves a chance to feed his family," Hank told James, when he expressed concern about how their customers might react. "You let me know who has a problem and I'll talk to them," he'd said. Now he better understood why Hank begged him to buy into the company. If anyone had found out about Hank passing, James could take over and keep the company alive.

"The secrets we keep from each other," James said, collapsing into a chair, his head in his hands.

"Born a Negro, lied and lived as a white man, and in the end, died a Negro all the same," Lance said, his anger growing.

"If your father is any example, there are a lot worse things to be in life than a Negro. You carry his blood in your veins. You shame him, you shame yourself." James said, without looking up. At that moment, Lance realized that to James Stephens and every other white person in Richmond, his father's blood made him a Negro, too.

Getting up from the table, Del said, "James, you go on home now. We be all right here. The boy's upset, he don't mean no harm." She helped James to his feet and walked him out to the back porch where they talked for a few minutes in low voices.

When Del came back inside, wiping her eyes with the corner of her apron she said, "Your father would never allow disrespectful talk, Lance. Never heard a harsh word come out of his mouth about a person's color."

"And now we know why," Lance said.

"Don't you go forgettin' who you are, Mr. Lance Henry Whitaker," Del said using his full name the way she used to when he earned her wrath as a boy.

"Who am I, Del? You tell me, because I'll be damned if I know. How can someone you think you know be so, be such a—," Lance searched for a word.

Before he could say something he would regret, Del said, "Tonight be raw with emotion 'cause you loved your Daddy. I loved him too. That ain't never gonna change. He is who he always was, the father who loved you, more'n anything or anyone and the man who did right by us all. A truth told don't change that. Learn the reasons why he was passin'. With the knowledge, come understanding, and then forgiveness."

"Why couldn't he just die with the secret, instead of leaving me and my mother to deal with it?" Lance said.

"Secrets like that don't stay secrets forever, Lance. The truth—it shows up in unpredictable ways. Like when a baby's born," Del said, remembering how frantic Hank had been the night Lance was born—worried about Miss Maggie for sure—but after she found out Mr. Hank was passing, Del knew he was also worried whether their child would be born with color. Now his son would have that same worry. Fate had finally forced Mr. Hank to give his son his birthright—one that the boy was unprepared to deal with.

"Your father asked me to keep some things for you," she said. "Didn't want your Grandmamma gettin' into them. Wait here and I'll fetch them for you." Del left the kitchen and returned a few minutes later with three leather-bound journals tied together with a maroon ribbon.

"These here belonged to your Daddy," Del said with reverence. "In his own hand he put down some of the things he wanted you to know, 'bout the past and how he reasoned things."

"He gave these to you to read?"

"No, he gave them to me to hold, should something ever happen to him," Del said, choking on the words. "He said he wrote these just for you, just for his son, and I would never betray his trust by reading what was not meant for my eyes. Your Daddy told me he tried to explain it all here," she said, patting the stack of journals and handing them to Lance.

Lance got up from his chair; took the journals from Del and walked toward the open back door. Del reached for him but he pulled away, so immersed in his own pain that he was blind to her suffering.

"Del, you pretty much taught me everything I know about life, maybe now you can teach me how to be a Negro," Lance said as he went through the door, "'cause I sure as hell am not white after tonight."

9

(I)

S HE HAD FRANCES CHANGE THE sheets but the scent of her husband's bath soap, shaving cream and hair pomade combined to bring him back into the bed they had shared for twenty years.

"How could you, you bastard?" she cursed him. "Oh, Hank," she cried clutching his pillow as she loved, hated, feared and missed him until she was finally exhausted enough to sleep. By dawn, she had accepted her husband's death but had not forgiven him. She had talked herself into believing that Richmond would ignore the inconvenient truth about her late husband. After all, she was Margaret Bennett Whitaker; the celebrated hostess of Richmond's prestigious West End. President of the Richmond Women's League and the West End Garden Society, and a member of the social committee for the Virginia Historical Society. The city of Richmond, the West End community and her friends could not do without her.

The next morning, she carefully did her hair and makeup and dressed in black. With dark circles under her red eyes, she planted herself in the drawing room to await the arrival of her society friends. Surely they would come offering condolences and baskets of home cooked food prepared by their household help. She deluded herself into believing it would not matter to them what Hank had revealed—she was still Margaret Bennett Whitaker, her friends would understand that she and her son had been done an injustice. They would help her go on with her life.

While Maggie waited, Charlotte paced the room. She knew the sympathetic callers Margaret expected would never come. She was pragmatic enough to know that with the news of Hank's heritage, her daughter and her grandson would feel the full savagery of Richmond's very civilized society. She didn't get to where she was today by underestimating the insincerity of their social class.

Where is Lance? Charlotte wondered. She did not want to upset Margaret by telling her the boy had not come home last night. She swept aside the fear that some racist hothead had hurt him to atone for his father's deception the same way she had swept up the glass from the rock that had been hurled through the kitchen window early this morning with the message, *Get Out Niggers* wrapped around it. She was afraid to leave Margaret in the house alone with Frances. If something happened, in her current state, Margaret couldn't deal with it and Frances wouldn't know what to do unless someone told her. Charlotte was not going to let fear paralyze her family. She would remain calm, wait for Lance to come home and then go downtown to Hank's office to talk with James Stephens about how Colonial Enterprises would provide for her family.

As much as she derided Hank about being a janitor, Charlotte knew the significant financial value of Colonial Enterprises. Without Hank at the helm, Charlotte would have to take control—other women in Richmond were heading businesses bigger than Hank's. Adeline Detroit Atkinson presided over the Hotel Richmond and even Maggie Walker, a Negro, ran a newspaper and was president of a colored savings bank in town. Margaret was in no condition to take over Colonial and Lance was too young and racially compromised. They would have to send him north to school, immediately.

When a car pulled into the drive, Maggie sat up in anticipation.

"Frances, the door," she called. But before the maid could reach it, Lance burst into the room.

"Good morning, Ladies," he shouted, "guess what I found out last night?

"Excuse us, Frances," Charlotte said, dismissing her just as Lance blurted out, "In addition to the fact that I'm a nigger – pardon me, a Negro. I found out that Del already knew about Daddy! Damned if Daddy told her but didn't tell us! Not a word to his wife or his son, but damned if Del knew! Birds of a feather and all that shit."

Maggie gasped at Lance's crudely delivered revelation. Charlotte's only thought was, *who else knows? Does the whole of Jackson Ward know now?*

Lance staggered to the couch, fell onto the cushions next to his mother, and dropped Hank's journals on the table in front of them.

"I got all the answers to our questions in these little volumes right here," Lance punched at the books with his index finger. Charlotte moved in to retrieve them.

"No, no, no, these are for my eyes only," Lance said, snatching the books from the table and stuffing them under his jacket. "Daddy and Del say so."

"You're drunk," Charlotte said.

"Yes I am, thank you. Seemed the appropriate thing to do under the circumstances," Lance said.

"Where were you all night?" his mother asked.

"Over on the East End, my side of town. I need to start getting used to my new status as a Ne-gro," he said, accentuating each syllable of the word. "Oh," he said putting his hand to his mouth. "I probably shouldn't even be sitting here all familiar with you fine white ladies. I best know my place—"

"Stop it," Charlotte cut him off.

"Stop what?" Lance asked. "Telling the truth? Just like my Daddy did last night. Whether you want to accept it or not, Miss Charlotte, my life has changed forever!"

"Go get cleaned up," Maggie said softly, as she pulled a handkerchief from her sleeve and dabbed at her eyes. "I don't want any of the ladies from the League to see you like this."

Charlotte looked at her daughter,

"Margaret, no one from the League is coming. We are on our own now," she said.

"They'll be here," Maggie protested.

"No, they will not," Charlotte, insisted as she walked to the door. "We are no longer the kind of people the League ladies talk to; we're the kind they talk about. Lance, please do as your mother asks; I'm going out, I have to make plans for our future."

(II)

"Where's Mr. Stephens?" Charlotte asked the weeping woman at the front desk of Colonial Enterprises.

"I'm sorry ma'am," she said, "We're closed today. Our founder died last night."

"Is James Stephens here?" Charlotte asked again, as if she had not heard the woman.

"Well, yes, but we're closed today. Mr. Stephens isn't—" Before the woman could finish her sentence, Charlotte walked toward the back offices.

"Which office is he in?" she asked. The young woman pointed toward the office with the name "Henry Whitaker" on the door. Charlotte opened the door without knocking.

James was sitting at the desk, his leather chair turned toward the window. He slowly turned around to face his unannounced visitor. The only time he'd met Maggie's mother was last night, yet there was something familiar about her. Now he was certain he knew her, but from where?

"Morning, Mrs. Bennett," he said, "I wasn't expecting you; I'm still trying to grasp what happened yesterday. I was planning to come over later today to see if Maggie needed my help—"

"I see you haven't wasted any time. You've already made yourself quite comfortable in Hank's office, rifling through everything," she said, looking at the open wall safe and papers scattered on the desk.

James stood up and handed Charlotte an envelope.

"Something to tide the family over until we have a chance to get everything here sorted out. I thought this might be helpful," he said, ignoring Charlotte's suspicions. Charlotte snatched the envelope from James. He watched as she removed her gloves, dropped them on the desk, opened the envelope and carefully leafed through the bills, mouthing the numbers as she counted the cash. He had seen her do that before; he remembered a white envelope, her long, tapered fingers opening the flap and leafing through the bills, mouthing the numbers.

It all came back to him in an instant. Now he knew when and where. He remembered her dark hair, long and luxurious, today restrained in a tasteful bun. Her body, though concealed by a fashionable high-collared dress, was still voluptuous. Her face was unlined after almost four decades and just as beautiful. Her hazel eyes were as fierce as he remembered them. He could see that she had no memory of him at all, but he knew her; a man never forgets the first woman he ever made love to.

(III)

Albemarle County, Virginia - 1892

He stood in the doorway, not quite sure what to do next. After a night of drinking with friends from the University, it had been easy to talk James Stephens into going to Sally's Cathouse, for the express purpose of losing his virginity.

"You must be the college boy," she said, looking up from her book. "Come in, close the door. Don't be afraid, I don't bite. Unless, of course, that's what you want," she laughed as she closed her book. "Cut off, I mean, turn off the lights over there," she said, indicating the switch for the overhead light near the door. "What's your name, college boy?" she asked as she stood up and draped a sheer red scarf over the lamp giving the room a rosy glow. She wore her silk robe open, revealing her naked body.

James swallowed hard; his mouth so dry that his lips stuck to his teeth making it hard to speak. She waited for him to say something but after a few seconds—that seemed like an eternity to James—she said, "I'm Little Cora. You don't have to tell me your name if you don't want to."

"James," he finally managed. "I'm James."

"Hello, James. You want something to drink before we get started?"

"Yes, please."

She walked over to a table where there was a bottle of whiskey, a decanter of sherry, and a pitcher of water. "Other than me," she said coyly, "what's your pleasure?"

"Just water, please."

"Some of my older gentlemen need a little something to keep up with Cora," she poured water into a Mason jar glass and handed it to him. She looked down at the bulge in his pants. "But from the looks of you, I think you gonna be alright."

As James drank the water in one gulp, she stood close enough for him to smell her rose-scented perfume. He could see her clearly, even in the room's dim light. *She's younger than me. I thought a prostitute would be older.*

"You don't have to know anything," his fraternity brothers told him. "These women are experienced. They know what to do and they know how to do it. You just lay back and let the magic happen."

As promised, Cora handled James's awkward inexperience with the finesse of a seasoned professional. She took the empty glass from him and put it back on the table. Then she turned to face him and slipped her robe from her shoulders, letting it drop to the floor. She was unaffected as his eyes widened, taking in her body. She was the color of fresh cream, with long, dark, luxurious hair, beautiful hazel eyes and delicate, sculpted fingers. Her body was girl-thin but her breasts were woman-full and he desperately wanted to reach out and touch them. James had never seen a woman so boldly naked before. He had never seen any woman naked before, except in pictures.

"What's the matter, college boy?" She stepped even closer to him. "Cora got your tongue?" she whispered in his ear, as she loosened his tie and threw it onto the chair. She unbuttoned his shirt and peeled it off with his jacket. Gently, she pushed him onto the bed and knelt down to remove his shoes and socks. Then she unbuckled his belt, unfastened his pants and pulled them down with his underwear, leaving them in a heap on the floor. James lay on the bed, naked, staring up at the fringed shade on the ceiling fixture.

"Oh, my," she said, commenting on what she had uncovered. Gracefully, Cora straddled him, her long hair falling around them like a curtain. She positioned herself on top and guided him into her.

"I want you to take it easy, or you won't get your money's worth," she whispered. "I'll move real slow, until you just can't stand it anymore."

James closed his eyes, the scent of her filling his flared nostrils. He understood why men pay for this. When he opened his eyes to look at Cora, her eyes were open, her face expressionless. Their faces were only inches apart, but she was looking past him, as if he wasn't there. Gasping with pleasure, James laced his fingers in her hair and tried to kiss her, but she turned her face away. All the while her body moved rhythmically, but not mechanically, her face showing none of the pleasure he felt. She was somewhere else altogether.

Later, when he reflected on the experience, James realized that what he saw on Cora's face was boredom. The fact that she could accommodate a man in the most intimate of acts, while

DONNA DREW SAWYER

remaining so detached, made him appreciate her skill, but he
also wondered whether a woman like that could ever love a man.

James gasped, and shuddered—he'd lasted as long as he
could, which wasn't long. As soon as he climaxed, Cora rolled
off him and sat on the side of the bed with her legs crossed,
gazing at the darkness outside the open window.

After a few minutes, without turning to look at him, she
asked, "So how was your first time, James?"

"Unbelievable," he said. Cora looked over her shoulder
and smiled at him. What a magnificently beautiful woman,
James thought.

"So you'll come back and see Little Cora?"

"I'd like to," James said. Pulling himself up on his elbows,
he reached out to touch her, but she got up and put her robe
on, this time cinching it closed.

"James, do you have something else for Little Cora?" James
sat up and pulled the sheet to cover his flaccid penis. Did she
want him again?

"My envelope?" she said.

"Oh," James leaned over and retrieved his jacket. He handed
her the white envelope the woman at the desk downstairs had
given him after he paid. Cora took the envelope in her long
fingers, turned it over and opened the flap. She counted the
money, mouthing the numbers. When she finished, she tucked
the envelope into her robe pocket.

"Can I, I mean, may I ask you a question, James?" she said,
in voice that sounded more like the girl she was than the bold
woman she had just been. "Would you recommend a book for

me to read, something that you read in college?" Her request surprised him.

"Women don't go to the University of Virginia," he said, looking around the room for the rest of his clothing.

"I know that. But if I was a man, what would I read," she answered.

James thought for a second, "Dorian Gray, maybe? Everyone's reading it," he offered.

"Is that the name of the book, or the author?" she asked.

"*The Picture of Dorian Gray*, is the title; the author is Oscar Wilde," James said, impressed that she knew to ask that question.

"That's what you'd recommend if I want to," she hesitated for a moment, "improve myself?"

"Sure," James said. "Wilde is pretty popular."

"Oscar Wilde, author," she repeated, making a mental note. "Thank you, James," she said, regaining her experienced demeanor. "I'll leave you to dress; my next gentleman is due in 15 minutes." She walked to the bedroom door, "Goodbye James, come back and see Little Cora again, okay?" Without waiting for his response, she closed the door behind her.

As James dressed, he noticed that there were books stacked carefully on shelves in the corner of the small room. She had all kinds of books – most of them old and tattered. She had used literature, history, math and science text books and discards from the library. James picked up the book Cora had been reading when he knocked on her door, "A Guide to the Manners, Etiquette, and Deportment of the Most Refined Society." *She's preparing herself for other things*, James thought. If he ever did come back to Sally's, he would bring her a book, but he was certain that if he didn't hurry, Little Cora would be long gone.

(IV)

"Mr. Stephens!" Charlotte slapped her gloves against the desk, bringing James back to the present.

"I'm sorry, what did you say?"

"I want to know what you were referring to last night when you said you were Hank's partner. Colonial Enterprises was Hank's business."

"It's our business," James corrected her. "Hank started the business, but we grew it together."

"What are you talking about? Hank owned Colonial, and now my daughter owns it. You're just an employee," Charlotte said.

"Mrs. Bennett, Hank asked me to buy into the business more than a decade ago. You don't have to worry, Hank and I made sure that if anything happened to either of us, our families would be taken care of."

"I don't care what Hank promised you."

"It's not a promise. I have a legal and financial stake in this business. I'll discuss all of this with Maggie and Lance after she's had a chance to—"

Charlotte cut him off. "You'll discuss it with me, right now. I will be handling my daughter's affairs from now on, Mr. Stephens; she is the rightful owner of this company. You will take your direction from me." James sat down in his chair as Charlotte continued. "I will make sure Margaret retains ownership of her husband's business. I don't care what you and Hank cooked up. You don't want to cross me, you have no idea what I am capable of," Charlotte threatened.

"Is that right, Little Cora?" James asked. "When was the last time you saw Sally? Is the Cathouse still in business? It's been a long time since you made me a man there. A woman like you is impossible to forget. How did you like that book I recommended? What was it? Now I remember, *The Picture of Dorian Grey*, seems you took it to heart," James said as he got up and walked around the desk to face her.

Charlotte could not remember any of the men from the brothel. She had sex with them—it was never intimate, just a simple business transaction. James Stephens knew her secret, and he could use it to inflict even more damage than Hank's revelation.

Taking Charlotte's hand, he said, "You have the most beautiful hands; they are what made me remember you." Charlotte snatched her hand away from James.

"I don't know what you're talking about," she said, hoping her composure would convince him but the fear in her eyes gave her away. The two eyed each other in a silent standoff. Charlotte's fingertips dabbed at the sweat on her upper lip. She felt her knees weaken; she stumbled to a chair. She couldn't breathe; the air in the room was gone as soon as James called her Little Cora. She'd spent almost four decades forgetting that name and that life. Flushed and coughing, she pulled at the collar of her dress. James poured a glass of water from a decanter and handed it to her.

"You changed your name. Charlotte, I like it, suits the new you. You've done alright for yourself, Little Cora."

"Don't call me that," she said in a harsh whisper.

"Do not threaten me, Mrs. Bennett, and do not try to interfere with the plans Hank and I made for our company. I assure you, your family is well taken care of." As Charlotte drained the glass of water, James asked, "Would you like something stronger?" Charlotte nodded. James took a bottle of whiskey from the desk drawer and refilled her glass.

"I suspect your daughter and grandson don't know about your former occupation, and no one has to know, if you respect my partner's wishes. Can you do that, Mrs. Bennett? I don't want to see Maggie or young Lance suffer any more than they already have. After Hank, your revelation might be more than they can handle."

Charlotte narrowed her eyes, "You can't prove anything. No one will believe you."

"No, I can't prove a thing, but Richmond likes nothing better than good gossip, especially in your social circle. The Whitakers and the Bennetts will be all this town talks about for a good long time. Let's work together Mrs. Bennett, for everyone's sake. I'll come by to talk with Maggie tomorrow about the business and what Hank wanted," James said as Charlotte regained her composure and stood up to leave. "Allow me to see you to your car."

"Don't bother," Charlotte snapped.

"Not a bother," James said as he followed her to her car parked in the alley next to the building. "Is there anything I can do to help with funeral arrangements for Hank?"

"Nothing," Charlotte said. "I have taken care of Hank Whitaker."

James opened the car door and offered his hand to help Charlotte in. "Then may I offer my condolences for your loss?"

"Keep them," Charlotte said, ignoring his chivalry. When she tried to pull the car door closed, James held it.

"Isn't it strange how the past is never really past, Cora? All through life we leave pieces of ourselves with others and we never know when, how or if those pieces will come back to us. We all have secrets Cora, some more than others. Your secret is one of my most treasured memories," James said as he closed the car door. "I'd hate to have to destroy you and my cherished memory of Little Cora."

Charlotte started the car and drove down the alley to the street; she could feel rage and fear building in equal measure. As she waited for the traffic to clear, she looked in the rear-view mirror at James standing in the alley. *That smug bastard*, she thought. Yesterday she was a pillar of Richmond society, now Hank and his partner James Stephens were destroying everything she had achieved since she clawed her way out of that cathouse. She'd managed to make it from a fifteen-year old prostitute to a wealthy man's wife by seventeen and a rich widow by thirty-five. She pulled her car onto the street and floored the accelerator. *Time to run again.*

(V)

Maggie sat at the dining room table where she had hosted her famous luncheons and dinner parties. She looked down at her reflection in the highly polished cherry wood, she didn't recognize the mournful version of herself looking back. Maggie had always delighted in the fact that a place at this table was one of the most sought after invitations in town. Today, the only people willing to sit at her table were James Stephens and her mother and they were here to help her process her diminished place in Richmond society.

"Maggie, you and Lance can't keep Hank's share of the business. I don't have a problem with it, but no one will do business with us if we're owned by a Negro and a woman," James said. "I've got enough to overcome now that they know about Hank. I'll be telling the truth when I say I didn't know he was colored." James was uncomfortable saying this to Maggie. "Your husband was always fair with me and I will be the same with you." James handed Maggie the agreement he and Hank had for the business along with the company's most recent audit. Either partner had the option to buy the other out, at 50 percent of the company's current audited value.

"Look through these, we should get this taken care of as soon as possible. Hank's revelation could be...." he searched for the right words, "very disruptive to my business."

"It is not your business yet," Charlotte bristled. James warned Charlotte with a quick glance. Charlotte took the papers from Maggie and started combing through them.

James opened his briefcase, took out a check and handed it to Maggie.

"This should be more than enough until Lance is able to find a way to make a living for the family. Even with the market crash up North, Virginia hasn't really been affected so if we can keep Hank's situation under control we'll all be okay. If you need more help, you can always count on me."

"Buy this house," Charlotte said, surprising Maggie and James.

"Momma, this is my home. I'm not selling my home."

"Margaret, you don't have a choice. Lance can't stay here. There's a covenant in the West End, whites only," Charlotte said. Maggie looked to James for support.

"I wish there was something I could do to help, but the One-drop rule doesn't give you much choice about the boy," James confirmed.

"He's lived here all his life!" Maggie cried. Charlotte ignored her daughter and focused on the benefactor.

"You want to help, Mr. Stephens? Buy everything, for cash. This house, the cars, Hank's business—we want it all in cash and the sooner the better, for all of us."

❧ 10 ❧

(I)

WITHIN THREE DAYS OF DYING, Hank Whitaker was in the ground and a bitter memory to the people he loved the most. They didn't talk about him—all they thought about was what he had done to their future. Charlotte, Maggie and Lance sat in the "Whites Only" waiting room at Richmond's Main Street train station. Every time a passenger came through the doors, Charlotte held her breath, afraid someone aware of Hank's secret would challenge their right to be there. She cursed Hank for putting her family's privilege in question.

Virginia's Racial Integrity Act against mixed marriages made Margaret a criminal and Lance a Negro and a bastard. These facts and the rocks hurled through their windows with hateful, threatening notes attached were enough to convince Margaret and Lance to leave Richmond. They boarded the train and took their seats in the "Whites Only" First Class car. When the train departed the station, Charlotte, Maggie and Lance all exhaled. They were fugitives, each in his or her own way. Lance was eager to end his short life as a Negro, Maggie would not pay for her crime of miscegenation and Charlotte's life as "Little Cora" was once again buried.

(II)

With Hank's money, Charlotte saw unlimited possibilities. Her mind reeled. There was a whole world out there; they could be whomever they wanted to be. They would take the train to New York, then book passage to Europe, and never return to this side of the Mason-Dixon Line. They would make a new life as wealthy expatriates; just like the stylish Americans she had glimpsed on her past trips to Europe. They would settle in Paris. No one there would know, question, or even care who they were. They'd be moneyed Americans, that's all. Hank's revelation and James Stephens' recognition had shaken her, but she was still on her feet; it would take more than two men to knock Charlotte Bennett down.

She looked down at her hands, tightly wrapped around the handle of the leather satchel, filled with the generous sum James Stephens had paid them for Hank's share of the business, along with the inflated purchase price James paid for the house and the car. *Guilt money*, Charlotte thought, *for stealing my daughter's business.* To that sum she had added her inheritance from her late husband. She had been a banker's wife and knew that financial institutions took a patriarchal attitude toward women so she held all of her assets in cash. Though she had no money in the market she knew that the financial troubles in New York would eventually affect the whole country. The cash gave her total control. With Hank's money, and her inheritance, they had enough to start over in a way that would attract the kind of people that attracted more money.

Hank ended up doing right by his family, Charlotte thought. For just a second, she felt a tinge of remorse over the last errand she'd run that morning. She alone had presided over Hank's burial. With the scent of freshly dug earth in the air, the two gravediggers lowered the plain pine coffin into the new grave.

"Are you sure you won't be wantin' a marker for the grave?" the undertaker asked her a second time. "Evergreen's sixty acres, Mrs. Bennett. If you ever want to find this grave again-" Charlotte shook her head, no, before the man could finish.

"Then will you be sayin' a few words before they close the grave?" he asked, hoping this woman was not as cold and heartless as she appeared. Again, Charlotte declined.

"Just cover him up," she said. "Cover him up good."

(III)

When Del did not hear from Lance or get notice of his father's funeral service, she put on her straw hat and took the streetcar to the Whitaker home, only to find Frances, Charlotte's longtime maid, packing up.

"They gone," Frances said, her words echoing through the nearly empty house. "Took the train out this morning."

"Took the train out to where?" Del asked, looking around at the wake of Hank Whitakers' life.

"North, I suspect. Didn't ask, since I ain't goin' with 'em," Frances said, letting out an exasperated sigh as she continued with her work. "After all these years, I am too old and too tired to put up with any more of Miss Charlotte's 'Frances do this, and Frances do that.'"

"What are you going to do now?" Del asked.

"They left me with a nice little piece of change for packing up, and all my years of service, and they *was* years of service I tell you. I saved a good bit, 'cause Lord knows I never had time to spend any of the little money I've been making all these years. Didn't get no house like you did," she said, her resentment evident. "But I'm gonna be comfortable, thanks for askin'."

Del ignored Frances' remark. She was hurt that Lance left town without telling her. "Did they already have the service for Mr. Hank?" she asked.

"Weren't no service that I know of," Frances said. "I'd ask Mr. Stephens, the one who worked with Mr. Hank? He bought the house, and the cars, and I think he gave them some travelin' money, too. Miss Charlotte sure was in a hurry to get outta here. You'd a thought she was the one with the secret." Frances paused. "You know about Mr. Hank passin', right?"

"I know," Del said.

"That's all folks talkin' about."

Del turned to leave, there was nothing for her here.

"Say, Del, almost forgot," Frances said, pulling a crumpled envelope from her apron pocket. Del recognized her name in Lance's handwriting.

"The young man gave this to me, asking if I would get this to you. I was gonna give it to Mr. James, so he could carry it over to Jackson Ward. No offense, but it ain't safe for a white woman in those parts."

Del ignored Frances' slight and took the envelope.

"You take care, Frances," Del said as she walked to the door.

"That's my plan."

Del waited until she was on her own back porch to open the envelope. Inside she found a letter wrapped around a few hundred dollar bills.

Del,

Please take care of yourself. I have my father's journals. Maybe one day, like you said, I'll understand and forgive.

Love,
Lance

≈ 11 ≈

Richmond to New York—March–June 1931

(I)

WITH THE TRAIN SAFELY OUTSIDE of Richmond, and encouraged by the gentle rocking of the coach and the warmth of late spring, the three travelers succumbed to exhaustion from the past few days. They rested fitfully, but easier, knowing the truth was behind them.

Charlotte awoke just before the train reached Washington, DC. She looked over at Margaret sleeping beside her, pain consuming her beautiful face. *This is why I never gave all of myself to any man,* Charlotte thought. *They use your body, take your soul and then betray you. Get over him,* Charlotte willed her daughter, but she knew that losing Hank, her home, and her coveted place in Richmond society had irreparably damaged her daughter. *She's like her father, never had to strive for anything. Nothing earned; everything given. Makes you weak.*

Walton Wainwright Bennett III, Charlotte's late husband and Margaret's father, was the weakest man she had ever known; which is why she chose him. Ten years her senior, his most attractive feature was that he was the son of a prominent Richmond banking family. Once they'd had sex, he never questioned who she was or where she came from, easing her transition from a young prostitute to rich man's wife. Throughout their marriage, she used her sexual prowess to control her husband. It was ironic that he died from a heart attack after sex, leaving her a very wealthy widow. At fifty-four she no longer sought or needed comfort or confirmation from men. Her solace and power were derived from the ability to control her circumstances. In most instances money, not men, proved to be her most reliable resource.

Charlotte watched Lance staring out of the window. She hoped he didn't intend to fulfill the promise he made to his father to find the Whitaker family. When she told Lance that they were leaving Richmond, he did not question her decision. All he wanted to know was when they would have his father's funeral.

"Where do you propose we have it?" Charlotte asked, neglecting to tell him what she had arranged for Hank's burial. "No respectable church in Richmond will allow it. Who would come? You? Your mother? Del? Now that James Stephens has what he wants, he won't bother. Hardly seems worth the expense or trouble for a man who did what he did to his family," Charlotte said. "I've already taken care of things, Lance. Nothing more needs to be done." She remembered how vacant his eyes were when he went back into his room to finish packing. She was grateful that he hadn't brought the subject up again. *Lance will be fine,* Charlotte decided, *we all will.*

(II)

From Washington D.C. to destinations north, passengers were no longer segregated. During the train's stop at Washington's Union Station, Negroes filtered into the empty seats around the white passengers.

A young Negro man startled Lance as he settled into the adjoining seat.

"Where are you headed?" he asked. A colored man addressing a white man, absent a direct question and neglecting to add "sir" at the end of his inquiry was dangerous behavior in Richmond. It took Lance a second to remember he wasn't in Richmond anymore and, he wasn't a white man.

"Uh, my family and I, we are on our way to New York."

"I'm on my way to Boston, I'll be a student at Harvard University in the fall," he said proudly. "Are you in school?"

"No, not yet," Lance said. "I'm accepted at the University of Richmond and Washington and Lee.

"I see," the young man said as he shifted in his seat then pulled a book from his bag. The mention of two of the South's most prominent segregated educational institutions made Lance's views on race clear.

"How did you come to go to Harvard? How can a Negro go to a college for whites? Shouldn't you be in a school for coloreds?" Lance asked.

"Harvard has been educating Negro men since 1870."

"Since 1870?" Lance repeated, perhaps in Richmond his exposure to what was going on in the rest of the world wasn't sufficient preparation for life anywhere else.

"If you'll excuse me, I have some reading to do," the young man said ending the conversation.

———⟫●⟪———

Lance surreptitiously watched the young man beside him, as well as the other colored passengers. *These Negroes are different* he thought; they dressed and even talked like whites. He had been around Negroes most of his life but they had been household help or the laborers his father hired in his warehouses. His parents hadn't raised him to revile people of color, he just never thought about them. Racist attitudes were prevalent among his peers so, like his friends, Lance assumed that all Negroes, with the exception of the few he knew personally—like Del—were ignorant, inferior, and irrelevant. *Now that everyone knows my Daddy's a Negro, do I have to be one too? What if I don't look for his relatives in Virginia? They don't even know I exist, they would never know the difference.*

Lance looked at his reflection in the train window. *I still look like a white man; I still feel like a white man. I only know how to act like a white man. That had been enough to make my father white to everyone, even my mother. Why can't I do the same thing?* Lance wondered. *What did Daddy say? He wanted my life to be as smooth as silk, that's what he wanted for me.*

The train lurched, forcing the young man's shoulder against Lance, who instinctively brushed off his jacket where they had contacted each other. The young student looked at Lance with disgust and muttered something under his breath as he gathered his things and moved to another seat.

Lance remembered what his father had said about not hating that he was colored, but hating the way he was treated because he was colored. It almost made him want to apologize to the young student for his insensitivity. *I don't know how to be colored,* Lance thought. He and the Harvard student shared the same racial heritage but even if he wanted to, Lance could not relate to the young man. *There's no advantage to embracing Daddy's heritage, finding his brothers and atoning for secrets and sins that were not mine. Why should I take on my father's burden?*

Lance straightened his jacket, rubbed his face with both hands and pulled them through his straight sandy colored hair. *I am white,* he told himself, *I've always been white and I'll always be white and I'll take every advantage that being white affords me.*

(III)

"Try the Waldorf Salad," Charlotte demanded as the family sat in the lobby restaurant of the Waldorf Astoria hotel. "It's a favorite of mine." After Walton's death, Charlotte had been a guest of the hotel whenever she travelled to New York; it was one of the few hotels that allowed a woman to register without her husband.

"You've barely eaten since we arrived in New York, Margaret. Lance, what else will you have?" she asked, looking around the restaurant to see if there was anyone worthy of her attention. "I hope you realize how fortunate we are. Everywhere you look there are people who don't have what we have. They lost everything when the Stock Market crashed. I never believed in the Market, I insist on keeping my money in cash, that's how we've managed to kept it all," she whispered sharing her great secret. She put a gloved hand on Lance's arm in an extravagant gesture. "Pour me another glass of champagne, darling." Like most of New York, the Waldorf Astoria ignored prohibition; after their ordeal, Charlotte was enjoying their freedom from Virginia's smothering rule of law.

Charlotte sipped her champagne in silence for a few minutes then said, "I want both of you to know that I've arranged everything. Without a stitch of help from either of you, I might add. I've made all the plans, shopped for everything we'll need and neither of you have seen fit to acknowledge my efforts. But tomorrow you have a chore. I want you to get rid of all of those old, provincial clothes you brought from Richmond. From now on we will be expected to keep up appearances." "For who?" Lance asked. "No one here knows or cares who we are, Charlotte." Since they left Richmond, she had insisted Lance call her by her first name, complaining that a young man calling her "Grandmamma" made him seem too young, and her too old.

"The proper term is 'for whom,' and I can assure you the right people *will* notice," Charlotte said, taking another sip of her champagne. "We'll be making our official debut in a couple of days," she said.

"What are you talking about, Momma?" Maggie asked.

"We leave for Paris, France, day after tomorrow," Charlotte said, beaming at her daughter and grandson.

"France?" Lance asked.

"Why not?" Charlotte asked. "If we are going to reinvent ourselves, let's really reinvent ourselves; get as far away from who we used to be as we can."

"I'm not sure I'm up to an overseas adventure," Maggie said.

"I'm not asking your permission, Margaret," Charlotte said and leaned into the table, continuing in a low, urgent whisper, "All you've done is wallow and wail over the legacy that husband of yours left you. If you had been more discerning, we would not be in this predicament, but no matter now. We are not going to sit here and wait for fate to take its course—we will set our own course."

As they had every day since Hank died, tears welled up in Maggie's eyes. Charlotte sighed, opened her purse and handed her daughter a linen handkerchief.

"Why not?" Lance said. "Let's go to Paris. I could use a new identity." Charlotte smiled as she looked around the nearly empty restaurant,

"Waiter," she called to the first server she saw. "More champagne, we're celebrating!" The waiter nodded and hurried to fill Charlotte's order. Though Lance and Maggie didn't yet know about it, she was also celebrating her family's newly acquired identities, courtesy of the United States Department of State. Though the U.S. had not required passports for its citizens since 1921, France required expatriates to have one. Charlotte had carefully filled out applications for her daughter and grandson and sent the hotel courier to expedite their new identification. On the paperwork, she made a change that she had wanted since the day her daughter eloped with Hank Whitaker.

The passports with their bright red covers arrived the next morning, giving worldwide access to Mrs. Margaret Bennett Withers and Mr. Lance Henry Withers. When the three of them boarded the French ocean liner, *Île de 'France*, for Le Havre in July of 1931, even if Maggie or Lance had wanted to correct Charlotte's final insult to Hank Whitaker, it was too late. By changing just a few letters in their surname, and burying the man in an unmarked grave, Charlotte had finally managed to erase all evidence of Hank Whitaker from the face of the earth.

☙ 12 ☙

Atlantic Crossing—Summer 1931

(I)

THE FRENCH LINE'S SS *Île de 'France* was the trans-Atlantic ocean liner of choice for first-class passengers who preferred the intimacy of a smaller ship. Charlotte was convinced that with fewer passengers in closer quarters, she would disembark with important and valuable acquaintances after their six days at sea.

Hoping to meet some of the famous passengers she had heard were onboard, Charlotte convinced Lance to join her on an exploratory tour of the ship. Maggie, claiming exhaustion, stayed in their two-stateroom apartment.

"I've heard people say that this is the most beautiful ship ever built by the French Line," Charlotte said, admiring the grand foyer that rose four decks high. Lance picked up one of the brochures that described the features of the ship.

"It says here that all the furniture and art are Art Deco style."

"I read about that new style of décor in *House Beautiful*."

"Introduced in France after The Great War," Lance read.

"Just like we will be," Charlotte laughed.

"Funny," Lance said then continued his narration of their tour from the brochure, "The first-class dining room is the largest of any transatlantic ship—three decks high with a grand staircase." Charlotte imagined herself making a grand entrance. When they toured the first-class library and salon, Charlotte also imagined having intimate conversations there with her new, well-connected friends.

"They have a state-of-the art gymnasium, a bowling alley and a shooting gallery. They even have a merry-go-round," Lance marveled.

"Aren't you a bit old for that?" Charlotte asked.

"Maybe not," Lance said, feeling more playful than he had in months.

"Let's go up to the sun deck," Charlotte said, hoping there would people she'd want to meet there.

The sun deck offered a spectacular view of the ship's distinctive red smoke stacks and they arrived just in time to bid Lady Liberty goodbye as the ship sailed out of New York harbor. Lance felt excitement displace some of his sorrow, and relief dislodge a bit of the resentment he felt toward his father. *Charlotte is right*, he thought, *a new identity is just what I needed*.

"Goodbye New York, goodbye United States of America," he said, realizing the momentous change he was making.

"Good riddance," Charlotte said into the wind as she turned her back on the coastline and looked toward horizon.

(II)

Lance had his father's lean six-foot frame, sandy hair, and now the same sadness in his green eyes. In just the past year his boyish looks had smoothed out into a handsome elegance that belied the fact that he had just turned eighteen. His polite manner, a staple of his Richmond upbringing, only enhanced his good looks. It took less than a day onboard for other passengers, especially the women, to wonder about the mysterious, well-dressed young man roaming the first class decks and salons. Even before his life became someone else's, Lance was mature beyond his years. He'd spent most of his time in the company of adults, and never much liked the behavior of his peers. In Richmond he had been so focused on the entrepreneurial life, eventually running Colonial Enterprises, that he had never considered anything else. Now he wasn't even going to college. His father's duplicity had taken all of that from him. He now hoped exposure to new people, places and ideas would help him find a new purpose in life. Maybe his plan was the same as his father's, just let life happen and hope it did not get ahead of him.

On the second day of the voyage, after learning that this was the young man's first trip abroad, the steward brought Lance several European magazines and newspapers to prepare him for what the continent could offer a young American with money. The cache included several issues of *In Transition*, an

English-language magazine published in France that reviewed current art and literature in Paris. The magazines featured the work of authors and artists Lance had never encountered in conservative Richmond: James Joyce, Pablo Picasso, Gertrude Stein, Man Ray, Marcel Duchamp, and others.

As he sat on the sun deck in the early morning, engrossed in the magazines, a woman took the deck chair next to him. Looking over at what he was reading, she said,

"Ah, you had better not let anyone see you reading such salacious material, young man. Magazines like that are inconsistent with the quest for ignorance that seems so prevalent at home these days. Those are the words and pictures of the Lost Generation, `la génération du feu, s'il vous plait`."

Lance was not sure if she was providing a warning or a reprimand, and the last part, what had she said in French? "The lost generation? The general de fue?" he asked, looking around to see whom else might be watching him mangle her words.

"Ah yes, the generation of fire," the woman said, ignoring Lance's imperfect French. "May I see who is in this issue?" She put her hand out, like a teacher collecting contraband from a guilty student. Lance complied with the mysterious woman's request.

While she scanned the magazine, Lance studied her. Her large slightly hooded green-grey eyes, upturned nose, full lips and cleft chin conspired to make her stunningly attractive. The wind swirling around the deck played with the mound of dark curls piled high on her head, succeeding only in extracting a halo of wisps which she periodically brushed away with her small gloved hand. She was small in stature like his mother, but there was a stylish simplicity about her elegant clothes and simple gold necklace and earrings. Both Maggie and Charlotte overdressed to make their wealth obvious and seemed to delight in taking the term bejeweled to the extreme. *Demitasse*, Lance thought as he watched the woman. The word he had only recently learned came to mind as he watched her examine the pages of the magazine with authority while keeping a running commentary. *Strong coffee in a small, delicately elegant vessel.* Years later, when he thought back on their first meeting he would remember how amazingly intuitive his first assessment of her had been.

"Oh my, James Joyce. His books are banned in the United States you know. Gertrude Stein, where do I begin with her and Alice?" she said in mock disapproval. She fanned the pages of the magazine, "Oooh, Picasso and Kandinsky, the work of my friends Pablo and Wassily, what do you think?" She held up a color photo spread.

Lance was not sure how to react. "Ma'am, I find it interesting, but I haven't had much exposure to art. Maybe you can tell me what you think."

"Only after we've been formally introduced," the woman said playfully, as she handed the magazine back to Lance. "I am Belle da Costa Greene. You'll find some of my fondest acquaintances in the pages of that magazine, every one of them a proud member of the Lost Generation. I love to see someone so young interested in the arts at any level. Tell me, who are you young man."

"My name is Lance Whit – ers. . . Withers," Lance said, stumbling over his new last name. "Lance Henry Withers. I'm, we're, my family and I, we're traveling to Europe, my first trip," he added, awkwardly. Belle extended her hand and Lance, not sure whether to shake it or kiss the back of it, jumped to his feet, took her hand and did both. Belle was charmed and amused.

"Do I detect the hint of a southern accent?" she asked.

Lance, unsure of how to respond, nodded slightly, "I live in New York, but my family is from the south," he lied.

"So, this is your first trip abroad?" Belle asked. "How exciting. This will be, oh my, I'm afraid I have made too many crossings to count. Perhaps I can tell you a little of what to expect. What are your interests? Literature, art, music, architecture, the food—oh, the food in Paris is fantastic! Tell me what you'd like to know."

"I'd like to know everything, Miss da Costa Greene. Tell me first about this Lost Generation of Fire you mentioned, and the things this magazine writes about?"

"First, you must call me Belle. Miss da Costa Greene is so formal," Belle said, flirting.

"Belle," Lance said, liking the name and the woman. "And I'm Lance."

"Now, that's better. I love talking about my bohemian friends," Belle said. "It's a dangerous move to get me started."

————◆————

For the next two hours, she held Lance's complete attention with her tales of expatriate and European artists and writers in Paris. Lance had read Hemingway and F. Scott Fitzgerald, and here he was talking with a woman who actually knew them. Lance had never seen a Picasso or a Matisse. Richmond's only museums were the conservative and narrowly focused Museum of the Confederacy and the Virginia Historical Society. Belle da Costa Greene gave Lance a new perspective on the colors and the lines that made the images in the magazine richer than his initial, shallow understanding. Belle told stories about the men and women who painted, drew, sculpted, wrote and collected art in Paris, enlivened by the city's politics and patronage as well as the *liberté, egalité, fraternité* that living in France offered. Belle and Lance made plans to meet again the next morning to continue their conversation.

On their third day at sea, Belle suggested that her young friend dine at her table that evening. Her interest in Lance now extended to an education of another kind.

"There are people joining me tonight that I know you will enjoy. They are friends who also love the arts. I think it will be nice to have another young gentleman at the table."

Belle Greene's written invitation to dinner arrived at the Withers' cabin before Lance returned from lunch. Maggie had once again taken to her bed, so Charlotte received and opened the envelope even though it was addressed to Lance. When Lance returned to the cabin, she greeted him with, "Who is this woman, and why is she inviting you to dinner? Do I know who this woman is?"

"I know who she is," Lance said, picking up the invitation from the table where Charlotte had dropped it. "This is addressed to me, and you opened it?"

Charlotte ignored Lance.

"Charlotte, why did you open this when it was clearly addressed to me?"

"It doesn't matter who opened it, you won't be accepting an invitation from a stranger. The wealthy have to be very careful," she added, picking up her cup of tea.

"She's not a stranger to me, Charlotte. I've already told Miss Greene that I will be dining with her and her friends this evening."

"Then I will decline on your behalf."

"Charlotte, you do not decide who I associate with. Please stay out of my business," Lance said as he took Belle's note and headed to his stateroom.

"Your business is my business," Charlotte called after him as he closed the door. She was not used to having her authority challenged by her grandson. She always attributed any behavior that was inconsistent with the way she wanted him to act to his father's negative influence. Since his death she had taken every opportunity to reiterate that point—as well as a great deal of satisfaction in confirming she had been right about Hank all along.

Charlotte rang for the steward. Encouraged by a generous tip, he was happy to share what he knew about Belle da Costa Greene, the powerful librarian for the Pierpont Morgan Library, and a bona fide member of New York's glitterati. The steward regaled Charlotte with society page accounts of Belle Greene's visits to the Opera, parties on the moneyed North Shore of Long Island, and her access to the wealthy families in New

York and abroad. Miss Greene was a frequent trans-Atlantic passenger and her many friendships and affairs with artists, writers, critics, and patrons in the art capitals of Europe were well chronicled. *Why have I never heard of this woman before?* Charlotte wondered. The steward had provided well known facts about Belle Greene but Charlotte needed more. An additional tip and his patron's eager attention was all it took to further loosen the steward's tongue and he shared the salacious gossip and innuendo that people in service always have access to. Though Miss Greene claimed that she was from a prominent family in Richmond, Virginia, he'd recently heard rumors, well founded, he assured Charlotte, that Belle da Costa Greene was really a light-skinned Negro passing for a white woman.

Charlotte knew Belle da Costa Greene was not from Richmond. She knew everyone who was anyone in that city. The woman was hiding something and that was useful information. Despite her questions about the woman, Charlotte marveled at Belle Greene's access and independence. Perhaps Miss Greene could offer them entre into the world of which Charlotte wanted so desperately to be a part.

Charlotte sent a note regretfully declining Miss Greene's kind invitation, she could not possibly let her grandson dine, unescorted, with strangers. Miss Greene replied with understanding and, as Charlotte had hoped, suggested that rather than decline her invitation, the rest of the family accompany Lance. She also mentioned that Mr. Walter F. Chrysler of Detroit and Miss Peggy Guggenheim of New York would be among the guests at her table that evening.

Charlotte was ecstatic. Her first invitation of the voyage, courtesy of her grandson, and he had achieved it without her assistance. Perhaps there was more than one way to elevate her family to grace and favor.

(III)

To Lance, the dinner conversation was more intoxicating than the champagne that flowed throughout the evening. Talk of European politics, the expatriate community in Europe, art, music, Belle's quest for manuscripts for the Morgan Library, economics, and banking swirled around the table at a dizzying speed. Lance was in awe of the knowledge, money and power present that evening. He did his best to keep up and, with what he'd learned from his recent conversations with Belle, he even managed to contribute to the discussion.

Charlotte knew the dinner guests at Belle Greene's table were the anointed and informed. This was not a Richmond society dinner party where she could dominate the conversation. Politics, business, regional and national events were men's talk in Richmond. Social gossip, gardens, fashion and decorating had been her purview. Intimidated by her dining partners, Charlotte was unaccustomed to being an observer rather than the center of attention.

Still depressed and mourning Hank, Maggie was barely able to maintain small talk with her dinner companions. When dessert arrived, she excused herself saying she was not feeling well. Believing the other guests would think poorly of her if she did not accompany her daughter, Charlotte offered her regrets and returned to the family's cabin with Maggie; however they both insisted Lance continue to enjoy the evening without them.

The group moved to the Grand Salon for more drinks, dancing and conversation until the early hours of the next day. At the end of the evening, Lance, ever the gentleman, escorted Belle to her cabin. Hours of chaste conversation and polite dancing would not satiate Belle's appetite for the young man, or Lance's curiosity about Belle.

"You're not a virgin, are you?" Belle asked, as soon as they were inside her cabin.

"No Belle, I'm not," he said, trying to keep his voice even.

"Not that it would be a problem," she said, setting her purse on a table, "I am an excellent teacher."

"And I have always been a gifted student," Lance said, as he watched Belle slowly take down her hair. Lance reached out tentatively touching her long fawn-colored locks. Belle leaned her head against his hand, her eyes on him.

"I like gifted students. Please make yourself comfortable," she said indicating the bed that dominated the stateroom, "I'll be with you in minutes." She kissed the palm of his hand, turned him around, and pushed him toward the bed.

Lance's mind was racing; he was not sure what to do. Wait for her to return? Undress and climb into her bed? Lay on top of the bed dressed or in some degree of undress or, naked? When Belle opened the bathroom door a few minutes later, Lance was sitting, fully clothed, in a chair next to her bed. Belle was naked, her long hair cascading over her breasts. She laughed as she approached him.

"Well, you don't look very comfortable."

"I wasn't sure what you meant. I did not want to be presumptuous," he stammered.

"Presume. Please," she said, as she helped him remove his jacket, starched collar and tie. She unbuttoned his shirt, revealing his toned, hairless chest. She ran her fingers across his smooth skin and sighed at the beauty of his youth. Lance needed no further encouragement, it took him mere seconds to remove the rest of his clothing and join Belle in her bed.

"I'd like us to enjoy each other," Belle said as she pulled Lance close. She drew in a long breath when her hand felt how glorious he was. "I want us to learn how to give each other pleasure," she whispered, knowing this would not be the last time they would be together. She guided him to places that excited her and reciprocated by exploring his body in ways that, she knew from her experience, he would appreciate.

Belle was not one of the shy, teenage southern belles with whom Lance had previously explored sex. She was confident and passionate, slowing him when his exuberance confirmed his sexual inexperience. Lance enthusiastically complied with her every request. He realized that sex with a woman was nothing like the blind, hurried, probing that boys and girls attempted to relieve their sexual tension. *Surely, this was not the same function*, he thought. *If this is sex, then I am a virgin.*

After she exhausted him, Belle let Lance sleep until the sun began to glow at the edge of the horizon. With a deep and full kiss that was yet another revelation to him, she woke him and whispered, "You must leave before we give the gossips more to talk about."

Lance pulled Belle close, invited by her open dressing gown. Belle watched him as he explored her with his hands and his eyes. She enjoyed the pleasure Lance took in her body. Belle was about to turn fifty, though she would only admit to being a decade younger and could easily pass for that. He made her feel young, something she longed to experience again. *We can give each other something*, Belle thought. *He needs my knowledge and experience, and I need his youthful admiration.*

"There is so much I'd like to show you, teach you," Belle told Lance, as she helped him dress.

"And so much I am eager to learn," Lance assured her. He would be hers for the summer, she decided.

"We will dine in my cabin tonight, we will be each other's dessert," she said as she turned him out into the hall and closed her cabin door.

One of the stewards startled Lance with a pat on the back; he hadn't noticed the man approaching in the narrow hall. What had happened to him in the last few hours? For the first time since the night his father died, he had not thought about who he was, where he came from or what he'd lost. He did not want to break the spell Belle had cast; he wanted this excitement and anticipation to last beyond a few hours. He wanted something to look forward to instead of looking back with regret on what had been his life.

Lance walked out on to the deck to watch the sun reveal itself. The air was damp, and he could taste the salt of the sea in the mist. He sat down on a deck chair and a steward hurried over to offer him a blanket to stave off the chill of the brisk morning. Lance refused; he could not feel the cold, just the warmth, the heat, the fire that was Belle da Costa Greene. Looking out across the water to the horizon, Lance thought he saw lights in the distance.

"How long before we dock?" he asked the steward.

"Oh sir, we have another three full days at sea. In a hurry, are you?" he asked.

"Not at all," Lance answered. "I want this journey to last forever."

(IV)

Charlotte and Maggie were in the onboard apartment's salon when Lance returned that morning. Maggie lay on the sofa with a blanket covering her. She chose to ignore the fact that her son had not slept in his own bed the night before. Charlotte took note and decided to take the matter up with Lance later.

"Come son," Maggie said, patting the sofa next to her. "Sit with me. Did you go dancing after dinner? When your father would take me out we would always go where they had dancing. He was a wonderful dancer, are you like your father?" Her voice caught in her throat and her eyes glistened with tears.

Lance quickly moved to another topic, "You know me, Momma, I'm a talker. I spent most of the evening with Walter

Chrysler. His father is one of the most powerful men in the country, owns a car company in Michigan, but they're moving the headquarters to New York, to what will be the tallest building in the world. Walter is going to manage the entire building for his father."

"He seems rather young for a job like that," Charlotte chimed in.

"He just graduated from Dartmouth, and he's going to Paris to buy art and have some fun before he starts work. He's invited me to spend some time with him in Paris and then visit him in New York. Everyone at the table last night is on a buying trip. Miss Guggenheim, she's from New York, collects modern art, and Belle, she's buying manuscripts for the Morgan Library."

"So it's *Belle* now?" Charlotte asked. Without responding, Lance got up and began grazing on the remnants of Charlotte and Maggie's breakfast service.

"I'm starving," he said, then continued to talk about his evening with Belle's friends.

Maggie watched her son, his enthusiasm, the way he could not stay seated when he spoke, how these new people intrigued him. He reminded her so much of Hank. She missed her husband, and the more she thought about what he did and the reasons for his deception, the less she blamed him. She no longer cared what the rest of the world thought about her husband, or her marriage. Hank had been a wonderful husband, and a good and generous man to her family, the people who worked for him and the community they lived in. He had given her an amazing son that they both adored. Tears spilled onto Maggie's cheeks in a steady stream.

"Momma, Momma, you've got to stop this," Lance said, wishing he knew how to help her heal.

"These are tears of joy, son," a half-truth. "I am so happy that you've found new friends. We could all use a distraction. I'm just happy for you, that's all."

Charlotte, watching from the other side of the salon, said, "Your Momma's tired Lance—you can fill her head with more tales later."

Lance took a handkerchief from his breast pocket and dried his mother's tears, then put his arms around her and planted a kiss on her cheek before heading off to his stateroom.

"He looks so much like his father," Maggie said as she watched him close the door.

"Don't start, Margaret," Charlotte warned. Maggie buried her face in the blanket to muffle her sobs. "It has been four months now. You need to forget Hank. He's gone, and I say good riddance."

"He was my life," Maggie said.

"I warned you, that first night he showed up on our porch like a stray dog. I warned you that he was not our kind."

"I don't care what you think anymore. I can't hate my husband just because he was a Negro. My son is a Negro too and I will never forsake my son. Momma, why did you teach me to be prejudiced?"

"I never taught you to be prejudiced," Charlotte said, surprised by her daughter's accusation.

"You allowed me to be that way," Maggie said. "You let me believe that Negroes were inferior, that because we're white we're better than everyone. But we're not, are we? It's because of Hank, a Negro, that we have all of this," she said, looking at the opulence around them. "It is because of Hank, a Negro, that I have Lance. Hank was the best thing that ever happened to me. I don't care about your rules anymore. I will not look down on my own son, or his father."

"They are not my rules," Charlotte said sharply. "I'm just forced to live by them, and if you truly love your son, you will too."

"I just want my husband back," Maggie moaned.

"That can't happen," Charlotte said impatiently, "So you had better pull yourself together and make something of the rest of your life, Margaret." Charlotte took her daughter's face in her hands. "You're still beautiful and young enough to marry again. If you keep the secret the Hank kept, you can give Lance a father and you'll find a husband worthy of both of you, but only if you play by the rules. Nothing but pain can come from Hank's confession, can't you see that?"

Maggie pushed her mother away and buried her face in her hands. She had spent half of her life with Hank, four months wasn't enough time to even begin to forget him. She thought about what Hank would have wanted. *He always wanted me to be happy*, she thought, remembering that the last thing he said was that he loved her. She could carry that love in her heart and still carry on. A few minutes later, when she raised her head, she knew what she had to do.

"Momma, for Lance and for you, I will keep our secret. I will play by your rules."

(V)

On the fourth day of the voyage, the choppy seas and cool, rainy weather kept most passengers in their cabins. Charlotte used the time to consider her next move. She thought about Belle Greene's behavior at dinner the previous evening—her attraction to Lance was obvious. Charlotte knew from experience what lust and seduction looked like. When Lance did not return to his bed last night, she was certain Belle had acted on her fascination. *Belle Greene and Lance shared a lot more than an interest in art*, she fumed. Being a pragmatist and an opportunist, Charlotte considered the value in Lance spending time with Belle and her friends. These were people she wanted her family to befriend—the renowned, wealthy and cultural elite. If Belle had bedded her grandson, there was not much she could do about it, except use it to her family's advantage.

After their three months in New York, Charlotte realized it would more difficult than she imagined to integrate New York society at the same level she enjoyed in Richmond. There she had successfully married her way into society. While money could call attention to them but it was not enough to gain them entrance to society on Belle Greene's level in New York and Europe. High society was still paternalistic—the only way in was on the arm of a husband or a father and they had neither method of access. If Belle Greene could provide Lance with introductions and affiliations, the family could do more than spend their money to glimpse high society, they could join it.

Yes, Charlotte thought, perhaps she could exploit Belle Greene's secrets and her salacious interest in Lance to her family's benefit.

———➤●◄———

"Where were you last night?" Charlotte asked Lance, as he was leaving the apartment later that morning.

"Charlotte, I am past the age of consent and as I told you yesterday, I want you to stay out of my business. Excuse me, I'm meeting Walter Chrysler for coffee," he said attempting to leave.

"Lance," she said grabbing his sleeve, "we need to talk about you and Belle Greene."

"I will not discuss her with you, Charlotte," he said pulling his arm away. "I can handle my personal relationships without assistance from you."

If Lance will not discuss this relationship with me, the lady involved might be more receptive, Charlotte thought after Lance left. She rang for the steward and asked him to locate Miss Greene. When he reported that she was alone in the First Class passengers' library, Charlotte dressed quickly and went to find Belle Greene.

———➤●◄———

Without an invitation, Charlotte sat down next to Belle.

"It was very gracious of you to invite us to dinner last evening. My daughter, grandson and I had a delightful time with your other guests. I hope you will forgive Margaret and me for departing early. Since the death of her husband, Margaret is rather frail."

Belle looked up from her reading, smiled, nodded graciously then returned to her book. Indifferent to Belle's desire for solitude, Charlotte continued, "Is it true that you are originally from Richmond, Virginia?"

Belle looked up from her book to see Charlotte waiting for her response. "Why yes, Mrs. Bennett, by birth and by breeding."

"I am originally from a prominent Richmond family myself. Perhaps our families are acquainted with one another," Charlotte said.

Belle closed her book and addressed her intruder. "I don't recall anyone in my family mentioning the Bennett name."

"Nor do I recall my family ever mentioning your family name; Greene, with an 'e,' is it? Is your Richmond connection through your mother or your father?"

"My mother. Now if you don't mind, I would like to get back to my reading," Belle said.

"What was your mother's maiden name? Perhaps we knew her by that name?" Charlotte continued.

"Mrs. Bennett, why is my genealogy of such interest to you?" Belle asked.

"I just find it fascinating that both of us are from Richmond. It's a very small, some say incestuous, social circle. It would be nearly impossible for our families not to have known each other." Charlotte paused, and then rose to her feet. "I will let you get back to your reading. My intention was not to disturb you, simply to thank you for your generosity. I'm planning to wire my dear friends in Richmond to tell them about your generous invitation and what a wonderful dinner hostess you were. Surely, one of them will remember you and your family from your time in Richmond. Please enjoy your day, my dear," she turned to leave, not waiting for an answer. After a few feet, Charlotte stopped and turned back to Belle, "Let me just say that you are looking particularly well-rested today. I suppose you already know that my grandson did not return to his own bed last night. At just eighteen years of age, perhaps his judgment about such things is not what it should be. I had hoped the lady, being more mature and certainly wiser, would have shown more restraint." Without waiting for a response from Belle, Charlotte quickly returned to her cabin.

Within the hour, the steward delivered a note addressed to Mrs. Charlotte Bennett:

> *Please join me in my cabin for lunch at 12:30 p.m. today. There are obviously matters of some importance you would like to discuss.*
>
> *Belle da Costa Greene*

(VI)

While Charlotte was out, Maggie had a chance to talk to her son alone. Over lunch, Maggie listened to Lance talk more about the world he was discovering through his new acquaintances. He had met Walter Chrysler for coffee that morning and they talked more about his art collection, the artists he knew personally, and what he hoped to acquire on this trip. They also talked about the social scene in Paris, and Walter invited Lance to join him to see some of the city.

"Walter and Belle Greene are staying at the same hotel we are in Paris, the Ritz," Lance said then took a bite of his *Croque Monsieur*. "I know this is just a ham and cheese sandwich but the way the French make it—"

"Lance, please don't talk with your mouth full."

"Sorry," he said swallowing. "I had no idea what we were in for when Charlotte insisted we leave Richmond but now I think this will be good for us. Maybe I'll buy some art and become a collector."

Maggie put her hand on her son's arm to get his attention, "I need to talk to you about your father," she said.

"What is there to talk about? He died," Lance responded.

"Yes," Maggie said, "He died and we've avoided talking about him because we were both hurt; he was taken from us so suddenly. I know I've been selfish, with my own grief. I haven't taken care of you at all," she spoke haltingly trying to keep from crying.

"I'm fine," Lance said, pushing crumbs around on his plate. "Charlotte said to forget him. Maybe we should just do that," he said, sounding like a hurt child.

"Can you forget your father, Lance?" Maggie asked. "You were so devoted to each other."

"He lied to me his whole life, to the people he claimed to love—he lied. What does that say about the man? The last thing we learn about him, the very last thing is that he was a nig—" Lance couldn't bring himself to say the word. "Yeah," he finished, "I have to forget him."

"Lance, please. Does it really matter what your father was? Isn't *who* he was more important? Your father was kind, he was loving, smart, hardworking. Remember those things about him, the important things. They're what made us love him."

"He also lied about who he was, where he was from. Every day we knew him, he lied to us. His whole life was a damn lie. Doesn't that matter?"

Maggie looked away for a moment. "It doesn't have to. We can forget about that part. It was seconds in an otherwise perfect life."

"Do you understand that my father took everything from me? My home, my name, my future? Colonial Enterprises wasn't just Daddy's business it was my future. I can't even go to college, what do I do with my life now?"

Maggie did not know how to respond to her son's valid questions.

"And look what he did to his brothers. We didn't even know he had a family. He claimed he was no one from nowhere and now we know that was a lie too. Should I do what Daddy asked me to do? Should I find his brothers, share what we have? He made me promise to find them, knowing that if I did it would ruin my life. He would have me live as a Negro, something he was never willing to do."

"He didn't want to ruin your life; he just wanted you to have family, your uncles to help guide you."

"The only thing a colored man can do is teach me how to be colored. I've never been colored, why would I do that now?"

"I don't know what to do, Lance. I don't know what's right anymore," Maggie said. Lance took his mother's left hand and fingered the gold band that Hank had placed there more than twenty years ago.

"You should take this off. You're not a wife anymore, and I am no longer my father's son. The people that we were no longer exist. I am Lance Henry Withers and you are Margaret Bennett Withers—we are what Daddy always led us to believe he was. We aren't from anywhere. We have no past, no provenance — all we have in the future."

Maggie thought about the question her mother always used to start her conversation with strangers, *Who are your people?* Charlotte would judge them based on the answer—that's what she did to Hank the very first time she met him. Now Maggie realized she and her son, for fear of harsh judgement, dare not answer that simple question.

Lance got up from the table, went to the window and looked out at the endless grey ocean.

"We may not know exactly where we're going, but I am not confused about who I'll be when I get there," he said. "I'm going to live like my father did, with all the privileges of a white man." Lance walked back to the table and knelt in front of his mother.

"We are the Withers family now. We left the Whitakers in Virginia. If we accept who Daddy was, and what his blood makes me, we lose everything. You know what a Negro's life was like in Richmond. As soon as our neighbors found out what Daddy was, what that made me, they hurled rocks through our windows delivering a clear messages about my future, 'No niggers in the West End' and 'Get out, nigger.' Your best friends acted as if you died along with Daddy. We will never get back everything we lost, but we can make a new start. My skin color gives me the advantage my father wanted me to have. His heritage was his secret, now it's mine and only by passing can I live fully with the legacy my father left me."

"What did you do with your father's journals, Lance? May I see them? Maybe they'll help me understand what happened, why he had to leave his family, where he was from, what happened to make him run from that life."

"I burned his journals," Lance said as he stood up and walked back to the window. "I didn't want to read his lies. I burned them so no one else would ever read them."

"Oh Lance, your father wanted you to know his thoughts, his history. You will regret what you did one day."

"I doubt that," Lance said as he turned to face his mother.

Maggie looked at her son, his eyes were cold, his mouth set. Everything that had happened since Hank's death was imprinted on his face. He was not who he used to be, and he was not who he would become. Maggie resolved to get stronger. She had to keep him from becoming bitter, cynical, calculating and cold; from becoming Charlotte.

"Lance, I know that we're on an abrupt, strange journey because of your father's death. I know you've only had Charlotte to rely on these few months, because of my selfish neglect. I'm sorry I haven't been available to you. Today that changes. I'm your mother, I love you, and I want you to grow into the best man you can be. Things will settle down. We will make a new home in Paris, just like we had in Richmond. We'll be a happy family again," Maggie said.

Lance heard his mother, but her words were just air. She had never really been there for him. She had abdicated that responsibility to Del, who had also betrayed him when she kept his father's secret. Lance resolved to never again depend on anyone; he would make his own way. He would design his own destiny and create his new life. Lance Whitaker died the same night his father did. Lance Withers was just coming to life.

(VII)

Belle opened a bottle of champagne while she waited for Charlotte Bennett to arrive. What havoc could this woman cause in her already tumultuous life? Would she really contact acquaintances in Richmond? If she did, the tale Belle had spun would surely unravel. There were already rumors about her ancestry. Once a whisper, they were now more audible than ever in New York society. She feared the talk would weaken her standing at the Morgan Library. After J. Pierpont's death, when Jack Morgan made her the first director of the Pierpont Morgan Library, she knew she was at the peak of personal power and influence. She also knew the appointment made her vulnerable. Exposing her lies would be costly to her and very valuable to her enemies. The social mischief Charlotte Bennett threatened could compromise Belle's glorious, privileged life. A few facts or fabrications placed in the right ears by the wrong person would fan the flames of gossip and she did not need that kind of illumination right now.

She knew her stunning looks and the small fortune J.P. Morgan left her would evaporate with time. Her plan was to retire from the Library in a few years, but in the interim, she needed to maximize her earnings and her value in the art world.

Yes, she slept with the young man. Lance was clearly past the age of consent. In Europe, such liaisons were an ordinary, glorious aspect of life. *Americans are so provincial when it comes to sex*, she thought as she poured herself another glass of champagne. Lately, her appetite for art and sex was voracious for the same reason – the opportunity to enjoy both was fleeting.

(VIII)

Charlotte knocked on the door of Belle's cabin at exactly 12:30 p.m. Belle Greene received her as a snake charmer would engage a cobra; cautiously, so as not to be bitten. Hoping to dilute her venom, Belle offered Charlotte a glass of champagne,

"To toast a new friendship," she said, as she poured the wine into crystal stemware.

"To a new alliance," Charlotte replied, as she picked up the glass and downed the contents with her eyes on Belle.

No amount of flattery will deter or distract this predator, Belle thought.

The two indulged in small talk as the steward served their lunch. After he excused himself, Belle asked, "What is it that you want from me, Mrs. Bennett?"

Getting right to the point, Charlotte said, "Is it true, what they say about you? Is it true that you are passing?"

"Again, my background seems to be of extraordinary interest to you." Belle said.

"Because I require your assistance with a similar matter," Charlotte said. "In some respects, I have taken my family as far as I can with my limited Richmond upbringing. That became apparent to me last night in the company of your fine friends. Due to my late son-in-law's duplicity—he was also passing—my grandson finds himself in a predicament similar to yours. His mother is too weak and broken by the revelation of her late husband's ancestry to assist in our family's advancement, so Lance and I must ensure the family's future." Charlotte took a sip of tea and nibbled for a moment on a petit fours that had been served for dessert.

"I could see at dinner last night that you recognize many aspects of my grandson's potential," she continued. "I would like you to help him maximize his potential, help him move, as you did, to the next social tier. You seem to have navigated it all so well. I need you to help him overcome disadvantages similar to your own. You can guide him, help him avoid the pitfalls."

"Mrs. Bennett, you don't know anything about me. Why do you think you can ask this of me?" Belle tried to gauge what Charlotte was prepared to do.

"You can teach Lance about the world you and your friends inhabit. Introduce him to people who can help him gain access into the same society you thrive in, so he can make his way as you have. You will do this because I can offer you the validation of the Richmond heritage you claim, and we both know, cannot confirm. I offer you confirmation in exchange for mentoring my grandson. And you will, of course, keep this arrangement just between us. Lance is never to know about it." Charlotte poured herself another glass of champagne and waited for Belle's response.

For a few moments, Belle could only stare at Charlotte in astonishment.

"You're blackmailing me, Mrs. Bennett?" she finally asked. When Charlotte did not answer Belle said, "I am fully aware of the talk that surrounds me. It does not deter my friends and, though it may fuel my foes, I doubt your confirmation or contradiction will have any effect on my life."

Charlotte put her glass down, folded her hands in her lap and looked down for a few seconds. When she looked up at Belle, her eyes had gone from merely cold to menacing.

"How certain are you of that statement, Miss Greene? As I mentioned, my son-in-law was passing, unbeknownst to my daughter and me. If I had known, or even suspected, I would have exposed him. So you see, I would have absolutely no qualms about exposing you, if I have to." Charlotte looked at

Belle, not wanting to miss her reaction. "You have no idea what I am capable of when it comes to preserving my family's future. My request is simple and costs you nothing. I have merely asked you to provide a few introductions for my grandson. You can do this for a young man you seem so enamored of."

Belle had already decided to indulge in Lance while she was in Paris for the season. His attention was flattering, especially as she drifted into middle age, unmarried and childless. Even without the threat and burden of this woman, after taking Lance into her bed, she wanted him. He was young, handsome, and eager to learn all that she knew about art and, as he demonstrated last night, the carnal aspects of life. He would not be her first protégé. What harm would it do to remain in his company while she was in Paris? It might benefit her reputation and Charlotte Bennett was right, Belle did not know what this woman was capable of.

"You leave me with little choice," Belle finally said. "However, did it occur to you to simply ask me to mentor your grandson, rather than make threats?"

"No," Charlotte said, in the same cold, flat tone that she had used to issue her threat. "No, it did not."

(IX)

Charlotte returned to the family's cabin, satisfied that the bargain she'd struck with Belle da Costa Green would benefit everyone concerned. She could not have crafted a more perfect scenario, especially since Belle had not challenged her. *Matters of race are so easily exploited*, she thought.

Lance was lying on the sofa reading in the apartment salon when she opened the door. "So there you are," Charlotte said, when she saw him. "What do you have there?"

"Belle shared this book with me. It's by an author she said is banned in America and some parts of Europe." He closed the book and showed Charlotte its spine. "D.H. Lawrence. Have you heard of him?"

Charlotte ignored Lance's question. She was still a voracious reader, at another time she might have been interested, but right now she had something more important on her mind.

"I know you had relations with Miss Greene," she said, as if she were talking about the weather.

"I've already told you I am not going to discuss that aspect of my life with you," Lance said.

Charlotte plowed on, "You think because you're eighteen you are old enough to conduct that part of your life without any advice from me. However," she continued, "there are things about your intimacies that we must discuss." Charlotte did not give Lance a chance to respond. "Your behavior last night confirms that you know how to perform the act. That usually comes naturally. Did your father explain how to protect yourself from fatherhood and disease? If not, I can find someone to explain things to you."

"That will not be necessary," Lance said.

"Well, at least he did that right," Charlotte said. "My concern is of course for your health, but also for your status.

If you father a child, even with a white woman, there is a chance—a very good chance—that you will have a Negro child." She paused for a moment to make sure the impact of her statement resonated, "You could be as lucky as your father and have a white-looking child, like yourself, but there are no guarantees. One dark-skinned baby could ruin everything for all of us," Charlotte said.

Lance remembered Del saying 'secrets don't stay secrets forever, like when a baby's born.' *Yet another consequence of my father's deception*, he thought, *one that will rule the rest of my life.*

"Thank you for everything, Daddy."

⤌ 13 ⤍

Europe 1931

(I)

L ANCE SPENT MOST OF HIS first year in Paris in the company, and the bed, of Belle da Costa Greene. He accompanied her to parties and salons with her artist, writer and musician friends. There were also moneyed art patrons from both sides of the Atlantic at these gatherings; always escorted by a contingent of gallery owners and art critics who influenced what treasures the wealthy bought while enriching themselves and their reputations in the art world. These were the people that helped fuel the frenzy of creativity in Europe after the Great War and Belle da Costa Green, as the director of the Morgan Library, with plenty of Morgan money to spend, was royalty within this aristocracy. She introduced Lance as her "young friend" and they both enjoyed the attention that they drew as an unlikely couple.

The primary reason Belle was in Europe was to acquire several illuminated manuscripts for an exhibit the Morgan Library was planning in conjunction with the New York Public Library. She spent long days doing research on religious art, attending lectures and buying at auctions. Belle's scholarly activities did not hold much interest for young Lance and left him time to explore his new home before meeting Belle each evening.

In Richmond, everything was familiar and prescribed; he'd been certain of how life would unfold without much input from him. In sharp contrast to his birthplace, acclimating to his new home forced Lance out of his cocoon of tradition and complacency. It was up to him to become whatever he wanted without the constraints and expectation of what he was supposed to be.

As he mastered the language and learned to navigate the city, Paris spiraled out before him visually and culturally, its history older but somehow more relevant than that of his birthplace. Paris never let him forget where he was from; the intersection of French and American history was everywhere. At 56 *rue Jacob*, a few blocks from where the family eventually rented an apartment, Benjamin Franklin had negotiated and signed the Treaty of Paris freeing the colonies from British rule. Lance often walked by the site on the Champs Elysées where almost two centuries ago, Thomas Jefferson lived as Minister to the Court of Versailles before the French Revolution. The Conciergerie, where Marie Antoinette spent her last days, still stood on quai de l'Horloge as majestic testimony to how the American Revolution helped to spark the will of the French people. The replica of the Statue of Liberty on Grenelle Bridge on the Île des Cygnes, an island in the river Seine, faced west to raise her torch to the American people. The statue was the twin to the majestic east-facing lady that had waved Lance goodbye as he sailed out of New York Harbor. Would he ever return to America? Or would he be a man with no home forever?

(II)

When Belle left Paris for several weeks to do more research and buying for the Morgan exhibit, Lance was left to discover other aspects of Paris. Walter Chrysler was still in town and Lance accompanied him on his eclectic and frenetic art acquisition sprees where he bought, traded and bargained for art like it was a common commodity. Unlike Belle who was academic and cautious in her approach—buying only what complemented or enhanced the library's collection—Walter seemed to have no specific acquisition strategy. He bought quality artwork on impulse and in great quantities with no qualms.

"Walter, I can't tell whether you collect for love or money," Lance said.

"Both," Walter replied, "Why buy one Cézanne when you can buy two and leverage that purchase to come away with an exquisite Tissot for nearly nothing?" As they sat in a gallery while the owner carefully wrapped Walter's latest acquisitions for shipping back to the U.S., Walter leaned into Lance to share a great insight. "I buy against the market. Before an artist is hot, or after, but never in the heat of it," he wagged his finger in warning. "Art is cyclical, like the stock market—well, the market before Black Tuesday. When everyone is buying an artist I sell, when everyone is selling an artist I buy. If you know art, if you have a good eye, great timing and the money to be patient, then you wait and you will eventually be rewarded. I let others pay a premium to be fashionable; I'm collecting for the long term."

"Anything in particular?" asked Lance whose knowledge of collecting art was limited to the Frederic Remington and Earl Bascom cowboy bronzes and prints his maternal grandfather once collected. Charlotte sold the collection in its entirety before her husband cooled in his grave.

Walter pulled out a gold filtered cigarette, put it between his lips without lighting it and leaned back on the elegant deep purple suede sofa that fit the art royalty that was the gallery's clientele.

"I want my collection to be encyclopedic, art from all over the world. One day I'll have my own museum," he said, draping his arm across the back of the sofa and tapping his fingers on the sculpted wood edge. "Being rich has distinct advantages, doesn't it?"

"I wouldn't know," Lance surprised himself by admitting that fact. Perhaps the champagne they had been drinking for the past couple of hours had lowered his guard. "I have an inheritance that won't last forever. I'm going to have to figure out something to do soon."

"In this Depression if you have anything, especially cash, you can figure something out. When I get back to New York, I'll be on the lookout for something we might be able to do together," Chrysler offered. "Remember when everyone is selling that's the time to buy."

At this point in his life, Lance was too pragmatic to be interested in investing any of his inheritance in art. He was learning from his new friends that you didn't collect art to make money, you made money then collected art, and right now, he was doing neither. He was postponing any decision about his future by spending his nights in the Creole and Caribbean clubs in Montparnasse and the jazz clubs in Montmartre with Walter and his friends. The club scene offered him escape from the constant burden Maggie and Charlotte had become. His mother and grandmother had done little to make their own friends. They didn't even try to speak the language so they avoided the French and found fault with everyone in the expatriate community. They expected Lance to be available to accompany them on all of their outings. Between Belle, Walter, his mother and Charlotte, Lance's only profession was escort and bon vivant.

(III)

With Belle out of town, Maggie was grateful that Lance spent more time at the family apartment.

"It is such a treat to have you join us for breakfast," Maggie said to her son who, like his grandmother, had his head buried in the *Paris Herald* and the *New York Herald Tribune* reading the latest news from the states.

"The Depression has hit the south hard," Lance said. "People are moving north."

"I guess we're not going home anytime soon," Charlotte added.

"What has that got to do with us?" Maggie asked, "We can afford to go back. We have enough money for a few years—especially now with everything so inexpensive."

"Money is not the issue, Margaret," Charlotte said. "What if we run into someone from Richmond? We cannot risk that, we don't know what is waiting for you and Lance. Staying in Europe is our only option." Lance hadn't bothered to respond to his mother and Charlotte returned to her reading.

Maggie had no interest in reading or hearing about the bad news from home. She was determined to go home soon, if not to Richmond, then at least to Washington or New York. *We are wasting our lives here*, she thought. She and Charlotte shopped and strolled – that is all they did. She hated seeing Lance stumble in from the clubs nearly every night, sleep until midday, then get up only to repeat the previous day's activities. *He should be in school*, she thought, then remembered the man her son was today had no records to prove he was anyone. No record of his birth, his baptism, whether he ever went to school. And the honors and accomplishments that had made his parents so proud were for a son who no longer existed. Maggie then realized she had no record of her marriage, the home she and Hank owned or her husband's life or death. She really didn't even really know who Hank was and it was obvious her son had no plans to keep his promise to find his father's family. *This existence is like vapor, a dream, there is nothing of the past that I can hold on to.* Maggie looked across the breakfast table at Lance and Charlotte. *They are all I have left in the world*, she thought. *I cannot lose one more thing, not one more thing.*

(IV)

When Belle returned to New York in the fall, she and Lance corresponded frequently about what was going on in New York and the mood of the country as the Depression tightened its grip. Belle's letters mentioned how tens of thousands were losing their jobs as banks and businesses failed. Even though the Morgan Library had a significant endowment, Belle now had to have every trip and purchase approved by the entire board of trustees. She didn't return to Paris until the spring of 1933. She was on her way to Venice, Milan and Florence to do research and to acquire several manuscripts for the Morgan Library holdings. Afterward, she planned an extended stay at a villa owned by a former lover who was also a renowned art critic. His art library and collection rivaled many academic institutions and she could justify her time there to the Library as a research trip. Belle's friend was in the United States indefinitely but he encouraged his friends to enjoy the villa in his absence.

"Would you consider accompanying me to Italy?" Belle asked Lance as they lounged in her bed during an afternoon of lovemaking. "You need to get out of Paris every now and then—there's so much more to Europe. We could leave in a few days and be gone for the summer. I have to return to New York in the fall and I don't know when I'll be able to come back."

"I was hoping you'd ask me to join you," Lance said, pulling Belle to him.

"I'm afraid you'll have to manage your own travel and accommodations, except at the Villa where we will be guests. The budget the Library has me on these days is not generous enough for two."

"Belle," Lance said, surprised that she would think he would agree to any other arrangement. "I am quite capable of paying my own expenses – with or without money," he laughed as he fondled her breasts.

He's lost some of that youthful innocence that was so attractive, Belle thought. There was a maturity—or was it arrogance?—that he had acquired since she last saw him. She had heard from friends that he had done some travelling with Peggy Guggenheim and still saw Walter Chrysler when he was in Europe. He was fluent in French now and knew Paris better than she did. However, Lance still seemed to be in search of who he would become.

"Should you speak with your family first?"

"I'll tell my mother and Charlotte that we're going," Lance said, letting her know that the familial cord had been severed.

———⟫●⟪———

In the family's large apartment in a Haussmann style building, in the heart of Saint-Germain-des-Prés in Paris' Sixth Arrondissement, the maid silently served the family croissants and coffee. Lance finished the newspaper before telling his mother and Charlotte that he and Belle were scheduled to leave for Italy by train the next morning.

"What are we supposed to do while you are traipsing around Europe with that woman?" Charlotte responded to Lance's news.

"Charlotte, you'll do what you normally do. You don't need me to enjoy the shops and museums. I'll be back soon enough."

"I'm not sure this is a good idea," Maggie said, always afraid something or someone would take him from her.

"I'm not a boy, Mother. You can't hold me by the hand forever. At some point, I need to make decisions more substantive than what bar to go to tonight and where I'll escort you and Charlotte tomorrow. I'm going to Italy with Belle. I will keep in touch as much as I can throughout the trip, I promise," he said, getting up from the table. "Who knows, I may even return a little wiser and with some idea of how I might take care of us in the future."

They had been living on their inheritance for more than two years. Lance still had not come to terms with his future, and how he planned to fulfill his financial responsibility to the family. He was still mourning his past. He hoped this respite in Italy would help him take his next broad step into manhood.

(V)

After visits to Venice and Milan, Lance and Belle settled in as guests, along with several other couples, at the Villa

I Tatti near Florence. It was owned by Belle's former lover, the renowned art historian, Bernard Berenson. The plan was to stay the summer, so Belle could do research in the Villa's extensive 140,000 volume library, write and relax from the stress of running the Morgan Library. They would return to Paris in late September and then Belle would go back to her work in New York.

They arrived at the Villa in time for dinner with the other guests and then retired to a suite of rooms that were, in Lance's opinion, grossly over-decorated.

"Is everything here religious art? I've never seen such grim works. Where's the vitality and vibrancy we saw in Paris? Could they have gotten just one more image of Mary and baby Jesus, a monk or a cross into the décor somewhere?" he asked. "I feel as if I'm being judged from every angle. It is just too much," he said as he draped his arm around a Bernini sculpture in the corner of their suite. Belle walked over to him and gently removed his arm from the shoulders of the marble bust.

"You could have damaged it, Lance. You don't really know what you're experiencing here do you darling? Taste is something one acquires with study and exposure. Yours is somewhat limited so I advise you to keep such opinions to yourself," she said. "I adore you for who you are, not for what you know."

The next morning while Belle slept in, Lance went down to the estate's Roman inspired pool for an early swim. Amid the columns on either end of the pool, Lance saw a man who looked to be in his late twenties, just finishing laps.

"You're new," he said in English with a thick Italian accent. "I'm Arturo, I saw you at dinner last night. And you are?"

"Lance."

"Lance. I like it—very masculine. Your real name?"

"Of course."

"Just asking. Who is your sponsor? Male or female? Not that it matters. It is better if you can accommodate both."

"My sponsor?" Lance asked as he took off the robe he wore over his swimming trunks and dropped it along with his towel on a chaise longue at the edge of the pool.

"You know, who did you have to fuck to get here?" Arturo laughed. Only then did Lance realize what he was asking.

"No, it's not like that," he said. "Miss Greene and I are friends. She's not my sponsor, I'm not her—"

"We're all whores darling; they pay, we play. You're young and pretty," he said, looking Lance up and down. "Very smart to take care of the body—it is your moneymaker," he added, playfully popping Lance on the behind with a towel. "Our bodies are all we have—they are certainly not interested in what is up here," he tapped a finger to the side of his head. "This is what holds their interest," Arturo said as he stripped out of his wet swim trunks and provocatively dried his privates before putting on a terry robe.

"Need to hurry back," he said as he gathered his things. "She likes Arturo in the morning too." As he started up the stone steps to the main house, he called back to Lance, "Save your money, darling. Our good looks won't last forever. See you at dinner."

Arturo's assessment stunned Lance just as Belle's remark about his taste in art had the previous evening. He dove into the water, slapping it with hard strokes, he powered to one end of the large pool then turned and pushed off with such force that he shot to the middle and surged to the opposite end to repeat the process. The more he thought about Arturo, probably not his real name, the angrier he became. Belle's comment about adoring him for who he was, not what he knew infuriated him in retrospect. *They all think I'm a gigolo.* He swam harder and faster, lap after lap, assessing who he had become in the past couple of years—a gigolo and a hanger on. The people he knew in Europe were not his friends, they were friends of friends. He contributed nothing to their existence; his absence in their lives would probably go unnoticed, yet these superficial friendships were all he had.

Finally exhausted, Lance pulled himself out of the pool and lay panting on the stone deck. When he finally caught his breath, he jumped up, grabbed his robe and, still dripping wet, ran back to the room.

(VI)

Belle was on the balcony overlooking the gardens, reading, her face shaded by a large straw hat. A tray with fruit, biscotti and coffee was on the table next to her.

"I had them bring breakfast," she said. "After last night I needed some sustenance." She laughed and looked up to see

Lance, still wet from his swim, dripping on the tile floor of the balcony.

"I was just informed that I'm your whore."

"Really?"

"Really," Lance said. "Is that what people are saying? Is that what you're telling them?"

Belle put her book down and reached out to him, "Dry your face, darling. Put your robe on before you catch a chill and sit. Have some breakfast before the coffee gets cold."

"Answer me, Belle."

"First you must understand that the sexual mores are different on the continent than they are at home. We are helping each other," she said. "And the truth is, dear Lance, that we *are* using each other. Not in the strictly transactional way some of the guests here are, but I am helping you to mature and you are helping me stave off middle age. My reputation is already established but it seems you are going to have to make the decision, as I once had to, to be the art or the collector."

"I don't know what you are talking about, just answer my question, Belle."

"I am answering your question," she said gently. "Listen to me carefully. This is important, this is me helping you. When I was about your age, I went to work as a library aid for Mr. J. Pierpont Morgan. He was a man of strong appetites—books, art, food, drink, money and women. He always had a harem of women. He was physically attracted to me and I could have easily exploited that attraction, but I'd seen Mr. Morgan's women come and go. I knew that as his mistress, I would be adored and well taken care of until another woman struck his fancy and replaced me. To an art collector, the most recent acquisition is the collector's favorite, until the next new acquisition comes along. Some older works you keep. They find their way deep into the collection and they are treasured but will never be what they once were. And some of the art you once loved you sell because it no longer fits your image or the themes within your collection. The collector makes those decisions—the art has no say in the matter. Expertise is always valued over beauty and the one with the expertise decides what beauty stays and what goes. For those reasons, I chose not to be the art, but the collector."

Belle paused, reached over, took her napkin and wiped a drop of water from Lance's face.

"You are quite special," she said. "You are a very good looking man and you are a joy to be with physically, but you also have an intellect; yet you've chosen to do little with that gift. I've seen how much you've absorbed about art in our brief time together. You already have a sense of it, you could develop a very good eye for art. Put some of your passion into training instead of floating about as you have the last couple of years. Consciously choose to use your attributes. You have the potential to be a great collector of art, knowledge and friends—but at this moment, darling, all you are is the art."

(VII)

For the rest of their time at the Villa, Belle began what she called "Project Pygmalion."

"So now you think I'm a gigolo and a cockney flower seller," Lance was only half joking. "Are you my Henrietta Higgins?"

"You are so far ahead of where Eliza started," Belle said. "I doubt my contribution will be that significant. I will point you in the right direction, you will find your own momentum. It will be easier for you to benefit from being part of the insular world of art and money—easier for you than it was for me. You will not be plagued with the same questions and doubts I had to endure as a woman. 'Who is she? Where is she from? Can she possibly know anything about art?' Even today, after I have proven myself time and time again, they still question. As a man, your intellect and authority will be readily accepted. However, you should still expect to be challenged by those educated far beyond their intelligence—the cognoscenti," she said in an ominous tone. "I am a little jealous of how much easier it will be for you but I will take pride in any role I play in your success." Belle took Lance's hand and led him into the Villa's extensive library.

"So Lance, we will begin, or should I call you my Eliza."

"As long as you don't mind being called Henry."

"Professor Higgins, if you don't mind," she said, closing the door behind them.

(VIII)

Lance had never seen Belle so excited; she bounced up and down as she waited for the train to pull into the station in Florence. At the moment the conductor Put the step to the car, a woman, much older than Belle, bounded off of the train.

"Gertrude!" Belle screamed, running to embrace the small woman with grey hair and dusty colored skin.

"My Bella," the woman said as the two wrapped their arms tightly around each other in an embrace that lasted several minutes and brought many tears. As the other passengers streamed around them, Lance stood awkwardly aside watching the reunion. Finally the two women stepped back to look at each other.

"Belle you never age, I hate you! You look as young as you did back in Princeton."

"And you are as beautiful as you always were," Belle said graciously. No one would believe that the two women were the same age; the years had not been as kind to Gertrude.

"And this would be?" Gertrude asked, looking at Lance standing near them.

"This is my protégée, Mr. Lance Withers," Belle said, putting her arm in Lance's.

"Your protégée," Gertrude repeated, then whispered in Belle's ear. "And the secret to your fountain of youth?"

Belle playfully nudged Gertrude.

"Lance, this is Gertrude Martins. A dear friend from my days at the Princeton library." The two women hugged again.

"We have not seen each other in twenty years. She lives fifty miles from me in NY and the only way I can get her to come and see me is to bribe her with a trip to Italy."

"Bribes always work," Gertrude said.

The plan was for Gertrude to stay for a few of days and then rejoin the church tour group she had abandoned to visit Belle. She asked Lance to call her Trudy. "I already look old," she told him. "I don't want to sound old too." Trudy loved to talk as much as she loved to eat and drink.

"These Italians," she said, pronouncing the word Eye-tal-eons, "really know how to live. Wine and pasta, pasta and wine. I could get used to this." Belle and Trudy had roomed together with Trudy's aunt when Junis Morgan, a Princeton man, introduced Belle to his uncle J.P. Morgan who hired her to help manage his growing collection. Belle moved to Manhattan, and Trudy and Belle's lives took different paths but the affection that they felt for each other never waned.

"We were both trained in the library by my aunt," Trudy explained.

"I thought you were students together," Lance said.

"Heavens no! Evelyn College for Women would never have admitted the likes of us," Trudy said. Belle, sitting beside her friend, gently squeezed her arm. Trudy immediately fell silent and took a sip of her ever present drink.

"Evelyn College for Women?" Lance asked.

"The sister school in Princeton. We could not afford to go there. We worked for a living," Belle said, making it clear there would be no more discussion.

DONNA DREW SAWYER

"Still do," Trudy said under her breath.

Lance felt like an intruder during their conversations about their days together at the Princeton Library. He started to spend more time in the villa's Library, walking the grounds or reading by the pool to give the women an opportunity to reminisce. Several times when he walked in on them in the midst of conversation, they immediately changed the subject, then invited him to join them. These women had secrets. He was curious, but because of his own history, he knew some things were best shared in their own time or not at all.

Lance made it his routine to swim first thing in the morning and since Arturo and his "sponsor" had already left the villa he now enjoyed his solitary early morning exercise. Belle's schedule of instruction often kept him in the library for hours each day so he treasured the time he had to himself during his swim.

On Trudy's last day at the villa, he left at his usual early time to swim but when he arrived at the pool the caretaker was doing maintenance and asked him to return later. He went back to the suite and let himself in. He heard Trudy in Belle's bedroom, the door was open, but they had not heard him return.

"Put your hat on, Belle. You'd better be careful or you going to end up looking like me," he heard Trudy say laughing. "You're getting too much sun, you're browning up."

"I am not," Belle said. "I just look healthy. I'm not as lucky as you. You were always lighter than me. I claimed to have the darker Portuguese blood, remember?"

"And my ancestors were from Southern Spain—more like southern Senegal. Look at us, same age and same story, except

I'm starting to look like I'm returning to the motherland. You won't be far behind me if you don't cover yourself from the sun."

"We're still light enough to pass," Belle said.

"They say as we get older we'll get darker. Soon we'll be two old Nigs who used to be white."

Lance quietly backed out of the suite and closed the door. He stood in the hallway, not sure what to do. When he looked up, Belle, in her dressing gown, was standing in front of him.

"I thought you went for a swim," she whispered.

"The pool, they're doing work. They asked me to come back…" Belle put her finger to his lips.

"You heard?" she whispered. Lance did not respond. Belle stroked his face,

"We'll talk later. After Trudy leaves. Give us a few minutes then you can come back," she said calmly. "You were not here, you heard nothing." Belle went back into the suite and as she closed the door on Lance, she called out, "It was nothing Trudy dear, just a breeze."

(IX)

At least forty, maybe forty-five Lance tried to guess Belle's age as he watched her sleep. It was hard to believe she was the same age as Trudy, who looked ancient to him. The early morning sun streaming through the bedroom window fell on her face illuminating the tiny lines around her eyes and her mouth. Without makeup, her face was a dull, dusty color; no rosy cheeks, well-defined mouth, bright eyes—any illusion of youth was gone. From her heavy breathing, he knew she was sound asleep but she clutched the satin sheet to her breast and turned away from him as though she could sense him watching her.

Lance got up slowly hoping not to wake her. He retrieved his robe and went down the hall to the bath. He thought about going for a swim, but changed his mind—even after a full night's sleep, he felt drained. Returning to their rooms, he stopped for a moment in the salon to look at the treasures from yesterday's shopping. Belle wanted them to talk away from the villa so they took Trudy to the train and after she departed to rejoin her tour group, they spent the rest of the day in Florence, shopping and talking.

Belle told him everything. That she was passing, that Charlotte had told her that he was passing and then blackmailed her into taking him on as her protégée. In the back of his mind he had wondered why a woman like Belle had such an enduring interest in him. *My grandmother procured a woman for me—what kind of a grandmother does that?*

Belle assured him that even before Charlotte threatened to reveal her Richmond background as a lie, she'd wanted to be with him for the summer. That explanation seemed too convenient. Lance felt sick, he went to the window, took several deep breaths of the clear Mediterranean air and then slid to the floor under the window. He could trust no one—not even his own flesh and blood.

He looked at the pair of Ferragamo shoes Belle bought yesterday and remembered how she insisted that he let her purchase a pair of Gucci boots for him. He had refused. He did not need Belle's money; he had money, for now. He did not need or want her sympathy. She had more to lose if her ancestry was revealed than he did. What he wanted from Belle was to know how she made her way to this grand life. He would leverage both of their lies to achieve the same results or better.

When Lance returned to the bedroom, Belle was just waking up.

"Come back to bed, hold me. Let's talk, we need to talk," she said. Lance climbed back into the still warm bed and took her his arms, her back to his chest, his head resting atop her soft mussed hair.

"I thought all night about what you told me yesterday," he said after several minutes of silence.

"I told you things that I tell no one, but you and me, we are two of a kind, you needed to know." Belle's voice sounded small, almost a whisper. She turned to face him, "You must never tell anyone that I am passing. People wonder, but let them. I tell everyone that my ancestry is Portuguese; if you are anything other than colored you are acceptable." A tear formed in the corner of Belle's eye and she turned away from him before it fell.

"How long have you been—Portuguese?"

"Since I was sixteen."

"What about your family? Did they pass for white as well?"

"I had to leave my family," Belle said after a few moments, "if I wanted to be free." Being free was something Lance never had to think about, as long as he stayed white he never would.

"I've always been white," he said. "At least I thought I was, until my father told my mother and me, along with the rest of Richmond, that he had been passing for twenty years. Then he died and left us to deal with the news. That's why we left Richmond."

"I know," Belle said. "Charlotte told me everything. No one will ever suspect that you are a Negro. Your mother is white, and so is your grandmother, they will be your insurance, no one will doubt you. Unless of course—"

"I've already been warned, several times. I could father a child that might reveal my ancestry."

"You're young," Belle said, facing him again. "You have physical needs. Satisfy yourself with women who have as much to lose from a pregnancy as you do. Women who already have children or marriages and lives they want to preserve. *Femmes d'une certaine age*, like me, women who have no interest in children. We know what to do to ensure there will not be conception and we know what to do if there is. So you know, London is the place to go to get things like that taken care of." Belle turned away from him to face the window and was quiet for several minutes, then she turned to stroke his face. "When there is chemistry, as there is between us, that is always the best of all worlds." Lance kissed her.

"You must not tell Charlotte that you know about the bargain. If she finds out you know, I'm afraid she will try to destroy me. I already have too many people eager to do that."

"She won't know from me," Lance said.

"That woman frightens me," Belle said.

"Me too." And they both laughed.

They lay quiet in each other's arms for a while then Belle said, "You'll need someone to confide in—a friend like Gertrude is to me. Someone who knows your truth and will keep it safe for life. I can be that person for a time but you will eventually have to share this secret with someone else," she said, for the first time acknowledging the difference in their ages. "People like you and me? We belong to no tribe—so we must be our own best friends. We have no family, no history, unlike art, we have no provenance."

Lance remembered telling his mother the same thing on their way to Europe.

"Passing does not make us white," Belle continued. "If we are ever discovered we lose everything. Whites will hate us for the deception and the advantages that we were never supposed to have. Colored people hate us for the very same reasons. That is how it is for me, and that is how it will be for you."

❧ 14 ❧

Paris to New York 1933 - 1938

(I)

"I T FEELS GOOD TO HAVE the sun on my face," Maggie said, tilting her head back to catch the last rays of the late fall afternoon as the family dined at the *Café de la Paix*. "When you're away, travelling, we take most of our meals in. It is wonderful to be out of the apartment."

"Not too much, Margaret," Charlotte said as she reached over and tapped the back of her daughter's head encouraging Maggie to shade her face under her wide brimmed hat. "You don't want to darken your skin," she cautioned.

"I'm the one with the problem, Charlotte." Lance said, "My mother is a white woman. Being colored isn't contagious, it is?"

"Don't be crass," Charlotte, snapped as she looked around. "You never know who is listening."

Maggie put her hand on her son's before he could respond, "Please, don't start you two. Can't we just enjoy our time together? We're all safe now, aren't we?" she said, looking to her mother and her son for confirmation.

As Maggie and Charlotte continued their meal, Lance ordered another glass of wine from the white aproned waiter and returned to watching the pedestrians stroll and the motor traffic jockey for position along the grand *Place de l'Opéra*.

"Paris, the city that gave me purpose," Lance said, breaking the silence at the table.

"Some purpose," Charlotte said, resentful of Lance's absence while refusing to accept that her bargain with Belle Greene precipitated the changes in her grandson.

"Lance is just doing what young people do," Maggie said.

"And the not so young," Charlotte added.

"You don't have any more travel planned, do you? Why don't you entertain your friends at home? Do you remember the parties we had in Richmond? It would be nice to entertain like that again," Maggie said. "I know the apartment will never be like our home in Richmond but it will have to do until we can go home. I'm beginning to get out more, explore, look for ways to make Paris home for now. Oh! Did I tell you, I looked for a church near the apartment? I went to a couple of services but I could not understand a word they were saying—the service was not like back home. It was in French—I had hoped they spoke English. Everything here is so foreign."

Lance laughed, "We, the Americans, are foreign, *Maman et Bonne-Maman*," he said as he kissed the back of his mother's hand and acknowledged Charlotte with a nod.

"What did you say? What does that mean?" Maggie asked, delighted by Lance's fluency.

"*Maman* means Mother and *Bonne-Maman* means Grandmother."

"Just call me, Charlotte; I don't want to be anyone's *bonne* anything," Charlotte said.

"Oh Momma, can't you just be gracious?" Maggie asked.

"I'm always gracious, Margaret. Even when everyone is trying to avoid talking about a young man's less than flattering behavior."

Lance knew it was time to escape. "Ladies, I will walk you back to the apartment," he said as he called the waiter over to settle the bill, "then I'm meeting some friends."

"Where to tonight?" Maggie asked. "I thought now that Miss da Costa Greene had returned to New York, you'd be spending more time with us."

"Belle has gone back to New York but Walter Chrysler is here for a time. He has invited me to join him, a friend from New York and some people they know in Paris to talk about putting our money together to buy distressed and foreclosed property in New York."

With New York real estate at a quarter of its pre-Depression value, Lance's friends assured him that a small investment would yield significant returns. Because of his fluency in French, Charlotte had empowered Lance to negotiate the lease on their apartment and the experience had piqued his interest in real estate. He was also keenly aware of what their lifestyle was costing them and that their money would only last a couple more years, at the most. He knew how much he could risk and what was at risk.

"Our money? You want to invest our money?" Charlotte asked.

"My money," Lance responded. "Half of my father's estate is mine."

"I won't let you squander—" Charlotte began.

"I've reached the age of majority, Charlotte. I don't need your permission."

"Twenty-one? You think you know enough to manage your own money?"

"Both you and my mother were married and running households in your teens. Surely, I can manage a small investment in our future. After all, the family is now my responsibility. I give you all the credit for knowing that staying away from banks was the wise move in this financial climate," Lance said and raised his glass of wine to Charlotte. With cash, they were protected, for now, but the Depression in Europe had finally reached Paris. Groups of homeless young men now gathered at entrances to the Metro to beg; every day their numbers seemed to grow. Families sold their belongings on the streets, children that had once been in school now begged alongside their mothers. Crime increased and the politicians used every opportunity to ensure their rivals were considered the cause while they offered salvation from the pain that had already spread across the city and out to the suburban and rural areas. The tensions resulted in sporadic and sometimes deadly riots and demonstrations. Unlike his friend Walter, whose family continue to make money, Lance knew his resources were dwindling—he was reminded of that every time he deposited a few francs into the extended palms of the less fortunate he encountered on the streets of Paris.

"How much are you planning to invest in this venture?" Charlotte asked.

"I have what I need," Lance said.

"What do you mean you have what you need? Where did you get it?"

"I took my share of my father's estate. Your inheritance and Mother's is still in the safe at the apartment."

"You will return everything you took—"

"Or what?" Lance challenged.

The tension between Charlotte and Lance had been building into a power struggle over control of the family assets. The revelation Belle shared made Lance even more resentful. He would not live on an allowance from his own money, doled out by Charlotte, after a thorough inquisition.

In addition to his long trip out of the country with Belle, Charlotte resented the relationships Lance developed outside of her influence. *So you're in charge of our affairs now?* She thought as she looked at Lance across the table. Her first instinct was to fight him but he had shown himself resourceful in the past and, he was right, it was up to him to provide for the family. Neither she nor Margaret had any prospects, no one they'd met in Paris had lived up to Charlotte's standards as a provider. Perhaps it was better to give him some latitude sooner rather than later. *Let us see what he's capable of.*

"As you said, it is your money. However, you will be at my mercy when it is exhausted."

"Thank you for your vote of confidence, Charlotte," Lance said of the response he expected.

Maggie had been holding her breath through the entire exchange. She hated the frequent flare-ups between the only two people she had on this earth; she tried to steer the conversation in a more amicable direction.

"Perhaps we can go with you and your friends tonight," she volunteered. "I'd love to meet them, see what it is you do when you're out. Perhaps Momma and I could even invest in your venture."

"We're meeting at a club in Montmartre. I'm not sure you'd be comfortable there," Lance said as he paid the restaurant bill.

"Is it one of those colored jazz clubs?" Charlotte asked. "Do you think it wise? You know, given your situation?"

"You're being ridiculous."

"Am I?" she asked, looking around to ensure no one was listening, "Most of them can tell their own."

Lance was as impatient with her constant warnings about his racial origins as he was her strangle hold on their finances. He leaned into the table and lowered his voice.

"Based on my Father's experience in Richmond I don't think that's the case. I may be the whitest colored person on earth, Charlotte. For most of my life I didn't even know I was colored. How is anyone else going to know, unless of course, I decide to end this farce and tell everyone?" He hoped to provoke a reaction. Charlotte did not disappoint, she nearly choked on her food.

Maggie patted Charlotte's back and handed her mother a glass of water.

"Lance, please. Stop antagonizing the situation," she said.

After Charlotte stopped coughing, Lance said, "My father's heritage does not ooze from my pores in the presence of other colored people so don't worry about my person or my purse."

He stood up, then helped his mother to her feet, slipping his arm in hers. Maggie, the peacekeeper, reached over and took her mother's hand as she stood. Then the three of them started their stroll down the boulevard toward home.

"So glad you could join me for dinner," Lance said. "We'll have to do this again very soon."

(II)

At the club, *Le Grand Duc*, that evening, Lance watched as nearly every celebrity or dignitary that came through the door jostled with the other patrons for the attention of a dark-skinned American at a table near the bandstand.

"That's Eugene Bullard," Walter Chrysler's friend, Nelson Rockefeller, said. "He was a pilot in the war; flew missions in the *Lafayette Escadrille*. Couldn't fly for America," he said taking a drag from his cigarette. "He's a national hero over here, won every military medal France had to give. He's a true celebrity."

"So it seems," Lance said as he sipped his drink.

"Would you like to meet him?" Nelson asked.

"Not really," Lance said, he'd rebuked Charlotte, but he did worry that something would give him away if he associated with Negroes, that somehow they might suspect he was one of them.

"What?" one of the Frenchmen at the table asked. "Surely you are not *un virage serré - cul américaine*. Nelson, what do you call it in English?"

"A tight-ass American."

"*Oui*, a tight-ass American that does not understand that *la crème* is always better *with le cafe*. Even in France, there are those who do not understand, but not here," he said, waving his arm to indicate the club and in a smaller gesture, their table.

"The French are curious and indulgent of people different from themselves. Africans, the Roma, American Negroes, Jews, the Chinese—all give Paris our exotic flavor, *c'est merveilleux, non?*"

"So all races are equal here in France?" Lance asked, already knowing that was not the case.

"Equal? *Peut-être pas complètement*, not completely. However, the French, especially Parisians, appreciate everyone's gifts. Have you seen *La Baker* at the *Folies Bergere?*" he seemed to swoon when he said her name. "Americans were too blind to see her so she came to us—we adore her. Now she is *un sauvage* all French men, and some women, would love to tame." If Lance had not had Belle's wise counsel, he might have believed the Frenchman's words made his family's reasons for fleeing Richmond less potent. Paris was certainly more diverse but for all of the *Liberté, Égalité, Fraternité* the French celebrated, it was still a white man's world. Negroes were not equal; they were just not as *unequal* as they were in America.

"I hear she does things that make men lose control," Walter whispered to Lance. "We should go."

When Lance finally did see Josephine Baker's show at the *Folies Bergere*, her performance and the audience's adoration triggered a feeling of discomfort that he had not experienced before. In Virginia he had been entertained by colored performers and never once thought about what their lives were like after the applause and accolades from an audience who reviled them. How did Negroes manage the duplicity of being lauded and disdained at the same time? Yes, the French loved *La Baker*; as a woman they desired her because they saw her, as his host that night at the jazz club explained, as exotic, "*une sauvage.*" They celebrated Baker's body and sexuality and Eugene Bullard's brawn and heroism, but neither of them would ever be the equal of their audience. Their race would always marginalize them. What had Belle told him? "Anything but colored is acceptable."

La Baker further confirmed his decision to continue to pass as white in France and forever. For all anyone knew, Lance Henry Withers was and always had been a member of the ruling class. Nothing he had seen or experienced on this side of the Atlantic or the other would ever make him relinquish that privilege.

(III)

Starting with the small investment he made with Walter and Nelson, and that he continued independently when they turned to other things, Lance turned the princely sum he controlled from his father's estate into a more than comfortable living for the family. By 1936, when he was about to turn twenty-four, he was in every sense, his own man. Belle's friends were now Lance's friends. He became the friend of a friend everyone who came to Europe wanted to meet and spend time with.

Now that he had the money to indulge in the same artistic pastime as his friends, he was still uncertain about what art to collect. Belle had tried to interest Lance in the antiquities and religious art that were her passion, but they just did not speak to him.

In the summer of 1936, Nelson's mother asked him to accompany her to London where she and a group of friends were looking for works to expand the collection of contemporary art for a museum they had established in New York. The political climate in Europe convinced Mrs. Rockefeller that there was trouble on the horizon and she wanted to make several purchases because she didn't know when she would have the opportunity again.

"There is just so much art to love here. You can't take a step without bumping into a canvas worth having," she told Lance. She encouraged him to take advantage of the surfeit of well-priced contemporary and modern art available on the continent.

"How do you decide? Where does a collector start?" Lance asked.

"With passion," Mrs. Rockefeller said without hesitating. Elegant and regal in the way only truly wealthy women are, she leaned lightly on a carved walking stick, drifting into the painting in front of them. "When you lose yourself in a work of art, you will have found your passion." She turned to face Lance. "Ignore the critics, the cognoscenti, the tastemakers; they only know what they love, or hate. I don't even listen to my husband and he pays for my indulgences," she said with a laugh, then turned serious. "Let your heart rule your head. Be it art or life, whatever touches you here," she said, pressing her bejeweled fingers to Lance's heart, "will always be right."

(IV)

Lance met Wassily Kandinsky, a Russian artist living in Paris, at a gathering at Gertrude Stein's apartment. He'd been a teacher at Germany's famed Bauhaus school of art and architecture until the Nazis raided the school in 1933. They displayed Kandinsky's vivid experimental compositions, along with work by artist Paul Klee and others, as degenerate art, then burned it. Kandinsky fled to Paris and continued to work. Lance visited the artist in his studio and listened to him talk about his work. The artist's complex and colorful compositions intrigued Lance. He gravitated to works that forced him to extract his own meaning from the canvas. He saw parallels between abstract art and his life. These works seemed to confirm for him that beauty can be found within chaos and not everything is figurative and representational. He had seen abstract works before, but now he saw it differently. Perhaps Belle's summer of immersion in the lessons of art and life had helped him mature enough to find the spark that he had been looking for. Lance developed an insatiable appetite for abstract art, particularly expressionism, and he developed a nearly infallible eye for an artist's best canvas, which he always secured at the most advantageous price. Lance bought and loved the more lyrical nature of these works by artists whose names were not as recognizable as Monet and Matisse. The bold works defined him—socially, culturally and financially, his collection was where Lance fully displayed his passion, it became the constant that helped him make sense of all that had happened to him—the loss of his father, his home and his identity. Like a hidden object in an abstract painting, Lance Henry Withers buried his secrets in his collection.

The art world began to take notice of the Withers Collection. His success in business complemented and supported his growing art collection, obscuring who he had been before the art cognoscenti discovered who he was now. Lance's popularity gave him the power to cull people, art and innuendo from his elite circle; he was in full control of his present and his future and, he had erased his past. Lance had taken the advice Belle gave him in Italy, he made his choice. Lance Henry Withers was now the collector—everyone and everything else was the art.

⁓ 15 ⁓

Spring 1938

(I)

MAGGIE'S DREAM OF HOSTING LANCE's friends never became a reality. She had worked hard to tastefully decorate their apartment to host the creative class. Instead, Lance used it as a warehouse for his growing collection. Canvases were carefully stacked against every wall in the apartment. He would return from trips to Italy, Belgium, Austria or Germany with crates of artwork then spend weeks in London on business deals. When he was at home, he spent most of his time behind closed doors in his office in their apartment.

Maggie's world contracted in direct correlation to Lance's expanding success. She never developed the stamina to keep up with Lance's new life. The few times he would invite her to stroll the boulevards, visit the museums, or lunch in the cafes now seemed to exhaust her and, after a while, he stopped asking her to accompany him. She suffered from recurring migraines, staying in her darkened bedroom for days at a time. Rather than go out, she preferred to spend time in the apartment's grand salon, peering out over the rooftops of Paris wishing for the past. She refused to read the news about the Depression in the United States. It was her way of believing that everything was as she left it. All she had to do was return with her son to resume the life she once had. But Europe was now deep in the Depression and Hitler, Franco and Mussolini were aggressively moving Europe to another war. Maggie was determined to go home. She gathered her courage and knocked on the door to Lance's office.

"Lance, we need to talk."

"Come in, come in," he said, jumping up to escort his mother to a chair. "Tell me, what do you need?"

"I think it is time to go home," she announced in as strong voice as she could manage. She steeled herself for his opposition unaware that he had been thinking the same thing.

"You're right."

"I am? Oh that's wonderful!"

"Just one problem, where's home? You can't mean Richmond. You can't go back to Virginia."

"It doesn't have to be Virginia. If we could just return to the United States."

"What about New York. I own real estate there, Belle's there and I have other friends and business associates who will be great resources for us. I think New York would be the best place."

"Oh Lance," Maggie jumped up and kissed him. "How soon—how soon can we leave?"

"Let's talk to Charlotte and then I'll arrange for an apartment and plan the travel. You can be strolling down Fifth Avenue within the month."

Maggie ran from the room screaming, "Momma, Momma! We're going home, we're all going home."

(II)

Charlotte surprised Maggie and Lance by agreeing immediately to return to the United States. Charlotte's lack of affinity for the French language put her at a social disadvantage their entire time in Paris. She managed only fleeting relationships with expatriate wives and widows and she was tired of the isolation. The Great Depression was beginning to ease under Roosevelt's New Deal, it was a good time to go home. It was also time for her to permanently step down and let Lance take control of the family—he had earned the right. He was still young, just twenty-five but his success had proven him a more competent provider than her bank president husband and Margaret's glorified janitor put together.

Charlotte looked forward to being a New Yorker. Unlike her last attempt to penetrate Manhattan society, she knew Lance's wealth and status in business and the art world would facilitate their acceptance. She would assume her role as the family matriarch and enjoy the sumptuous life that she created. *I could not have planned this any better,* Charlotte thought, taking credit for her grandson's success. It had been her idea to take the family to Paris. Her wise assessment of financial institutions had kept their inheritance safe. She was the one who convinced Belle Greene to make the introductions that led Lance to the people who would make him a success. *Yes,* she thought, *it is because of me that we are enjoying this great triumph. Now it is time to go home.*

(III)

Lance suggested his mother and Charlotte check into the Hotel Ritz so that he could have the apartment packed and shipped. He stayed at the apartment to supervise the move. Within two weeks they were in Le Havre boarding the ship for the voyage home. Lance had their luggage delivered to the ship so that all they carried aboard were their things from their stay at the hotel. When they arrived at their cabin there were only accommodations for the two women.

"They've made a mistake," Charlotte said, looking around for Lance's stateroom.

"There's no mistake," Lance said. "I'm not making the crossing with you. I'm staying in Paris."

"You can't stay, you must come with us. There is no reason for you to remain here, not without your family. We are all each other has, Lance." Maggie pleaded with her son.

"*Maman*," as he now called her, "please, this is where I belong. I've arranged an apartment for you and Charlotte in the Murray Hill section of Manhattan. You will love it there, I promise."

"You are supposed to be with us. You have to come home!"

"I am home. I don't think I'll ever live permanently in the United States again, but with both of you there and because of the business I'm doing in New York, I'll be back and forth. Soon there will be airplanes that can fly across the Atlantic. We'll never lose contact, you'll see."

"Lance, how can you stay? Europe is a tinderbox. Leave now, everyone says so. The ship is full of Americans. Even the Europeans are leaving. You cannot stay here. Leave with us or we all stay!"

"*Maman*, nothing will happen in Paris—the Germans will never march down the *Champs d'Elysées*. Please don't worry, I am safe here. This is my home now," he said remembering that he once thought of Richmond as home. He had outgrown and discarded the person and the persona that arrived in Paris in 1931. Now he disdained the south and its culture. He had pushed the West End, Colonial Enterprises, Del, even his father so far into the past that he found it hard to recall the life he once had. It had not been easy to let it all go. His father's journals haunted him. He had even tried to contact Del the year after they arrived in Paris. He wrote to her and gave the letter to Belle to mail from New York, using the Morgan Library as the return address, just in case. The letter was returned unopened. He never attempted to reach anyone in Richmond again. Paris was home and he was not about to leave. His mother and Charlotte were very much the same people they had always been, but he had grown to be a man. It was time to put some distance between them.

"So you are abandoning us," Charlotte said, exacerbating Maggie's hysteria.

"I am not abandoning you. I'm a man now; it is time for me to live my life – not yours. I will always take care of you, no matter where I am. I've arranged everything in New York. A chauffeur will meet you when you dock, take you to the apartment. I've even hired staff to look after you. I wrote Belle and told her you're coming. She will help with introductions so you can make new friends. All you have to do is relax and enjoy. Get to know the city so you can show me around when I come for a visit."

"And when will that be?" Maggie asked, trying to make him commit to a date.

"We'll see, Maman, we'll see," Lance said, wrapping his mother in his arms and kissing the top of her head. "You will heal better in the United States. No more migraine headaches, nothing to be anxious about. It will be easier in New York, everyone speaks English."

———◆———

Maggie clung to her son, showering him with kisses and tears until he was the last visitor to leave before the crew removed the gangplank. From the deck of the ship, Maggie waved to Lance as he stood on the dock. Through tears, she blew heartfelt kisses that her only child playfully pretended to catch. As the ship slipped into the early morning fog, and the distance between them grew, she could no longer see Lance. She had lost the two most important people in life—her husband and now her son. Neither would be coming back to her. She had nothing left. Maggie looked toward the shore. She thought she saw the dock again and where Lance had been she saw Hank, standing tall and strong, beckoning to her.

Maggie returned to the cabin where Charlotte was relaxing with a magazine and a cup of tea.

"I had a feeling he was staying," Charlotte said. "The ruse of checking us into the Ritz so we could not see what he was doing reminds me of something I would do. Your son is clever."

"I've lost him," Maggie said.

"You haven't lost him, he's just exercising his independence, Margaret. Remember when you did the same thing?" Charlotte said, reminding Maggie of how she had eloped with Hank. "Relationships between a parent and a child change with time; the boundaries of your influence diminish. You have to accept that. I did."

"Did you, mother?" Maggie asked.

"What is that supposed to mean?" Charlotte asked.

"It is not supposed to mean anything," Maggie said, wondering whether she could have kept her son if her mother had not pushed them out into a world that was so different from everything they knew.

"Margaret, we are better off than we've ever been."

"Are we?"

"How can you ask that? We thrived during one of the worst times in history. You have everything a woman could ask for. Why don't you see that? It has been more than seven years and you are still mourning that pathetic excuse for a husband."

"Don't say that," Maggie shot back. "If you had ever loved anyone other than yourself you'd understand why…" She didn't finish the sentence, trying to explain her love for Hank to her mother was a waste of time and energy.

"Are you finished?" Charlotte asked. "I will ignore your ungrateful, disrespectful outburst because you are upset about Lance."

"Yes, that's it. I'm upset about Lance." Charlotte returned to her reading and after a few minutes of silence Maggie rose from the sofa and headed to her stateroom. "I won't be joining you for dinner, I don't have much of an appetite," she said.

"Suit yourself," Charlotte said. "Evelyn Cumberbatch is also aboard and she has asked us to dine with her. I will convey your regrets. Rest, you'll feel better in the morning." When Maggie reached the door to her stateroom, she turned back to her mother.

"This did not work out the way I wanted it to. I thought there would be more time with them," she said.

Charlotte looked up from her magazine, "I think things worked out just fine, Margaret."

"Momma," Maggie asked, "have you ever needed anyone?"

"What a question," Charlotte said. "Get some rest, you'll feel better in the morning."

"Did you love my father?"

"As much as I could," Charlotte said, without looking up.

"I love you, Momma," Maggie said. Charlotte looked up just in time to see her close the door. She didn't bother to tell her daughter that she loved her too.

(IV)

Maggie went to the desk in her stateroom and wrote a long letter to her son, then sat on the side of the bed until she heard her mother leave for dinner. She rang the steward and asked him to post the letter on the first mail back to France.

"Will you do me a favor? My mother is in the dining room. Please ask her not to wake me when she returns from dinner. Let her know I've already gone to bed."

After the steward left, Maggie rummaged through her toiletries until she found the bottle of medicine for her migraine headaches and a vial full of sleeping pills. She poured all of the pills into a glass and added the entire bottle of the potent migraine medicine. While she swirled the glass to dissolve the pills, she thought how wonderful it would be when she was finally with Hank again. *Lance will take care of Momma*, was her last thought before she drank the entire contents of the glass.

(V)

When Lance returned to his apartment in Paris after seeing his mother and Charlotte off, there was a package there from

Belle in New York. Inside was a Monopoly board game. The accompanying letter read:

Dearest,

I received your letter letting me know that Charlotte and your mother are on their way to New York. As you well know, your grandmother scares me to death! However, as a favor to my favorite protégée (I'm blushing) I will have a small reception for them so they can meet a few people here in the City. I will contact them with the information you sent me to set a date once they arrive.

No doubt you've noticed the present accompanying this letter. The Monopoly Game is all the rage here in the US. I thought it fitting for you, in real estate and art, as you are quite the tycoon these days, gobbling up all of the great modern art and undervalued real estate on the market. I don't dare let on that I know you as well as I do (again, I'm blushing) for that knowledge leads directly to questions about how you know what artist to buy before the rest of us have an inkling. I am lost when they start talking real estate – but just in case you want to share I've been asked to inquire about the location of New York's next upcoming neighborhood for savvy investors. My Love, you are now quite the collector – and to think I knew you when you were just the art!

I do want you to think seriously and soon about following your family back to the States. You and Peggy Guggenheim are the last of my original group there I believe. Peggy will not leave, she is furious because the Louvre won't hide her art in their secret refuge – too contemporary they say. You, dear, may have the same problem – remember, the Germans have already burned the work of two of your favorite artists, Klee and Kandinsky! If you won't think of yourself, think of your collection, please! I know when we were in Italy I was wrong about Mussolini, but I am right about Hitler – Germany and now Austria will not satisfy him.

Send word and I will be happy to help you look for suitable housing for you and your collection – not that you need real estate advice from me!

In the meantime I beg you to remain safe and vigilant.

Affectionately,
Belle

Lance smiled thinking back on who he was when he met Belle da Costa Greene—a lost and traumatized eighteen-year-old who fled Richmond clinging to Charlotte's coattails. Today, he felt older than twenty-five. He'd worked hard to be the man Belle wrote about in her letter.

His acquaintances were educated men and women; he gleaned everything he could from them and then learned more. He would never be a university club man like his Ivy degreed friends—he never felt the need to be. He didn't require that kind of group acceptance and social confirmation. He liked being independent, it was safer. He was comfortable with the quiet reputation he'd built among high-end investors as a result of his financial success. His collection provided entrée into the most élite group of serious art collectors. The exclusivity of these worlds offered him the protection of limited scrutiny, especially in Europe. New York was too close to whom he used to be, one glimmer of recognition from someone in his past life—an old acquaintance of his father's or one of his mother's League ladies shopping New York—could bring the world of Lance Henry Withers crashing down around him. The word 'whom' made him laugh as he remembered how Charlotte corrected his grammar at their departure lunch at the Waldorf in 1931. *Just seven years but a lifetime ago*, he thought. Now he could give Charlotte lessons in manners and decorum.

"I am my own man," he said aloud. *Everyone else believes it*, he thought, *even if I don't.*

(VI)

Arrived. Settling in. Please come soon.
Love, Maman

Lance received his mother's cable the day after she and Charlotte were scheduled to arrive in New York. Two days later a long rambling letter from his mother arrived. As he read it he realized how distraught she was about their separation. *Why was she surprised that he was ready to strike out on his own, that's what men did.*

Maggie's letter repeated several times how much she loved him, how much she loved his father and how she missed the life they had in Richmond. *That was almost a decade ago,* Lance thought. *I don't know why she can't let go of the pain and move on.*

In her letter, Maggie asked Lance to promise her one thing,

No matter what happens in your life, mine or hers, I'm begging you to take care of my mother. Please keep her with you always, she is your only connection to your true past. Please do not tell Momma that I asked you to do this for me. She pretends that she needs no one but she loves both of us and wants the best for us, even though she has difficulty showing it. She will not be able to live without you in her life.

Why would she ask him this? Of course he would take care of them, why would she ever question this? He would talk to her about it when he went to visit them in New York.

(VII)

In August of 1939, Lance received a letter from Charlotte notifying him that she had booked a trip to New York for him in early September. Initially he considered ignoring her demands and staying in Europe but all the expatriates he knew seemed to be making plans to return to the United States and they encouraged him to do the same. A friend in the U.S.

Embassy warned him that the government was planning to order all Americans to leave France. Passage to the States was becoming impossible to get so Lance relented, packed his art collection and the contents of his apartment and shipped everything to New York.

On September 1, 1939 the Nazis invaded Poland. The morning of September 3, 1939, Lance Henry Withers boarded the *SS Île de'France* on route to New York with 1,776 other passengers, 400 more than the ship usually carried. Ironically, the same ship that brought him to France would return him to the United States.

Just a few hours into the voyage, the captain announced to the passengers that Great Britain and France, in response to Hitler's aggression, had declared war on Germany. The *Il de France* was the last ship to leave France before the outbreak of the war.

(VIII)

Charlotte was there to meet Lance when the ship docked. "Where's *Maman*?" he asked looking around for his mother.

Charlotte put her hand on his arm, her eyes welled with tears. "My dear Lance, I have something terrible to tell you."

In the back of his mind he knew something was awry when Belle wrote to tell him that only Charlotte came to the reception she planned for his family. He assumed that *Maman* was once again feigning illness to avoid social events. The letters he received from her throughout the year he remained in Paris, dictated to her secretary, assured him that she was on the mend and seeing him would put her back in great form.

Now Charlotte was telling him that his mother had been gone for more than a year.

"She took ill on the voyage to New York…the ship's doctor did everything he could but she could not be saved," Charlotte told him through what seemed like a fog.

"Why didn't you tell me?" was all he could manage with the shock of the news.

"She made me promise not to tell you anything until you were safely home. She did not want you to carry any guilt for what happened to her. The letters I wrote in Margaret's name were to bring you home. I was desperate and alone," Charlotte began to sob.

"What about the letter she wrote during the voyage, did you write that one too?"

Charlotte looked up, dabbing her eyes with her handkerchief. "Letter during the voyage? I didn't write you during the voyage, only when we arrived in New York, as your dear mother asked me to."

His mother's request in the letter he received a few days after she left France now made sense. *She killed herself,* Lance thought. She had been wanting to since his father died.

"Where is she buried?" Lance asked as they rode to Charlotte's apartment.

Charlotte hesitated for a few seconds. "We had to cremate the body…the condition it was in when we docked…" she didn't finish the sentence.

They were silent until they arrived at his mother's apartment.

"I'm going to a hotel. I need to be alone," he said. What he really needed was to be away from Charlotte until he could purchase a home for himself. He would honor his mother's request and keep Charlotte with him as his permanent guest. He would make sure she was cared for, but he would do everything he could to keep their lives separate, for as long as she lived.

(IX)

In April of 1940, German forces invaded Norway and Denmark and in May, Germany began its assault on Western Europe. On June 14, less than nine months after Lance left Paris, the German Sixth Army marched down the Champs Elysees after the French government evacuated Paris and declared it an open city. The French surrendered to the Germans on June 22.

Part Two

Abstract Expressionism

Movement in painting originating in New York City in the 1940s. It emphasized spontaneous personal expression, freedom from accepted artistic values, surface qualities of painting and the act of painting itself.

❧ 16 ❧

New York—Winter 1948

"I DON'T THINK WE HAVE ANYTHING for you," the kind-faced young girl said from inside the warmth of the service entrance. "I think the kitchen is all staffed up," she added, looking at the pale teenager dressed in a heavy sweater and a shawl on a twenty-degree New York winter day.

"You eaten today? You look pale as a communion wafer. Wait here a second. Let me get you a little something from the kitchen. Don't move now, I'll be right back," she said, leaving the door open enough for Emma George to see down the long hall and feel the warmth inside. *Inside, if I could just get inside for a few moments.* She took a small step across the threshold to get closer to the warmth of heat and people. She had been out in the cold and by herself since she left Ellis Island over a month ago.

Emma heard a commotion and a woman's scream. She saw the girl who had asked her to wait at the door run past the hall and then she heard another woman shout, "Don't touch me. Don't you ever touch me!" Emma took another step into the hallway, curious but mostly cold, just as the kindly young woman came around the corner and back into the hall.

"Can you help me? Help me get the wench up and back to her room," she said without charity. Emma came inside and closed the door behind her. She dropped her satchel on the floor and followed the girl.

"She doesn't like me to touch her. I'm not *white*; maybe she'll let you because you are."

"Let me help you up, ma'am," Emma said, reaching for the elegantly dressed older woman sprawled on the floor. She allowed Emma to help her up while the girl brought over a wheelchair.

"If you'd just use the chair, Miss Charlotte, you won't fall."

"Mind your mouth, you gal," the old woman said to her. "My nurse is here now and she'll tell Lance what you did to me, won't you, dear?" Emma had never heard venom and honey flow from the same mouth in one sentence. "Take me to my room, dear. This has been all too much for Miss Charlotte. I need to rest." Emma looked at both women, not sure what to do.

"Do not look to her for direction," Charlotte said. "She takes her orders from me *and* from you, that's the natural order of things. I told Lance bringing them into the house was a bad idea. I would never allow that in my house. Out in the garden, the garage, the shop—but never in the house," Charlotte said, staring directly at the girl who, though young, looked strong enough to snap the old woman in two without breaking a sweat. "I told Lance," Charlotte continued, "they will steal you blind. They'll tell your secrets." The girl's facial expression never acknowledged Charlotte's insults, she simply turned and started down the hall, indicating Emma should follow with Charlotte in the wheelchair. The three of them entered a small elevator, the girl pressed the button and impatiently waited for the elevator to rise to the next floor. When the door opened, she exited first and Emma followed as the old woman continued to heap insults on the poor young woman. When they arrived at the door to an opulent suite of rooms, Charlotte addressed the young woman as if she were a wayward animal.

"Shoo now! What you hanging around here for? You've done enough damage," she said to the girl who couldn't have been much older than Emma, but showed a maturity that Emma wasn't sure she could have managed. "Now, help me onto the bed, dear," she said sweetly to Emma, "and sit with me while I nap."

There was a flickering fire in the room's fireplace, lace curtains on the windows and rugs layered upon the carpet that covered the floor. The upholstered chairs had embroidered doilies on the arms and the backs. The old woman's bed was covered with a silk comforter. Emma was overwhelmed by the warmth and beauty of the room. Was she was dreaming? A hard bench at the ferry station could not inspire a dream like this.

"Stay here. I'll look in on you in a few minutes," the girl whispered to Emma as she left the room, leaving the door ajar.

"Tell me your name again, dear. I'm forgetful these days," Charlotte said, her watery eyes on Emma.

"I'm Emma, ma'am. From London, Richmond-upon-Thames. I came to the U.S., well here to New York because, because—well I had . . ."

"We're from Richmond," Charlotte said, then clapped her hand to her mouth. "Lance has forbidden me from telling anyone that, so it must be our secret. We're just two girls from Richmond," she whispered, then laughed. Charlotte handed Emma a book from her bedside table, "Read to me, from this."

"*East Side, West Side* by Marcia Davenport," Emma read aloud.

"I know it's not Shakespeare, but sometimes I just love a really good story and this one is about our people, New York Society. I know its fiction, but I've been told I'll recognize some people I know," Charlotte said.

"I don't read all that well, ma'am," Emma said self-consciously.

"Don't be silly, the British are all very well read. I've been across the pond too, dear. Actually, I've made several crossings, and for a time, I even lived abroad. That was before the war of course . . ." the old woman said, trailing off. After a few minutes of silence, Emma started reading as she had been told. Before she reached the second page, she could hear Charlotte snoring softly. Not sure what to do, she sat in the chair looking around the room. If she could just sit here for a while, rest and finally get warm.

From the time she left England to today, she had been cold, hungry and alone. There was nothing left for her in London, or what was left of the London she used to know. The blitz had taken everything: her mother, her father, her dear brother Philmore, her home and her job. The house and garden in Richmond-upon-Thames where her family had been in service for generations was destroyed. The Master and his family retreated to their estate in the country, leaving the servants in London to fend for themselves. *Displaced person.* That's what they called her when she applied to come to the United States. There were rich people in America, they still had their houses, and they would need staff she reasoned. Emma knew how to cook, clean and care for those who don't do those kinds of things for themselves. She would make a new life for herself in America.

A soft knock on the door brought Emma back. The girl motioned for her to quietly come with her. Once outside the door she said, "I'm glad you were here. I'm the only one downstairs right now. My mama's the cook here and today's her market afternoon. The old woman gets like that sometimes, we don't pay her no mind. My mama says you'd think she was a southerner or something. She says that's the way they are back where we're from in North Carolina which is why she moved us to New York."

"Who does she think I am?" Emma asked, wishing she could be that person.

"Her personal maid up and quit earlier this week and she's been even more addled than usual ever since. As long as she doesn't have to deal with my mama or me, she's happy—only wants to deal with white folks. I hope you don't mind me sayin' so, I'm just speakin' the truth."

"Does she need another maid? I can do that too. I do more than kitchen work."

"Well, I'm not the one hiring, but wouldn't hurt to ask. What's your name?"

"I'm Emma George. From London, England. My family's been in service . . ."

"Slow down, Emma George, this ain't no interview. I'm just Mina, I help my mama out in the kitchen when I'm not in school. I go to the culinary arts school, but I'm gonna be the chef here one day. You'll have to see Mr. Lance, Miss Charlotte's grandson. This here is his house. But first let's get some food into you. You're wasting away before my very eyes."

———❖———

Emma George arrived at 580 Park Avenue in February, 1948, and never really left. Lance Withers hired her on the spot. All civility in his relationship with Charlotte ended the day he returned to the United States from France. He could not forgive Charlotte for hiding his mother's death from him, but did as his mother asked him to—he kept his grandmother with him. He'd purchased a city estate in Manhattan, a home and grounds large enough to keep Charlotte under the same roof but out of his sight. As long as he could pay someone to fulfill his mother's last request, he was happy. At seventeen years of age, Emma had the youth and patience to deal with Charlotte Bennett's demands. Eventually she became the only one who could.

Emma thrived at 580 Park Avenue. In her mind, taking care of Charlotte Bennett was a small price to pay for a clean, warm place to sleep, food, a fair salary and a family in the other members of the staff. A life of security at 580 Park Avenue was more than she had dared hoped for when she sailed for America.

≈ 17 ≈

New York 1950

T HE ELEVATOR OPENED TO A face Lance Withers had
seen before. Startled, he hesitated for a few moments,
as the other New Yorkers also waiting for the elevator
streamed around him filling the car.

"There's still room, sir," the operator said. "You going up?"

"Yes. Yes," Lance said. "Sorry."

"Not a problem, I'm here every day, eight until six, travelin'
the same route—you can catch me goin' up or comin' down,"
the man said. Some of the passengers tittered at the operator's
joke. Lance stepped into the elevator and tucked in behind the
man. He was as close to him as he had been several times at
the clubs in Montmartre. He was older now, they both were.
Lance was thirty-seven so this man had to be in his mid-fifties
if Lance remembered correctly. His hair was grey now but he
stood tall and straight in his Rockefeller Center uniform. No
medals for valor or gold braid decorated his uniform, but he

wore it with the same *élan* as when he was the celebrated black fighter pilot for the French Military's Escadrille Flying Corps.

"Which floor, sir?" the operator asked, turning to face Lance as the first group of passengers left the elevator.

"The sixty-fifth. Not afraid of heights are you?"

"Me? Not at all, sir," the operator said. "I've done some of my best work at six thousand feet. Eight fifty ain't nothin' to me."

Now Lance was sure. It was him—Eugene Bullard—the celebrated "Black Swallow of Death," the World War I fighter pilot and recipient of France's highest military honor, the *Croix de Guerre*. When the elevator arrived at the 65th floor, Lance was the last passenger.

"Here you are, sir," Bullard said as he opened the elevator door.

"Thank you," Lance said. Before stepping out of the elevator, he extended his hand to shake Eugene Bullard's hand, something he never had the opportunity to do in Paris. Lance gripped Bullard's hand; he looked down at their clasped hands—Bullard's dark, fleshy and strong—the hands of the boxer he had once been. Lance's white and manicured—the hands of a man who had and never would work with anything but his mind.

"Well, you're quite welcome, sir," Bullard said, surprised by Lance's gesture. When Lance stepped off the elevator, he started to walk away, but turned abruptly to face Eugene Bullard as he was closing the door to elevator.

"I remember you, from Paris, I remember you," Lance said in French. The elevator door was halfway closed but Bullard opened it again.

"Do I know you?" he asked in French.

"No," Lance said, returning to English. "We never really met. But I was in Paris, before World War II, and I remember you."

"That was more than a lifetime ago. No one knows that man anymore," Bullard said like a man who had long ago accepted how life worked out, then he closed the elevator door.

But for the color of his skin he might have been a celebrated hero in the country of his birth. Lance knew that the color of his skin had protected him, giving him the opportunity to fulfill his potential despite the fact that he shared Eugene Bullard's heritage. *I'm not the man I was in Paris either,* Lance thought. He watched the floors light up in the elevator's overhead panel as the car descended with a glimmer of his glorious past inside. The promise of Paris seemed longer ago than a lifetime to him too. With Belle's death a month earlier and Paris now overrun with GIs and a younger generation of expats, there was virtually no one from his time still there. Everyone had returned home to do other things and now Lance Henry Withers was a reluctant New Yorker.

He had turned his real estate investments from the time of the Depression into the more formal Withers & Associates, an exclusive private investment limited partnership with Lance as the controlling partner. Throughout the last two decades he had made himself—and the few investors he had allowed to buy into the fund—very, very wealthy men. He was at the RCA building to meet with his old friend Nelson Rockefeller and his banker brother, David, to talk investment strategies and look at Nelson's recent art acquisitions.

Lance, still the collector, was the founding chair of the City's newest museum, The Manhattan Museum of Modern Art. He achieved the distinction the way most wealthy people do, with money and the loan of several of the jewels from his collection to open the Museum.

Nelson was still a trustee of the Museum of Modern Art—the museum his mother, Abby Aldridge Rockefeller, had founded. Walter Chrysler, as he said he would, opened his own museum in Provincetown, Massachusetts. Lance, Nelson and, on occasion, Walter sometimes competed for the same art for their respective museums. Their rivalry was friendly but serious, often driving up the price of art when it became known that the three were interested buyers.

Lance's business and social life were insular and inter-changeable. In his world, money bought everything—his mansion on Park Avenue, art, access and anonymity. While he maintained friendships with the sons of titans and a few of their friends, they were not close relationships. Nelson Rockefeller was serving on presidential commissions and planning to run for governor of New York State. Walter continued his habit of making substantial purchases in art as well as glass, books and stamps. Unlike these men who enjoyed being in the public eye, Lance tightly controlled his world and remained outside the limelight his friends cast. By many standards he should have enjoyed his life, but Lance Henry Withers still feared that someone, somehow would uncover the secrets and lies that were the bedrock upon which he had built his success. Though race relations were not what they were in the thirties, in 1950, racial discrimination was still rampant in business, housing, jobs, education and the art world. It wasn't until he returned to the United States that Lance realized how deeply his father's revelation had scarred him—and still had the potential to take everything from him, again. The only way he could ensure that would never happen was to tightly control every aspect of his life, ensuring that no one would ever know that he had a life before the one he had now.

Lance had not taken Belle's advice to find someone who knew his secret, so he carried that burden alone after she died in May. She had been ill for a while and they had seen each other infrequently. Now that she was gone he felt the loss deeply. Charlotte was the only person who truly knew who he was. She was not his confidant, but he knew his secret was as safe with her as it had been with Belle. Charlotte was the only person who wanted to keep his race a secret more than he did.

⟜ 18 ⟞

New York 1960 - 1965

(I)

"Richmond-upon-Thames, is that correct? I once knew people in Richmond, the one here in the United States," Lance Withers said, without looking up. Emma perched on her chair across from his desk, eyes riveted on him.

"I don't know London that well, but Paris, have you ever been to Paris, Miss George?"

"Once, sir. Before I came to America, I accompanied my former missus. We were there just before the war." Lance was half listening to Emma as he leafed through her personnel file.

"So you think you're ready to be assistant House Manager? How long have you been with us, Miss George?"

"Twelve years in February, sir. I started as Miss Charlotte's aide."

"Twelve years," he said, still distracted by the paperwork, as if Emma only existed in the documents in front of him.

"Mr. Withers," Emma said, tired of talking to the top of Lance's head. "Mr. Withers, I'm right here. You can ask me anything that's in those papers."

Lance finally looked up. "Of course, I'm sorry. Yes, I remember when you came. You've changed." In twelve years, this was the first time he really took the time to notice her.

"I've grown up some," Emma said, but it was evident to Lance that she had not just grown, she had blossomed. "And I'm a citizen now," she added, proudly.

"Well, congratulations. That's an achievement," Lance said.

"Thank you, sir. Now, about the position?" Emma launched into a rambling pitch for the job as the house-manager-in-training. "I manage the first floor housekeeping staff now, coordinating with the kitchen, engineering, and any event staff. I know the scope of the work, having worked closely with your house manager, Daniel. He has given me his recommendation. I believe you have a copy there. If not, I have a carbon copy here that he gave me and I can assure you that I am ready to take on additional responsibilities, and I will in no way neglect my responsibilities with Miss Charlotte . . . "

At that point, Lance raised both hands, palms up, in surrender.

"May I get a few words in here?" Lance asked the now red-faced Emma. "Daniel told me he wants to retire in a couple of years. He is extremely impressed with you. He tells me if he can work with you, you are the best person to succeed him. He says your best qualification is that you get along with Charlotte."

Emma tried, but could not suppress her grin.

"It's fine, it's fine. We all know she's more than a handful," Lance said, laughing.

"She and I understand each other," Emma said. "She's just afraid, that's all."

"We're talking about Charlotte Bennett here. I've known her all of my life and I have never known her to fear anything or anyone."

"That's what she wants you to think, sir. She knows I understand her fears."

"Well, you must be the first to have that distinction. On that basis alone, you deserve a promotion."

"Yes, sir," Emma said, fearing she had said too much.

"So, you want this job, Emma George?" Lance continued, "In addition to dealing with Charlotte and Daniel, you will now have me to answer to. Are you up for that?"

"That and more, sir," she said, looking directly at him.

Lance clearly saw the woman the girl had become. *She's not afraid to go after what she wants*, he thought. Her intensity unnerved him a little. "Fine, so you'll train with Daniel. He will work out the compensation details and let me know," he said, extending his hand to shake on the agreement. Emma stood, grasped his hand firmly and gave it a good downward snap that surprised Lance. *Strong and confident*, he thought.

"You won't regret this, sir," Emma said, backing out of the room.

"I don't expect to, Miss George."

Lance called after her, as she turned into the hall. "When was the last time you were home?"

"This is home," she said without hesitation, then closed the door behind her.

(II)

For Lance, it started as lust, but he knew how to control that and for years, he did. With Emma's new responsibilities came their frequent meetings on household matters. More contact meant more opportunities to savor the smell of her hair when she sat next to him, the way she bit her lower lip when she pondered a question, her quick wit, her innate wisdom, and her willingness to challenge him. He admired her courage in dealing with vendors and her compassion with the staff—the only family she had.

Because of Emma's efficient preparation for their meetings on house matters, they always concluded their business early, leaving time to talk about other things.

"Miss Charlotte wanted me to read to her every day. The war put an end to my studies, so my reading was just awful. I practiced and practiced, read anything and everything. Miss Charlotte said to me, 'Don't just read, study!' So I did, through six years of night school to earn my degree from City College. Miss Charlotte had my diploma framed so I could hang it in my room."

"No, I never thought about leaving once I graduated. Why would I? Your household is like running a small business. I doubt that working anywhere else would be quite as wonderful."

"Now that I have a U.S. passport, I want to travel when I have time off. I've already been to the villa in Jamaica with Miss Charlotte, and I want to see how they rebuilt London, but I'm not quite ready to go back yet. It's still too painful—I lost so much in the war."

Emma spoke to Lance with ease, while managing to maintain the appropriate distance between employer and employee. Lance found it more difficult to maintain that distance. The more he learned about her, the more he was intrigued and looked forward to their next meeting.

Emma was not the kind of woman Lance was usually attracted to. His fascination with mature women started with Belle da Costa Greene and remained throughout his life. After his physical relationship with Belle ended, he continued to fulfill his need for sex and companionship with strong, mature, independent women of means. Some of his companions were rich in knowledge, others in connections, and every relationship benefited both Lance and the lady in some tangible way. The reciprocity proved useful in helping him keep his personal life private, and his sexual encounters discreet. Women his age and younger wanted commitment, marriage, and children; things that Lance Withers could not, would not, give.

Emma George was not fashionable, and she was young— nearly two decades younger than Lance Withers. She always wore plain navy or black conservatively styled business suits, a white shirt buttoned to the neck, and low-heeled black pumps—a work uniform she told him she modeled after the one her mother wore when she was in service. Lance imagined she had at least a week's worth of the outfits hanging in her closet waiting to be marched into service. Her skin was pale, as if she still lived under London's cloudy skies. She wore her black hair pulled back, in a tight, severe bun at the nape of her neck. A halo of curly wisps always managed to work their way loose, giving a hint of the beauty that she suppressed under her occupational attire. She wore no jewelry, except a watch, which she checked frequently, and no makeup except for a touch of lipstick. Emma was determined efficiency in a delicate, porcelain package.

Though he tried not to, Lance found Emma's strength and independence attractive. He knew enough wealthy men and women who indulged in unwise relationships with household staff; those assignations always ended badly for everyone. He tried to think of Emma as he did his priceless art collection—something to be treasured, but not touched.

≈ 19 ≈

Spring 1965

(I)

"SO WE'LL MEET AT ONE—NO, one-thirty—and from there we'll go to W&J Sloane's to see the furniture. Sheila will be joining us," Lance said, laying out his plans for the day.

"Sheila, the decorator?" Emma asked, hoping he would not hear the disappointment in her voice. She had hoped it would be just the two of them.

"I'm not taking the car this morning, so have Charles bring you when he picks us up from lunch. I have to make a quick stop at a gallery on Madison then we'll head over to Sloan's on 38th street," Lance said, then thought, "Why don't you come early and have lunch with us at 21? Sheila can tell us both what she has in mind for the staff quarters—you'll want to have a say on that won't you?"

"I'd like to, but I don't want to intrude on your lunch."

"It's a working lunch, Emma. You won't be intruding, you'll be working. I'll see you at noon then, 21 Club, Charles knows where it is," Lance said as he headed out of the door.

As Emma watched him cross Park Avenue, Mina, who now ran the kitchen came up behind her.

"What are you lookin' at Emma?"

"I just saw Mr. Withers off."

Mina looked out the door to see Lance Withers walk-running across Park Avenue. "Wherever he's going he's excited about gettin' there."

"Probably meeting Shee-la," Emma said, saying the name the way the woman pronounced it.

"Damn, you don't like her, do you?" Mina said as they headed to the kitchen.

"I'm just tired of her disrupting my house," Emma said as she took the kettle from the stove, filled it at the sink and then put it back on for tea.

"Oh, so this here is your house now?" Mina teased.

"You know what I mean. Every time I get a room in order, she changes another. Here comes Sheila," Emma said, mimicking the woman's contrived way of floating and walking, "in her tight little suits, gaudy and no doubt expensive jewelry and her endless measuring, furniture rearranging, color swatching and fabric draping."

"And she does a whole lot of Sheila draping on Mr. Withers too," Mina said as she moved items from the refrigerators to the stainless steel prep table to begin the day's meals.

"You noticed that too? I do not understand what he sees in that woman, He could do better," Emma said.

"I see," Mina said, smiling.

"You see what?"

"Look over here a minute," Mina said, squinting as she looked at Emma. "Yep, you got the green eye."

"What are you talking about Mina? My eyes are brown," Emma said, pretending not to understand.

"Uh huh," Mina said. "Don't be thinkin' there's more to your relationship with Mr. Withers than there is, Emma. That's how you get your heart broken *and* lose your job. Mr. Withers doesn't disrespect his staff like that. All the years I been here he never has. You been here long enough to know that too. Ain't like what you told me went on where your Momma and Daddy worked over there in London. No one here asks for or gets those kind of special favors. Mr. Withers don't fraternize with the help, so you best use those moony eyes I seen you give him on someone else."

The kettle began to sing and Emma pulled it from the stove, poured the hot water into her teacup and plunged the infuser in.

"Why you don't just use a tea bag I'll never know," Mina said.

"I'm British," Emma responded. "We respect tea."

"You're not British any more, you're an American now!" Mina reminded her of her recently earned citizenship.

"Yep, working on that American dream," Emma responded. "A husband, a house, two kids and a car."

"Well, I got the husband, three kids, too much house and a temperamental car. I also got the bills and the worry that go along with it so, I don't know how much of a dream it is," Mina said.

"But you also have the love that goes along with it, don't you?" Emma asked.

"That I do, that I do," Mina said with a smile. "Don't know where I'd be without Charlie and my boys. Emma," she continued, "you be careful. Don't go pretendin' this here is your house, your home, all you got. We all love you here but you gotta have something for yourself. You a good lookin' woman. You go out and find a man to give you those two kids, the home and that car if that's what you want. What about that Ed, the guy that works night security? He's a nice looking Irishman, told me he's planning to take the police cadet test—wants to become a detective like my Charlie. I seen how he looks at you—why don't you talk to him? You need to make more of an effort, for your own sake."

"I know," Emma said as sipped her tea. "Ed seems nice enough. He's asked me out few times. Nothing special, for a beer and a hamburger. I had a good time."

"Emma, Ed could be the one. Mr. Withers is not an option if only because Miss Charlotte don't want no woman gettin' with Mr. Withers. I've seen her work on 'em until they give up and go. Only one Queen Bee in this house and that is Charlotte Bennett," Mina added.

"I know that too," Emma said. She sipped her tea in silence while Mina began washing and chopping vegetables for tonight's dinner.

"Well, at least I'm going out to lunch today," Emma said.

"Now that's a start. With Ed?"

"No, Mr. Withers—he's taking me to 21." Mina eyed Emma but made no comment. "It's a business lunch with Sheila and Mr. Withers," Emma conceded. "I've never been to the 21 Club before. I don't know, maybe I should cancel. I'm not exactly in the 21 Club crowd."

"It's just a restaurant," Mina said, "You know how to eat, just go there and eat. What did Mrs. Roosevelt once say, 'Can't nobody disrespect you without your permission.' Withhold your permission, Emma, and just go."

(II)

When the car pulled up in front of the restaurant, the doorman greeted Emma as if she were a regular.

"Miss George, how nice of you to join us today. Mr. Withers told us that Charles would be bringing you. Mr. Withers and his other guest have not yet arrived, but your table is ready. Allow me to escort you in." Emma was surprised Mr. Withers had called ahead to let the restaurant know she would be joining them; the greeting and hospitality helped to calm her.

Seated at Mr. Withers' table, she looked around at the fashionably dressed women and prosperous looking men and she felt self-conscious in her standard black business suit uniform. She had put on a little makeup today, something she rarely did since she spent most of the day with her staff and not out in public. She put her hair in a French twist instead of her usual bun and she wore the small gold earrings Miss Charlotte had given her for Christmas last year. As she waited for Mr. Withers, she decided Mina was right, she would make more of an effort with her appearance and she'd find someone with whom to share her life. She would start with what she wore to work. *Perhaps it's time to update the outfit and my life*, Emma thought. Just then, Lance Withers entered the restaurant with his arm around Sheila's waist. When he saw Emma, he removed his arm, took Sheila's elbow and guided her to the table.

"Emma," he said, "glad you could join us, sorry to be a little late."

"We got tied up," Sheila said as she flashed Lance a look that left no question as to what delayed them. Sheila then turned her attention to Emma, "I know you're glad to get out of the house for a change. And lunch at 21! This must be a *real* treat for you. Lance and I dine here all the time, don't we darling?"

"I thought we could go over the design schemes together since Emma will be implementing everything and I wanted her input on the staff quarters," Lance said ignoring Sheila's pettiness.

"Oh, of course, the staff quarters; that would be your area of expertise wouldn't it, dear?" Sheila said, fixing a patronizing gaze on Emma who looked back at her with a stiff smile. Fortunately, the waiter arrived and Emma didn't have to respond.

After they placed their orders, Lance suggested that they talk about Sheila's recommendations for the staff rooms on the upper floor of the house.

"We can do something appropriate, down market, wood—maple or pine maybe? No upholstery of course. Simple single bed, a chair, small chest of drawers, that sort of thing. I think we can put two people in each room and that would create space for the gymnasium you must have, Lance."

"What do you think, Emma?" Lance asked.

"I think it sounds like prison," Emma said. "Mr. Withers' staff works hard. They are on their feet most of the day and sometimes on call twenty-four hours when we have guests and events. They need and deserve a private, quiet, comfortable place whether they live in or out. It doesn't have to be opulent but it doesn't have to be austere either." Emma turned to Lance, "It should reflect you, your house, your values Mr. Withers."

"They're servants," Sheila said, appealing to Lance.

"They're people," Emma said firmly.

"Emma knows better than I do what's best for the staff. She's the reason we have so little turnover and I have no complaints about what she's advocated for them in the past. So, what are we talking about to upgrade the rooms as Emma suggested?" Lance asked.

"Lance, are you sure you want to accommodate servants and lose your gym? Everyone is putting a gym in these days—that's the perfect place for it, Lance darling," Sheila cajoled.

Lance shot her a look that let her know that she was being inappropriate. "I'll defer to Emma," Lance said. "She manages every aspect of 580 Park Avenue."

"Apparently she does," Sheila snapped just as the waiter returned with their meals.

The three made polite small talk through lunch. Several times Sheila tried to exclude Emma from the conversation but Lance always brought the topic back so that it included the three of them. When she realized that she was not making progress in her attempt to make Emma disappear Sheila excused herself to call ahead to Sloane's so they could pull some items together for them to look at.

When she returned to the table, she perched on her chair saying, "Lance dear, the salesman at Sloane's that I work with is only there until 3 today. I think I'll go directly over there to see what they have for the staff rooms, since we are going with what Emma wants. Why don't you take Emma with you to the gallery, that might be exciting for her. You don't really need my input. Who knows, Emma might have an opinion on art as well." Sheila dabbed her mouth with her napkin and rose from the table.

Lance got up to help her with her chair. "You take the car," he said, "Emma and I can walk to the gallery. It's just across Fifth, then Charles can come back and pick us up at the gallery."

"Whatever you say, Lance, dear. I think I have an idea of what you're looking for and I'll be ready when you and Emma arrive."

"Thank you, Sheila," Emma said.

"Miss Vaast," Sheila was quick to correct her. Emma watched Sheila undulate out of the restaurant clinging to Lance. *Shee-la Vaast, sounds like a stripper*, she thought, and then started to laugh. When Lance returned to the table, Emma was still chuckling.

"What's so funny?" he asked.

"Oh, nothing, Mr. Withers," she tried but couldn't stop laughing.

"Okay, are you going to let me in on the joke or not?"

"I'm sorry, it's just her name, I didn't know Sheila's last name until just now. It just struck me as funny, that's all."

"I know," Lance said, "She's one of New York's top decorators, but I swear her name sounds like she's a Times Square stripper."

(III)

Emma lay in bed trying to recall every detail of the day. Their lunch at 21 where he defended her from Sheila. Their walk to the gallery. Exploring the art with Mr. Withers as he told her about the artists and asked which paintings she liked.

"They are paintings, not pictures," he told her, and encouraged her to express her opinion and invited her to use his library to learn more about art and artists. He even purchased one of the paintings she admired, *The Flower Stand* by Childe Hassan.

"Let's hang it in your room so you can enjoy it every day," he suggested. "American impressionists are regaining favor these days. You have a good eye; this painting might be quite valuable in a few years. Good choice, Emma."

Emma buried her face in her pillow; *how could I have embraced him? But he put his arms around me and pulled me closer, or did I just image that?* Emma rolled over, sat up and turned on the light to look at the Hassan hanging on her wall. "I love it," she said aloud. "I love him too." She put her hands over her ears trying to drown out her mother's words ringing in her ears. *There are rules Emma, when you are in service there are strict rules about relationships. There is the front of the house and the back of the house, and nothing in between.*

↶ 20 ↷

Omaha, Nebraska to
Montego Bay, Jamaica to New York
November 1965

(I)

A NEWLY MINTED MILLIONAIRE FROM OMAHA, Nebraska, of all places, out-maneuvered Lance Henry Withers. He had underestimated the man; having his bid rejected in favor of a rookie investor was something people would notice. Lance had always been the youngest and the sharpest of his contemporaries. They used to call him the *Whiz Kid of Wall Street*, but at fifty-two, he was no longer a kid—was he also losing his edge? Lance could feel the hot breath of the next generation on his neck. The children and protégés of his peers were now anxious to put their Ivy League MBAs up against his street smarts. Lance had no heir to pass the baton to, and even if he did, he was not ready to relinquish his title.

Once the textile manufacturing company accepted the Omaha kid's final bid, Lance's acquisition team wasted no time getting out of the Nebraska winter. After months of flying back and forth to try to revive this deal, they were eager to return to the comfort of spouses and children. Lance decided to spend another night in the hotel in Omaha to avoid the two women he lived with. Charlotte was as demanding and possessive as ever, and Emma would never be his to possess. He'd stayed in Omaha during the months of business negotiations to help suppress his attraction to Emma. Hard work and a little distance had always quelled a romance he wished to avoid; however, his self-imposed exile had not had the effect he'd hoped for. He missed Emma.

He ate his room service steak and looked out of the window at the flat, bleak landscape of winter in Omaha, knowing that the same grey of the season waited for him in New York. He clicked on the television and flipped channels until he landed on an old James Bond movie filmed in Jamaica. As he watched Ursula Andress emerge from the Caribbean Sea in a skimpy white bikini, he asked himself, *why should 007 have all the fun?* The island was just the tonic he needed. *I'll go to the villa in Round Hill*, Lance thought. *Some sun, Appleton rum and a beach full of bikini-clad women, that's what I need.*

(II)

Lance bought the Round Hill villa in Jamaica so that Charlotte could spend the winters away from him. If Charlotte hadn't decided to take a cruise with her friend Mrs. Cumberbatch and encouraged Emma to use the villa for the three weeks she would be away, it might never have happened.

Emma went to Round Hill to make her final decision about leaving 580 Park. She had been dating Ed McKenna steadily the last few months; she knew it was time to either commit to him or end it.

Emma often accompanied Charlotte on her winter vacations to the villa and over the years, she and Winsom, Withers' long-time Jamaican housekeeper, had become friends and confidants. In her youth, Winsom had survived a crush on the dashing Mr. Withers. Now happily married and immune to his charm, she was the perfect person to counsel Emma.

Away from Lance Withers' world, and with Winsom's wise counsel, Emma could clearly see that to have a chance at a life of her own, she needed to leave her existence at the edges of Lance Withers' life. She'd spent enough time longing for a man she could never have. At thirty-three years old, she was running out of time.

Feminism and the Women's Liberation Movement were gaining traction, women were considering their options beyond the roles of wife and mother. Emma had been liberated since she was sixteen years old. She was used to making her own living and structuring her life on her terms. What she had not experienced was the intimate constraint of loving someone and having them love you back. She had lost her mother, father and brother, Philmore, in World War II. If she wanted a family she would have to create it, starting with a man to love her and give her the children she wanted. If she stayed at 580 Park Avenue that love and that life would never happen.

(III)

Lance had never seen Emma wear anything other than her work uniform. She stood with her back to him, wearing white shorts and a bikini top the colors of the hibiscus and ginger flowers that she was arranging in a vase. She was bronze, down to her barefoot toes, from the week she had already spent in the Jamaican sun. Her hair, tied back by a colorful scarf, cascaded down her back. *She's even more beautiful,* he thought, standing just outside the kitchen door listening to Emma and Winsom chatting.

Winsom turned, surprised to see him. "Good Lord Mon, you give Winsom such a fright! Why you be lurkin' like some such lizard," she chastised him. "Mr. Lance, this be your house, when you come, you make yourself known. We were not told to expect you!"

"Sorry, Winsom, I flew down this morning. I didn't know anyone was here. You're supposed to be on vacation aren't you? And Miss George, when did you…?"

"Mr. Withers, I had no idea that you—Miss Charlotte told me to use the villa since there wouldn't be guests while

Winsom was on vacation," Emma said. "I'm sorry, if I had known you were coming . . ."

Lance interrupted her. "I could really use a cup of coffee," he said, animating both women into action and keeping Emma from saying anything that might ruin this moment for him.

"Right away, Mr. Lance," Winsom said, pushing Emma aside to make coffee in the small kitchen. "Winsom make you lunch as well."

"Just the coffee is fine, Winsom, I can go down to the restaurant for something to eat," Lance said, never taking his eyes off Emma while she smoothed her hair and folded her arms across her chest in an effort to cover herself.

"No, Mr. Lance. I fix your lunch. Rest yourself down by the pool and I bring you what you like. Go now, I say. No talk of restaurants while Winsom is still here!" With Winsom, one did as one was told. *Who works for whom?* Lance thought as she ushered him out of the kitchen and planted him in a chair on the patio.

Lance sat by the pool, looking up at the kitchen window and wondering what to say to Emma, other than the inappropriate, "Please stay."

With her trademark efficiency, Winsom reappeared in a few minutes, "I bring the coffee as soon as it brew. Lunch be right on its heels," she said.

"Is Miss George still with you in the kitchen?" Lance asked.

"No sir, as soon as you leave she make herself scarce. Shall I call her?"

"No, no. I'll find her," Lance said. Winsom returned to the kitchen and Lance sipped his coffee, trying to convince himself to do what he should, not what he wanted.

(IV)

Emma was almost finished packing when she heard a knock on the bedroom door. "Come on in," she said, calling from the bathroom as she threw the last few things in her bag.

"Is he still eating lunch? Before he finishes, I need to be gone from here. I cannot believe this! I finally get everything straight in my mind and he shows up and confuses me. We had it all worked out, didn't we Winsom? I knew what I had to do—what my Mum used to say, there are rules, there's the front of the house, the back of the house, and nothing in between. Clear boundaries, the way it has to be. When I saw him—damn it, he never comes here. Made me start wanting the impossible again. You're right, Winsom, there's no future there. I just wanted these three weeks to get used to the idea, then I could go back to New York, resign, and start my new life. I *never* should have accepted Miss Charlotte's offer. I'll find a hotel in Montego Bay . . ."

"That's not likely, given we're coming up on a holiday," Lance said. Emma ran out of the bathroom to see him standing near the open door to the bedroom. Her hands flew to her face and she dropped onto the sofa in the room.

"Stay," Lance said, "I'm going back to New York this afternoon. This is your vacation. Tell her she's earned it, Winsom," he added as Winsom walked into the room.

"You've earned it," Winsom said, realizing that she'd interrupted something.

"Mr. Lance, your lunch be ready." Lance walked over to Emma, took her hands from her face and placed them awkwardly in her lap.

"You stay. I haven't even unpacked. No worries," he said. "I've got a car waiting to take me to the airport. Thank you for lunch, Winsom. Have wonderful vacations, both of you."

(V)

Emma sat in the great room of the villa listening to Billie Holiday sing the blues. She had downed nearly half a bottle of rum. She had to drink more, she was going for drunk. She'd made a fool of herself in front of Mr. Withers. *All I had to do was turn around for a second and I would have avoided confessing that I was in love with him. Did I say I loved him?* She couldn't remember and it didn't matter; she had said enough. Emma laughed at how ridiculous it was to think Mr. Withers would see her as anything other than staff.

A burst of thunder and a flash of lightening made her jump. *Get up, if I drink any more I'll be sick, then I'll have to clean that up too. What the hell,* she thought, and poured herself another drink.

The storm intensified and the canvas curtains that protected the open-air room during severe weather billowed and flapped in the wind. Rain, or what the Jamaicans call liquid sunshine, spattered onto the marble floors. She watched the growing pool of water, *I should clean that up. I'm the help, back of the house, at your service Mr. Withers.* Tears filled her eyes, "I've wasted so much time," she sobbed. "Thirty-three years old and I have nothing to call my own—no family, no home, no life outside of ..." Peals of thunder and flashes of lightening were no competition for Emma's sobs. Before Mr. Withers showed up unexpectedly, she'd decided to resign; but she also knew she could change her mind. Now, she didn't have a choice, she had to leave. *I could stay in Jamaica, find work at one of the hotels on the island.* The thought of putting distance between her, Lance Withers, and everything she knew made her cry harder.

A bolt of lightning finally snuffed out the electricity, as it had been threatening to do all evening. Emma continued to drink in the silence and the dark, as she waited for the resort's generator to start up. Through the billowing canvas, she caught a glimpse of headlights on the road outside, and then heard footsteps running up the walk. Just as she was about to feel afraid, the generator kicked in, illuminating Lance as he stepped into the room. Emma held her breath.

"Everything out of Sangster was cancelled. I tried to get a flight to anywhere, Emma. I didn't want to come back here. I knew if I did I might—"

"Might what?" Emma stumbled getting up from the couch.

Lance put his suitcases down. He could see that she'd been drinking and crying. *Was that Billy Holiday playing?* He knew he could easily pull them both into something that could be wonderful or disastrous.

"I'm soaked, I need something to warm me up," he said. Emma held up the bottle of rum. "I was thinking coffee. You could probably use some too," Lance said, moving toward the kitchen.

"Mr. Withers, do you know how to make coffee?" Emma asked. Lance thought for a second, and then realized he had never made coffee in his life.

"I didn't think so," Emma said when he hesitated. "You change out of your wet clothes and I'll make us both some coffee, how about that?"

(VI)

"So you're resigning?" Lance asked, taking a sip from his mug of coffee as they stood in the small galley kitchen, "When were you planning to tell me?"

"I'd just decided," Emma, said looking down at her bare feet. They stood in silence for a few seconds while the storm outside provided an ominous soundtrack for their strained conversation.

"This afternoon, when you said you knew what you had to do, is that when you decided?" Lance asked.

"I had to figure out whether the next seventeen years of my life are going to be the same as the last seventeen."

"Were they so bad?"

"No, no, Mr. Withers, I didn't mean to imply they were. This job has been everything to me. When I showed up on your doorstep with no place to go, you saved my life. When you made me major domo, you gave me a profession. I owe you so much and I'm grateful. It was a hard decision to leave, but it's time."

"Don't—" he paused to clear his throat, "leave."

Emma looked up at him. "It's time," she repeated. "I've spent most of my life making a home for you and Miss Charlotte, and I forgot to make one for myself."

"You once told me that 580 Park was your home," Lance said.

"You remember that," Emma said, smiling at the memory.

"And I remember when I hired you. You were just a girl, and when you asked for the major domo job, I remember thinking—when did you become this, this beautiful woman? And I remember—" The wind howling outside blew open the kitchen window shutters. The rain poured in. Lance and Emma raced to the window wrestling side-by-side to close the shutters against the elements. When they finally secured them, the two were soaked to the skin. Emma grabbed a dishtowel and tentatively dabbed at rain dripping from Lance's face before handing the towel to him and grabbing another to dry herself.

"What did you mean by front of the house, back of the house, nothing in between?" They were facing each other in the kitchen's narrow aisle.

"Just something my Mum used to say," Emma said, wondering if there would ever be another opportunity to tell him how she felt. She had already told him she was leaving, and emboldened by remnants of the rum, she decided she had nothing to lose.

"No, what it means is that I have to go because I have feelings for you that are, oh hell, I'm just going to say it. I've been in love with you for so long," she confessed. She tried to read his face, looking for a reaction to her confession. Lance said nothing; his face gave her no clue as to how he felt about what she'd just said. "I know that was inappropriate, unprofessional, even ridiculous, but I've gone and done it now, haven't I," Emma said, ringing the towel in her hand into a tight knot.

"So, I guess I have to do something about this now," Lance said, still giving her no indication of what he was thinking. He reached over and took the knotted towel from her hand.

"You've worked for me long enough to know that I have a strict anti-fraternization policy in my household, Miss George," he looked down at the towel now in his hands. Tears started to well up in Emma's eyes as he continued. "I want you to know that you have been a valued employee, but because of what you just said to me the professional relationship we've enjoyed all these years can't continue. Miss George, you are officially terminated." When he looked up, a slight smile inched across his face, "Now that you are no longer an employee, I am free to tell you I am also inappropriately obsessed with you." He paused long enough for her to take in what he had said before he took her in his arms and kissed her.

(VII)

When Emma opened her eyes the next morning, Lance was staring at her, his face just inches from hers. Her first thought was bliss; she had fantasized about being with him so many times, but this was not a dream. She sat up in disbelief, not knowing whether to laugh, cry, run, or stay. Lance put his arm around her waist and pulled her to him.

"This is the part where we don't know what to say to each other," he said.

"I'm not sorry," Emma said. Lance let out a breath he didn't realize he was holding, and pulled her closer.

"Neither am I," he said. She lay back down on the bed, Lance's chest nestled against her back. His hand brushed against her breast and she stiffened slightly. He kissed her shoulder, the lobe of her ear, then whispered, "Emma." She wanted to respond but saying *Lance* aloud seemed strange. She was struck by this ridiculous conundrum—when you're lying naked after making love to the man who has been your employer for almost two decades, what do you call him? She tried to suppress a laugh but she couldn't.

"What?" he asked.

"I was trying to figure out what I should call you," she said turning over to face him. "Mr. Withers doesn't seem appropriate in this situation, does it?"

"Try Lance," he said.

"Lance." The name seemed odd on her lips and to her ear.

"Say it again," he said.

"Lance."

"That's who I am now. I am Lance and you are Emma. Not Miss George—Emma, the woman I have been thinking about in inappropriate ways for quite some time now."

"Lance," she said again. Pressing her naked body against him she asked, "How inappropriate?"

(VIII)

Emma drew her finger lightly across the sheen of sweat on Lance's forehead. It was well past noon, after the drenching rain from last night the island sweltered in the Caribbean sun. Even with the sea breeze blowing through the mostly open-air pavilion and ceiling fans swirling above, the bedroom was warm with the salty aroma of sweat and sex.

"We're going to have to get out of bed at some point," Lance said, his eyes still closed.

"I suppose," Emma said. He opened his eyes to see her forehead, also beaded with sweat, damp, dark curls framing her face. *So young, so beautiful.* Lance thought. *Too young, too beautiful,* he thought again.

"Stop frowning," Emma said, tracing his lips with her finger.

"Was I frowning?"

"What were you thinking about?"

"You."

"Wow, didn't last long," she said.

"You said you love me," Lance said, turning serious. "How do you know that?"

"I just do," Emma said.

"How do you know with such certainty?"

"I've seen so many women come and go in your life; surely there was someone you loved," Emma said.

Lance took a few moments to answer, "No, I never let a relationship get that far, I'd always end it before it got to that." He sat up and looked through the open window to the blue Caribbean Sea, perfectly framed by palm trees and Jamaica's cerulean sky.

Emma sat up and turned his face to hers. "Why? Why did you always want to end it?"

"I'm not sure. What about you, have you been in love before?"

"I tried, but you were always in the way. You were the measure of every man and no one seemed up to the challenge."

"You told me you loved me so easily."

"It wasn't easy but it was worth the risk," Emma said.

"Why?"

"Do you want me to innumerate all of the things that are—what did you call it earlier—inappropriate?"

Lance got up without answering her question, walked into the bathroom and closed the door. Emma pulled the sheet up to her chin, suddenly conscious of how exposed she was. She closed her eyes tightly and rolled over in the bed facing away from the bathroom door. *I said too much*, she thought. *Presumptuous, too honest, stupid*—she berated herself.

"Emma?" She hadn't noticed Lance return, "Sorry, bathroom break," he said as he sat down on the bed and took her hand, "Be patient with me," he said. "I'm not certain what I'm doing, being here, like this, with you. I know this is wrong but somehow it doesn't feel that way. I can't tell you I love you. I've been selfish all my life, I'm not sure I'm capable of—" he didn't finish that thought but said, "I want to find out what happens next—for us."

"Well, that's something isn't it," she said.

"It is," he said. "For me, it's something."

(IX)

"So how do you like your coffee?" Lance asked as he helped prepare their breakfast of fresh fruit, eggs and toast. It was the first time he had helped to prepare a meal; he liked sharing the unfamiliar task with Emma.

"No coffee for me, I hate coffee," Emma said, screwing up her face in disgust.

"You had coffee last night."

"That was for medicinal purposes if you recall."

"I see," he smiled remembering last night. "How can anyone hate coffee? Especially this coffee, Jamaican Blue Mountain. Next to Ethiopian coffee, I think it's some of the best in the world. I love coffee."

"I know, I'm the one who keeps the coffee larder stocked—here and in New York."

"Oh, right," he said, remembering she had the advantage of knowing most of the mundane details of his life. He had much to discover about Emma George.

"So your preference is tea."

"I'm British, remember? Strictly tea, a love Miss Charlotte and I share," Emma said as she opened the tea caddy, choosing a package of Earl Grey.

"Tell me something, why do you seem to be the only person on earth who gets along with Charlotte?" Lance asked, in awe of Emma's ability to deal with his formidable grandmother.

"I understand her because we have a shared experience."

"What experience could you possibly share with my grandmother?" Lance asked as they carried their breakfast to the patio.

"We understand loss," Emma said not looking at Lance. "Miss Charlotte lost all of her family when she was twelve, and had to make her own way. I was sixteen when I lost everyone, my mother, father and my brother in the London Blitz. Something happens to you when there's no one to look out for you; when you are all you have. Miss Charlotte and I understand the fear of vulnerability."

Lance sat back in his chair. "Charlotte, vulnerable? You're kidding, right?"

"No, I'm not. People deal with the fear in different ways. Miss Charlotte keeps everything in here," Emma said putting her hand over her heart, "to keep from being hurt. That's why she keeps people at arm's length. I have a special place for her in my heart because I understand she fears losing everything, again. I had to find a way to manage that same fear. Instead of putting up barriers, I tore them down; I forced myself to be fearless. When I got on that boat and came to New York from London, I was a war orphan, I was the only one I could count on. I was then, and I am now, all I really have in the world."

"You still feel that way?"

"I have to," Emma said. Her answer made him uncomfortable.

"What am I? Vulnerable or fearless?" he asked.

"Both," she said. "You're like Miss Charlotte, erecting barriers to keep anyone from knowing the real Lance Henry Withers. I believe you're fearless in business—you know money gives you power—it is the way you put distance between you and everyone else. But your art collection is the biggest barrier. All the emotion you don't show people you put into your collection. I see the way you collect —you fall in love with each piece, and the way you care for it—I've seen you, what's the word, commune with it."

"What are you talking about Emma? I enjoy my collection-"

"No it's more than that. The way you look at a painting – like you're pulling something from it or being pulled into it – one or both, I don't know. I think that's the only time you let all of your barriers down, where you reveal yourself. You also use art to keep people focused on what you have, not who you are."

Lance looked away from her. "So you've spent the past seventeen years analyzing me."

Emma got up from the table, walked over to him, taking his face in her hands. "I see you; without the art, the money, the power, the privilege. I see you, Mr. With—Lance," she said, still getting used to calling him by his first name. "And I'm not afraid of what I see."

"Maybe you should be."

"I know how to take care of myself. I'm good at it. I'm fearless, remember?"

(X)

"You're going to wear that? You look like a rich tourist." Emma, in cut-off jeans and a bright cotton sleeveless shirt, made a face as Lance came into the living room.

"I am a rich tourist," he said as he patted his pocket looking for his sunglasses.

"No, for the next two weeks you're not. You're just a guy, not the gentry. Get rid of the Rolex, those fancy leather sandals, the silk shirt and linen slacks—they all have to go. The places we're going, you wear jeans and a tee shirt, sneakers or flip flops."

"I don't wear jeans or tee shirts. I wear shoes or Italian leather sandals. I don't even own that other kind of attire," he said as if she'd asked him to go into Montego Bay naked.

"Attire? Good Lord Mon!" she said, invoking the island dialect. "Work with me here. Surely there is something in your closet that does not scream, 'Hey, over here, rich guy!'"

She took his hand and led him back into the bedroom. Rummaging through his closets, she dismissed outfit after outfit, then turned to him with her hands on her hips.

"I'm renowned for my impeccable wardrobe," Lance said. "I learned about fashion when I lived in Paris."

"Paris can't help you here. Don't move," Emma said as she headed toward the service area of the house. She returned with a pair of cotton khakis and a bright green, yellow and red Jamaican flag tee shirt.

"You and Kingsley are about the same height, he's thicker around the waist, you'll need a belt. We'll have to make do with the shoes, all I could find were work boots and your feet are a couple of sizes larger than his," she said, then added, "and for that I'm grateful." Lance laughed, enjoying this Emma. She began unbuttoning his shirt.

"You want me to wear my gardener's clothes," Lance said.

"Just for today, I don't think he'll mind. They're clean— Winsom washed before she left and I'll wash them before they get back. He'll never know."

"You're kidding, right?" Lance asked.

"I'm not," Emma said. "We'll buy you some 'relaxed attire' at the market but in the meantime these will do."

"You want me to wear the gardener's clothes?" Lance asked again as Emma pulled the tee shirt over his head and stood back to admire the effect, then handed him the khakis.

"I want you to experience this island like you're a part of it, not *apart* from it. Eat a little *ackee* and *saltfish*, drink Red Stripe, listen to reggae, get some sun on that pasty skin, dance on the beach—you dance don't you? If not, maybe we'll smoke some ganja—that'll loosen you up," she said, assessing his new outfit. "You can keep the sunglasses and we'll get you a hat, no one will recognize you—not that any of *your* people will be where we're going."

"Emma, let's just stay here and enjoy each other; order in, go out on the boat, visit some galleries."

"That's what Mr. Withers would do but you're Lance, you're still Lance right? He's with Emma, on *her* vacation. Trust me," she said, planting a kiss on his lips. "You are about to have the time of your life."

———⟫●⟪———

Emma showed Lance another side of Jamaica and life. He'd been coming to the island for more than a decade and had rarely been outside of Round Hill's guarded compound. Instead of dining in the island's best resorts and restaurants, she took him to the open-air markets where they ate from carts and shopped for food that she showed him how to cook. He was even surprised to find some interesting art among the local artists selling their work on the streets.

Emma didn't drive and Lance had not driven a car in years but after several harrowing attempts, he finally mastered driving on the left side of the road. They visited Ocho Rios and climbed Dunn's River Falls, ate jerk chicken, peas and rice and drank Red Stripe at rustic local restaurants that Lance declared better than the faux island fare at the starred restaurants he usually frequented. They swam naked in Negril and made love on the beach. He bought a hat, several pairs of jeans, tee shirts, even flip-flops.

For two weeks they were consumed by the intimate excitement of the present. Thoughts of what came next were always on the periphery but they did not talk about how, or if, they would go back to being who they used to be. Their unspoken pact was to stay in the perfection of who they were at this time and in this place.

The night before Emma was scheduled to return to New York, Lance lay awake watching her. She slept so peacefully, he had never been able to sleep like that. *Do you rest easy when you face your fears?* Was being fearless the secret to her strength and her compassion? He was in awe of her courage. He had spent most of his life being afraid of everything and everyone. These past two weeks showed him that in his cloistered existence he had missed so much.

At the same time, their adventures had confirmed the choice he had made to pass. In Montego Bay, Ocho Rios, and Kingston and everywhere on the island in between he was fully aware of the racial advantage of being white. Jamaica was a country of black people but the most prosperous on the island were white tourists and the Jamaicans who ensured those tourists were not touched by the poverty and pathos that existed in the real Jamaica.

Lance thought back to that night in Paris when he watched Josephine Baker perform for white men who only saw her sexuality; they didn't see the woman, they only saw how she pleasured them. Lance had only experienced how Jamaica pleasured him; until now he had never seen its people. He secretly shared their heritage and nothing else. He felt as he had that night in Paris, disconnected from everyone and everything—like his father and Belle Greene warned, he belonged to no one and no tribe.

What if Emma could really see through all the barriers I've erected? Is my secret still worth protecting? What would happen if I took down that final barrier and revealed everything to Emma? For the first time in thirty years, he considered the prospect. He closed his eyes and pulled the sleeping Emma close, his breathing matching hers.

"I'm not the man you think I am," he whispered into her dark curls. "I never have been. You know me better than anyone and you don't know me at all."

(XI)

Emma left the island first.

"When I see you in New York, we will work things out," Lance said, kissing her goodbye as the taxi driver loaded her bags into the car. He held her close, stroking her hair. When she started toward the waiting car, he held onto her hand, taking her in as if it would be the last time he would ever see her.

"I'll see you at home," Emma said, as she slid into the backseat of the taxi.

"I'll see you at the house," he answered. With those words, Lance burst the bubble that they had lived in for the past two weeks. Emma knew "house" meant something very different from "home." Five-eighty Park Avenue was the house they both lived in, but not together, and Emma did not know if there was any place the two of them could make a home. Lance was the front of the house, she was the back of the house, and now there was nothing but heartache in between. He was already pulling away.

Lance gave the driver instructions and enough money to ensure that Emma had an escort to the gate, and onto the plane. Lance closed the door and stood aside as the car started to pull away. She and the driver heard Lance shout "Emma!" when the car was a few feet down the road.

"Stop the car!" Emma screamed at the driver. Not waiting for the car to come to a complete stop, she opened the door, jumped out and ran back to Lance, who scooped her up in his arms.

"Everything that happened here was real, do you know that?" he asked, holding her so tight that she could barely breathe. The tears Emma had been able to avoid were now streaming down her face. "We will work this out, decide what's next," Lance whispered, as if trying to convince both of them. Emma held him, her eyes closed, imprinting how his body felt against hers. She reached up and stroked his face with the back of her hand.

"Forever, I will love you forever," Emma said, and kissed him so deeply she felt like she was drowning. Then slowly, reluctantly, she pushed him away. She turned and walked quickly to the waiting car. Without looking back, she got in, slammed the door closed and said to the driver, "Go! And don't stop for anything."

Lance was rooted in the middle of the road where she'd left him, her scent still with him, and the warmth of her kiss still on his lips. He stood perfectly still, a single step would shatter the last two weeks. He watched her taxi wind its way down the hill and along the road until it disappeared, never realizing just how far it would take them from each other.

⌁ 21 ⌁

New York—November 1965 - February 1966

(I)

"I'VE NEGLECTED EVERYTHING BUT YOU for the past couple of weeks, my business partners are not happy. I should be back in New York in a couple of weeks."

"I'm not going anywhere," Emma told Lance when she called the villa to let him know she had arrived safely, "I'll be here."

Lance wasn't sure why he lied to her. He could return to her now. He could tell her the truth about who he was and what that meant. He had never been this close to sharing the facts of his life with anyone other than Belle. But he did what he always did—he pulled back. It would be three months and as many continents before Lance returned to New York. He flew to Europe, then Mexico, then back to the Caribbean, slipping back into the man he was before his time with Emma.

He needed to think about what had happened to him, why she had made him consider doing something he had spent his whole life resisting. He regretted not heeding Belle's advice, he needed to talk this out with someone who knew his truth, but he had no one he could confide in, he belonged to no tribe. *Ah Belle, I need you*, Lance thought missing her. The only other person who knew his truth was Charlotte, and despite what Emma said about her, Lance knew she was not someone he could confide in.

So Lance did what he always did when he was trying to solve a problem—he returned to his lifelong mistress, art. With her, he was the powerful Collector, always in control. As he toured studios and galleries, talking with artists and gallerists, he was preoccupied with the prospect of life with or without Emma. Was he willing to risk everything, all of the secrets he had buried, for what would be a difficult life for both of them? She would always be the maid who married the millionaire. He recalled the merciless way the media savaged the kitchen maid who wed one of the Rockefeller heirs. Emma told him she was fearless, but could she withstand that kind of hell?

Then there was the age difference, he was almost two decades older than she was, he would be a cliché as well. If they had children and they bore signs of his hidden heritage, would she love them without reservation? Would he? It was impossible for him to consider all of the implications of loving Emma; but he did love her, he was sure of that now. But was love enough? No matter how much art he bought, or how much he tried to dissuade and distract himself with business and even other women, he always came back to Emma.

With no clear answers, but determined they could resolve everything together, Lance called Emma to tell her he would be home in a few days. He left several messages, which she did not return. When he finally arrived at 580 Park Avenue, Mina told him that Emma had been gone for more than a month. It never occurred to him that Emma would not wait for him.

"She just left, Mr. Withers. She didn't say anything to anyone," Mina told him. "She and Miss Charlotte had dinner together, and the next day Emma was gone. We're all trying to figure out what happened."

"What did you do this time?" Lance said, bursting into Charlotte's room.

"What did I do?" Charlotte retorted. "What did *you* do? You took advantage of that girl in Jamaica. Don't look so surprised. It was all over her when she got back here. At first I didn't know it was you until your secretary told me you flew to Jamaica after you left Omaha. I already knew she was there. Why couldn't you just leave her alone?"

"You don't know what you're talking about, Charlotte."

"I know you compromised that poor lonely girl."

"Charlotte, what did you do to her? Why did she leave?"

"You acted like a damn fool, Lance, but I took care of it."

It took Lance just two steps to cross the room and grab the old woman. "What did you do, Charlotte?" he bellowed.

"Don't you talk to me that way, Lance Henry Withers. Your cavalier behavior put us all in jeopardy. I wasn't going to let some fling with the housekeeper change our lives. What if you'd gotten the woman pregnant? Do you think for a moment our friends would be eager to accept a colored child you fathered with the housekeeper? Think with the right head, Lance."

Lance let go of Charlotte and dropped into a chair, his face in his hands.

"What would you have me do, Lance? Tell her the truth? If you loved her so much what took you so long to get back here? Why didn't you tell her who you really are?"

"What have you done?" Lance was nearly frantic. "Where did she go?"

"I have no idea," Charlotte said, straightening the sleeve of her sweater where Lance had grabbed her. "I told her there was no chance that you would marry her, and that I would not allow it. You two had your fling, and now it's over. After that, she left. Not sure exactly when she left, she just took her things and slipped away."

Charlotte did not mention that she told Emma that it was Lance that wanted her to leave—making her believe that he didn't have the courage or the decency to tell her himself. She also neglected to tell him that Emma left him a note:

"Lance, I think we both knew we could never work. I just wish you had told me. Still, I wish you well.

Fearlessly, Emma"

When Charlotte found the note, she destroyed it.

Lance looked up at Charlotte. "It wasn't a fling. I love her."

Charlotte was unmoved. "You say that now, but later you'll thank me. I just did what was best for all of us. She couldn't stay here. She was smart enough to know that—for that I give her credit. I won't have that kind of thing going on in my house."

"Your house? Who are you to make decisions about what goes on in *my house?*" Lance shouted.

"But for me you would have none of this, Lance Henry Withers," Charlotte said fingering the strands of pearls she still wore every day, "I plotted and planned to get this life, this house and everything in it for you. Do you thank me? No, you detest me for it. What were you going to do with that poor woman? Marry her? Keep her and any black babies you'd have with her hidden away?" Charlotte said, lowering her voice for the last sentence.

"Charlotte, I have lived with that threat for so long. It is 1966, none of this matters anymore."

"It matters to people like us," Charlotte assured him. Lance laughed at the hypocrisy of their lives. "Like us? We're not even people like us, Charlotte. We just pretend to be. You of all people know Lance Henry Withers doesn't really exist. He was never born. He is one of your creations."

"Yes, I may have fabricated Lance Henry Withers, but *you* brought him to life," Charlotte said triumphantly. The old woman walked over and closed the door to her suite. Eighty-nine and still formidable, she stood over the defeated Lance, "Tell me, Lance. What is it exactly that you hate about me?"

"I don't hate you, Charlotte. I hate the things you do. I'm fifty-three years old and you are still interfering, trying to control my life."

"The things I've done, I've done for you. I made your grand and glorious life possible, Lance. When your father made certain your only future was that of a Negro in the segregated South, it was Charlotte that made sure that didn't happen. I kept this family financially solvent, even during the Depression. I took the family to Europe. When you needed contacts and seasoning, I was the one who *asked* Belle Green to take you under her wing. When your mother was sick, I took care of her because you were too selfish to leave your life in Paris."

"You can stop the martyr act. I know exactly what you've done, Charlotte. I know everything," Lance said, opening the dam on more than thirty years of truth and hurt. "I know my mother killed herself because she thought she'd lost everything. You never understood. My mother loved my father. She loved him, Charlotte, but you never let up on him. No matter what he did, how successful he was or how much his family loved him, he was just 'the janitor' to you. What did you call him on the night he died? A nigger? She loved a nigger more than she loved me or you!"

"You're a cruel bastard," Charlotte said, her eyes welling with tears.

"It seems to run in the family doesn't it?" Lance said. "You wanted to have this conversation, Charlotte, so we'll have it. Here's more truth," he said, moving in to confront the old woman. "You took control of me and my mother and all of my father's money as soon as he died. We were still in shock but before my mother and I knew it, you had my father's body removed from the hospital and buried. No funeral, no flowers, no regrets. You treated him like a mongrel dog," Lance said, wincing in pain from the memory. "And you never even bothered to tell his wife or his son when or where he was buried. You changed my name and my mother's name without our knowledge or consent. I know you threatened to blackmail Belle if she didn't, what did you call it, *take me under her wing*?"

"And you benefitted from everything I did *for* you, not *to* you," Charlotte said.

Through gritted teeth, Lance continued to list his grandmother's grievous acts.

"You prostituted me with your little bargain with Belle Greene. You didn't tell me my mother had died; for more than a year after she killed herself you sent me letters and wires as if they were from her. You did the same thing to my mother that you did to my father. You never gave me a chance to say goodbye." Lance said, the pain of both losses still palpable.

"I was afraid you wouldn't come back from Europe if it was just me," Charlotte wailed.

"You threatened and controlled me with the fear of who I was and how loving someone, anyone, would ruin my life and so I never loved or was loved—until Emma—and now you've destroyed that, too." The hate welled up in him. He wanted to hurt Charlotte for all the years he allowed her to hurt him. When she began to whimper in fear, he was unrelenting.

"Do you know why you're here, Charlotte? Why you've lived in my house all of these years? It would have been so easy to . . ." He didn't finish the sentence, he was afraid of what he might say. "Before my mother killed herself, she sent me a letter. She said, 'If anything ever happens to me, please take care of my mother. Keep her with you, no matter what.' She said that we were each other's only connection to our true past. She asked me not to forget that she loved you, and that she loved me. She wrote, 'Despite everything, remember Hank, the husband and father we both loved.'" Charlotte's face contorted in pain at the thought of her precious daughter's love and generosity—qualities she knew were not her nature.

Lance sat down on the bed, exhausted by all of the old memories.

"Belle Greene once told me to find someone who knew my truth. Someone I could confide in. All these years I kept everything inside and then I found Emma, I was going to tell Emma. I wanted to know what love without secrets and lies felt like—I've never known that kind of love. I'm certain you don't know either," Lance said. "Look at us, Charlotte, we *are* all each other has; you are the only one who knows my truth. You let Emma leave both of us because you were afraid her love for me would take something away from you. The sad thing is that she loved you, too." Lance got up to leave the room then stopped, turning to face his grandmother he said, "I'm done, Charlotte. I can't take anymore of you. I broke my promise to my father, now I'm going to break the one I made to my mother. I can't be around you anymore. I'll find Emma, but we won't come back here. I've got to find her or I'll end up just like you." Lance moved to the door.

Charlotte reached out and grabbed his coat to stop him. "We're more alike than you know," she said.

Lance turned around to see tears streaming from Charlotte's eyes. She took a linen and lace handkerchief from the wrist of her sweater and pressed to her cheeks and nose.

"I was born Cora Ann Cox, in 1877, in Enfield, North Carolina," she said haltingly, speaking barely above a whisper. "I was the light-skinned daughter of a black woman who didn't have the right to say no to a white man. I was my mother's shame, and I was nothing to my father," she said spitting the word "nothing" out like a mouthful of bile. "My husband never knew. Your mother never knew. I don't even know why I'm telling you."

Lance could only stare at her. *My God*, he thought, *so many secrets*. Charlotte's confession explained so much about the woman he had known all of his life, and hated for most of it.

"I hated your father because his truth was the same as mine, and he threatened the existence I struggled so hard to escape. My daughter and I achieved the ultimate advantage over segregation—we *were* white! I did whatever I had to do to keep my secret. When my sister-in-law, Elsa, found out about my past I threatened to kill her if she uttered a word to anyone. She knew I meant it too, that woman went to her grave with my secret. Your father's confession could have destroyed everything—for me, for your mother and especially for you. I was the only one who knew that you were more colored than white, and I did what I had to do to keep you from the hard life of being a Negro in America, an existence that you don't know anything about because you've always lived the privileged life of a white man. But I knew," the old woman said, shaking her fist, as if at God. Lowering her head and her fist, she said in a near-whisper, "I knew because before I was Mrs. Charlotte Bennett, I was Cora Ann Cox, one of old man Cox's nigger bastards—hated by white folks for having the black blood of my mother, and by black folks for having the white blood of my father. But I showed them," Charlotte said, her lips a thin, hard line. Her eyes, no longer tearful, were narrowed into slits of determination.

"I did the only thing a girl could do on her own to make her way. Night after night, I spread my legs for strangers and I learned that sex and knowledge were powerful currencies for a woman. Back then there were no feminists, or Black Power, or any of that—I was colored and I was female and I was a bastard—but look at me now. I showed everyone who said I was nothing! I showed every goddamn one of them."

(II)

Albemarle County, Virginia—1890

Cora could feel his eyes on her as she scrubbed the kitchen floor on her hands and knees. She tried to ignore him by keeping her eyes on her work, rhythmically moving the scrub brush in circles the way her mother had taught her. The man was standing in the doorway watching her every move. She didn't dare look up at him, she hoped by ignoring him he would go away.

"Hey little gal," he finally said. "You workin' up a nice sweat there, little gal. I'm enjoyin' watchin' it make rivers between those pretty little titties up under your dress there," he teased. Cora grabbed the front of her dress and turned her back to him.

"Hey Sally," he called to the woman escorting him to the bedroom upstairs. "What about this young thing here?"

"Oh, Mr. John, she's just a baby. She's here with me for safekeeping. I got an experienced girl for you right upstairs." Sally pulled at his arm but the John didn't move.

"I want this one," he said. "I'll pay you extra for this one." To Cora he said, "Ever had a white man before? I'll bet you'd like it, I know I'd like you." Sally made eye contact with Moses whose bulk and blackness kept all the Johns who came and went from being any more unruly than Sally wanted them to be.

"Come on, Mr. John, you don't want no trouble here. She's not a working girl," Moses said, standing between the man and Cora, blocking his view.

"Alright, alright," the John said. "I came here to get laid, not to get laid out," he was the only one who laughed at his joke. "Sally, think about putting that one to work. I'd pay you extra for some of that," he said as he ascended the stairs.

"Don't you worry none, little Cora, I be here when you need me," Moses said, returning to his post on the front porch.

Cora sat back on her heels in the middle of the wet floor pulling her dress tightly around her as if it could protect her. She felt even more vulnerable than the day her father sent her here.

"I'm sorry 'bout your mother," Mrs. Cox said as she put Cora in the wagon that day. "You can't stay here, Mr. Cox wants you gone. Maybe if your momma hadn't died giving birth you could stay, but with her and the baby gone, Mr. Cox thinks it best you go too."

"Where am I goin'? Why can't I stay here? I won't be no trouble. Momma taught me to be no trouble."

"You gonna go stay with your Aunt Sally, your momma's baby sister. She lives up near Charlottesville. Hear she's got a fine house with plenty of room. You can get some more schoolin' there, have a city life. Maybe find a nice husband and not have to work the fields for a livin'. Be a good life," the woman told her husband's twelve-year-old daughter. That was a year ago and Cora hadn't been to school a day since.

Mrs. Cox had been right about one thing, Sally did have a fine house. During the day the house was quiet. Sally's "roomers" slept in, read, and went shopping. At night they went to work; they were high-yellow colored girls servicing white men in one of the most renowned brothels in the county. Cora's job was to help the girls prepare for their customers; press their hair, wash and iron their fine clothes, change the bed sheets and keep the house clean. She did all that in exchange for a small room off the kitchen, three meals a day and the tips the girls gave her for little extra things she did for them. Cora never gave up hope that one day she would thrive in the city, but as long as she was under Sally's roof, Cora believed the only way she would thrive or survive would be to lie on her back for strangers.

(III)

"How much money can you make bein' with men?" Cora asked Iris, one of the prostitutes that had taken a motherly interest in her. Cora was sitting at Iris' dressing table, playing with the bottles and jars of perfume and makeup.

"Don't you get caught up in all this," Iris warned. "I was 'bout your age when I found my way here, now it's all I know. What am I gonna do when all that there face paint don't hide that I'm an old girl? Then none of these here men will want Iris, they'll be wantin' something fresh and new – like you."

"Couldn't you just get married to one of the men before you get old?" Cora asked.

Iris laughed, "No man, black nor white, wants this cow now that they had all the milk. Moren' likely, I'll be doing what you're doin' now, taking care of the girls still young enough to make men ask for them," she said, taking a long drag on her cigarette and blowing the smoke out slowly as she thought about the truth she'd just told.

"You can read, can't you little Cora?" Iris asked.

"Went to school through almost 6th grade," Cora said proudly.

"Then you count on that kind of learnin', not the education you get workin' what's between your legs."

"I read books all the time. You don't make no money readin' books," Cora said.

"Some women do," Iris said. "I've seen them in Charlottesville in their fine homes with servants and husbands attendin' to them. They found their refinement in book learnin', little Cora. You could be a teacher. You halfway there cause you can read. Those books that Miss Sally keeps in the parlor—they just decoration to me but you can get the learnin' that's in 'em, then you can teach me and we can both be ladies." Iris got up from the bed and did an elaborate curtsy that sent young Cora into a fit of giggles. A moment later, Iris turned serious. She stood next to Cora who still sat at her vanity. For a few moments she looked at their reflection in the mirror. Iris picked up her hairbrush and began slowly and lovingly brushing Cora's long black hair, tears filled her eyes.

"If you brush your hair one hundred strokes at night it will shine like a new penny," Iris said "My Mama used to tell me that." She was silent for a few minutes then she said, "Little Cora, what we do here is kill dreams. Women don't get to decide much in this life but we can still dream. Don't let no one take that from you. Don't let dreams go so easy—don't do that to yourself. You're a looker that's for sure and right here, right now, men who can't get a looker like you on their own are willin' to pay to pretend they can. Make 'em pay with a ring, not a few dollars a couple times a week. Iris can tell you smart and strong too. Put the looks, books and the 'bilities God gave you together and use your gifts to find another way."

(IV)

"Charlotte, Charlotte, where'd you go?" Lance asked. Charlotte blinked looking at Lance as if she had never seen him before, "Charlotte!" he said, shaking her.

Charlotte flinched. "Don't hit me, please don't let him hit me. Moses!" she screamed, "Moses help me!"

Lance grabbed her by the shoulders to steady her, "Charlotte, I'm not going to hurt you."

"Lance?" she asked, "what are you doing here?" Charlotte was shaking; Lance embraced his grandmother for the first time in thirty years. Charlotte initially stiffened, unaccustomed to kindness in their contact with each other, then relaxed into her grandson.

"I loved you more than any of them," she whispered. "My mother, my husband, even my daughter, I love you more than any of them. After everything I'd been through I didn't think I could love like that, until you were born, Lance, until you."

"Why me Charlotte?" Lance asked.

She was silent for a few moments, then said, "Because I had to make sure you got the freedom and the future none of the rest of us could have. You were born white and male, that gave you the power and authority to make life lie down before you. Your father almost took it from you, but I got it back. Whatever I did wasn't to hurt anyone, I did what was necessary to make sure nothing and no one stood in your way. I was the only one who knew everything—what it was like to be nothing and believe that's all there is. I was the only one who had seen it all. You would have better. I had to make it better for you, otherwise there was no point to it at all. I just wanted, I just wanted—"

"What we all want Charlotte, to be loved and accepted," Lance finished her thought. "You're safe now, okay? We all are," he said, more tenderly than he knew he could be. Charlotte clung to him, crying tears that went back seven decades.

She is still running from her past, just like I am, Lance thought. He couldn't hate Charlotte anymore. She had given him a gift tonight, a glimpse of what his future would be like if he did not have the courage to love Emma. All the fear, hate, and loss would fester until he ended up like Charlotte—alone and afraid.

When Charlotte had exhausted herself Lance said, "We will keep each other's secrets," remembering what Belle had told him so many years ago.

He helped Charlotte to her bed and when she was settled, he took her hands in his. Spotted with age, her skin was pale, and transparent enough to see her veins filled with the blue blood she aspired to. *This is what we use to divide us from one another*, he thought, running his thumb over the back of Charlotte's hand, tracing the raised veins set against the pale skin that made her heritage invisible. He put her hands to his lips and kissed them. Charlotte gasped, pulled him to her and kissed her grandson for the first time in decades.

"I buried them together," she said. "Your parents, I did that for my daughter. Evergreen Cemetery in Richmond. I buried them there, together."

Lance sat with her until she fell asleep. He left Charlotte's room thinking how close he was to her fate, but Emma could save him.

(V)

Lance had no idea how to find Emma. As far as he knew, her whole life had been 580 Park. He knew she had no family in London. He interrogated the staff and searched her office and her room. The only other place he could think to look was where they had been together. He flew back to Jamaica, hoping Winsom could tell him where to find Emma, but even when he threatened to fire her, she claimed ignorance. Soon after, Winsom left the villa at Round Hill and went to work for another family.

Even a private detective could not find Emma. Lance replayed their last moments together in his mind and wondered if she ever intended to be at the house when he returned. "Forever, I will love you forever," she'd said. Had she meant he would be in her heart forever, not in her life? After a year of searching and waiting, he stopped looking, and settled back into his old life, a life that now did not suit him quite as well as it had before.

⤻ 22 ⤻

March 1969

(I)

C HARLOTTE BENNETT DIED IN HER sleep three years after she sent Emma away. The funeral was in the main chapel of Saint Thomas Episcopal Church on Fifth Avenue. A few of Lance's artist friends, some of his business associates, and the house staff were sparsely scattered throughout the large chapel. Lance sat alone in the first pew reserved for members of the immediate family. As the service started, a woman walked to the front of the church, stood for a second looking at Lance and then eased in the pew across the aisle from him. Dressed in black, she looked straight ahead throughout the service. When she did look Lance's way again, he was looking at her. The two held each other's gaze for a few seconds, then Emma looked away.

When the service was over, Lance left the church with the processional, accompanying Charlotte's casket as they loaded it into the hearse parked in front of the church. It started to rain, lightly at first, then a driving rain scattered the last few mourners.

Emma had wanted to see Lance; she didn't know why because from the moment she left him in Jamaica, his actions made it clear that he was done with her. Knowing that was painful, never seeing him had been even more painful. *Today was a mistake*, she thought as she struggled to put on her raincoat standing under the eaves at the top of church steps.

"May I help you with that?" he asked. Emma was surprised to see Lance reaching out to help her with her coat, she had not noticed him come up the steps. After her coat was on, he lifted her hair out of her collar and smoothed it from behind.

"Don't," Emma said, taking a few steps away to avoid his touch.

"Thank you for coming," he couldn't think of anything else to say and he couldn't say what he wanted to. *Where have you been? Why didn't you wait for me?*

"Of course," Emma said. "I was surprised when I heard. I thought Charlotte would live forever. The last time I spoke to her she sounded fine…"

"The last time you spoke to her? When was that?"

"About a month ago."

"You were in touch with Charlotte all this time?"

"She hired a private detective to find me. After that, she would call me every now and then. She even visited us a month after—"

"I hired the detective. How'd she? All this time, Charlotte knew where you were?" he said, cutting her off.

"I asked her not to tell you. There was no point. You were married. I was married."

"I never married."

"But Charlotte said—"

Lance just shook his head. *Until the day she died*, he thought.

"But you're married?" he asked.

"I am."

"Who is the lucky man?"

"Someone I knew, for a while, before you." Emma said as a car pulled up in front of the church. Before she could say any more the driver laid on the horn.

"I've got to go, my husband," she said nodding toward the car.

"I'd like to meet him," Lance said.

"Why? We're not the kind of people you would know, Mr. Withers."

"Emma, don't."

"I've got to go," she said, moving toward the steps.

"You don't have an umbrella, at least let me walk you to the car." Trembling, she tried to keep from touching him as they walked to the waiting car.

When they were within a few feet, a small boy opened the window and shouted, "Mummy. Hurry, I missed you."

Lance looked at Emma.

"My son," she said. "Our son, my husband and I."

"Emma, move your ass," her husband called out to her. "I've got to get to work." He yelled something at the boy who closed the car window and slumped in the back seat. Before Lance could say goodbye, Emma bolted from underneath the umbrella, ran to the passenger side of the waiting car and ducked in. She was barely in the car when it pulled off, but not before Emma's husband gave Lance a look of pure hatred.

Lance watched the car with Emma and the life she always wanted slowly make its way down Fifth Avenue in the rain. He remembered watching her car leave in Jamaica. This time she had not told him that she would love him forever.

"I will love you forever," he whispered as the car disappeared down a side street. Lance turned and walked alone to the limousine waiting to take him to the cemetery where he would bury Charlotte along with the secrets of their past.

(II)

That night's beating was the worst.

"Feel better now that you've seen him?" he taunted her when he got home from work. He removed his shoulder holster and laid it on the sideboard. Ed was still working security having failed the police exam for the third time. She asked him several times to leave the gun at work for Philmore's safety. He never did. Ed liked wearing a gun, it made him feel powerful, invincible. He'd even bought the boy a toy gun, it was one of the few times he played with Philmore, showing him how to hold the gun, aim and pull the trigger.

"Bang, bang. You're dead," Ed would say, pointing the gun at the boy. "Now you do it," he'd urge Philmore.

"Bang, bang, you're dead," Philmore would say pointing the gun at his father.

"Now shoot Mummy," Ed would say, but Philmore refused. "Don't be a sissy," Ed would taunt him, "Shoot Mummy."

"No!" Philmore would tell his father, "I only shoot bad guys."

———————

When Ed came home that night he was already drunk and still drinking. Seeing Lance and Emma together that afternoon had agitated him. In the four years of her marriage she had made just one slip. They were making love and she called him Lance, he never forgot it and never let her forget it.

"I work two shifts to give you and the boy a roof over your heads and put food on the table and all the while I know you're fuckin' that old man in your dreams, the great Lance Henry Withers." Emma knew to ignore the insults. If she kept her mouth closed sometimes he would calm down.

"What do I get for it?" he said, taking another swig from the pint wrapped in a brown paper bag. "What do I get for it?" he grabbed her arm and pulled her to him.

"Please," she begged. "Don't wake my boy. I'm not fuckin' anyone but you Ed."

"If you hadn't gotten knocked up – I wouldn't be stuck with a frosty bitch like you. I'd be beddin' some wild Irish rose, like my brother's wife."

Emma pushed him away.

"You and your precious boy. He's my boy too but you won't even give him my family name. What kind of bullshit is that?"

"I told you, I wanted to name him after my brother—to honor my brother killed in the war, I wanted him to have the George family name."

He shoved her to the floor. "Fuck the George family," he said, staggering to the kitchen. "Where's me dinner?"

"Right here," she said, scrambling to her feet to take the plate of stew out of the oven where she had placed it hours ago to stay warm.

He pulled the foil off of the plate and looked at the dried up meal. "You expect me to eat this shit?" he said, shoving the plate across the table so that it splattered to the floor.

"If you'd come home on time, you could have eaten with…" He slapped her across the face before she could finish the sentence.

"Don't," she said. "You hit me again and we're leaving,"

"Where you gonna go? Back to Lance Withers' big house? Think they'll take you in again? Not after I get finished with you," he said, raising his hand.

———>●<———

"Hi Mummy," Philmore said, rubbing his eyes as Emma crawled into bed with him after cleaning the blood from her lip and applying cold compresses to the bruises on her face.

"Go back to sleep, Philly boy. It's not time to get up," she said, hoping the swelling on her face would go down a little before morning.

"Okay, Mummy," he said barely awake, "Love you."

"Love you too, little man, now go back to sleep."

When she heard the boy's breathing even out and she was sure he was asleep, she put her hand over her mouth to keep her crying from waking him. Ed was right, she had nowhere to go. As soon as they were married he refused to let her work, now she and her son were completely dependent on this violent man. Whenever she threatened to leave he'd beat her until she was ashamed to go out in public. Three years of this was enough, she had to get away.

Why had she settled for this man? Had Ed really been her best option? After Philmore was born something in him changed. He was jealous of any attention she paid the boy. He accused her of flirting with other men; the butcher, the building superintendent, the pharmacist anyone that said a kind word to her or to Philmore was suspect. But Lance Withers was the real thorn. Emma never said anything to anyone about the two weeks she spent with him in Jamaica, but that time with the man she loved was never far from her thoughts. It was like Ed could sense there was someone between them. She tried to talk to Ed about her time at 580 Park Avenue, she wanted to share that important part of her life with her husband. But Ed resented being reminded of what she had accomplished there.

"Workin' for rich folks don't make you one of them, Emma. What you got now is as good as it's gonna get for you. You're a working stiff's wife and our son is going to be a working stiff like his father. Stop with the castles in the sky, Emma. Your feet are on the ground now, get used to it."

Ed wanted the life he'd always had, the same life his Irish immigrant parents had. Emma wanted more. He wanted her to be what he called *the little woman*—to worship him for providing for his family like his Ma worshiped his Pa. Emma could not be that woman. She hated the Hell's Kitchen tenement where they lived. She tried to nudge her husband into wanting more out of life.

"What if I get a teaching job once Philmore starts school? With my salary we can move to a better neighborhood, maybe Queens. It's better for families."

Ed took the suggestion as an insult. "So you don't think I'm a good enough provider? If this place was good enough for me Ma then it's good enough for you."

"I want more for our family, Ed."

"You can want all you want. Getting is something I control, and I'm fine with the way things are."

Emma had not risked everything to come to America to live Ed McKenna's meager mundane life. If she and Philmore stayed with him, their present would be their future. After Lance Withers' rejection, she'd hastily taken the easiest path out of his life and that had been Ed. He had pursued her relentlessly, he had been great fun the few times they were together and there was no denying he was incredibly good looking. She liked Ed. She knew she didn't love him, but believed that with

Lance Withers out of the picture she could grow to love him. She never did.

Life had not worked out as Ed planned either. Before he was ready he was a husband and then a father. He couldn't pass the written part of the Police exam, so he couldn't achieve his dream of being a cop. Emma offered to help him study for the exam but he refused.

"I don't need your pity, Emma." After three tries he gave up, started drinking heavily, coming home drunk almost every night from his job still working night security. Drinking made him angry and irrational and Emma was the enemy.

I never should have married Ed, she thought as she lay in the dark next to her son. I should have had my boy on my own. He was the one good thing in her life and only she knew that he was Lance Henry Withers' son. Emma would never tell Lance that he was Philmore's father, she vowed that the day she left 580 Park Avenue three months pregnant. She couldn't trust Lance to love her or their son. He hadn't even had the decency to tell her they would not be together, he had Charlotte do it.

Emma remembered telling Lance when they were together in Jamaica that she was fearless; that she could take care of herself. Emma thought of how all of that had changed in four short years; now she was just fearful. She almost smiled at the irony of it all but that would only open the cut on her lip again.

She looked over at the son she and Lance had made together. "Philmore, such a big name for a little boy," she whispered. She needed to get him away from Ed McKenna, she needed to find a way to get them out of the mess she had gotten them into.

(III)

Emma began asking around the apartment building to see if anyone needed help with laundry or ironing. For five dollars a load she washed and ironed, sometimes twenty loads a week. She would babysit kids in the building as long as their parents picked them up before Ed came home from work. She scrimped on the allowance he gave her for food, buying enough for Ed and Philmore; she would eat whatever they left on their plates. Her weight dropped but her spirits began to soar. She kept her mouth shut and did what she could to avoid both sex with her husband and his beatings.

A neighbor, believing she was being helpful, told Emma that she had seen Ed visit the woman in apartment 6D several times when she knew the woman's husband was out of town. Emma wanted to hug the woman and say thank you, but she restrained herself. If Ed wanted someone else maybe he would let her go.

It took her a year to save enough money to leave. Mina, who was now Executive Chef at 580 Park, helped her find a furnished room in Queens with a woman would could baby sit Philmore so Emma could work during the day.

"Do you want me to talk to Mr. Withers about you coming back here? The man that's got the job now is no major domo – more like major don't know. Mr. Withers is gonna let him go soon as he finds someone else. You could get your old job back, Emma. Just think, we could work together again, just like old times. I know Mr. Withers would want you back, let me mention it to him," Mina said. "I don't care if he finds out that I lied to him when I said I didn't know where you were. Back then I had to choose the lesser of two evils and I was more afraid of what Miss Charlotte would do to me if I let on that I knew where you were. She would have made it so I would never work again."

"They say you can't go home again," Emma said.

"Who's they?" Mina asked. "You got a better idea?"

"Maybe after I get settled, Mina. I've got to make a place for my boy first. Then I'll come and talk to Mr. Withers."

(IV)

Ed left unusually early to work an overnight shift one night in late March of 1970. It had been twenty-two years since she left London, and now Emma was leaving another war torn existence, her marriage. She had a little more than eight hours to disappear before he would return. She pulled her suitcase from the back of the closet and filled it with the few things she planned to take—just some clothes for her and Philmore. She left their suitcase by the door and went to wake her son. Before she could arouse the boy she heard the front door open. She ran to the living room, Ed was holding the suitcase.

"Where the hell do you think you're going?"

"Ed, you don't love me and I don't love you. I don't want anything from you. I just want to take my son and go." Ed opened the suitcase and dumped its contents onto the floor.

"He's our son and you ain't goin' nowhere, Emma."

"Ed, please let us leave. You can see the boy anytime you want, just let us leave. You're not happy, why don't we just end this before things get worse?"

"Sure, I'm supposed to just let you walk outta here. Have everyone sayin' Ed McKenna's not man enough to keep his wife. You're not going anywhere Emma, if anyone leaves, it'll be me, but I don't leave because I understand I got an obligation, even if you are one ungrateful bitch."

"Ed, I appreciate everything you've done for us. I do."

Ed took his coat off, un-holstered his gun and laid it on the sideboard.

"No you don't, Emma. When you got knocked up, I did the right thing by you. You think I was ready to get married? I was still havin' a good time. You were just a good reliable piece of tail to me," Ed walked over and grabbed Emma's behind, "That's all you ever were."

Emma pulled his hand off of her.

"I go and do the right thing; marry your sorry ass and then you go and get all virginal on me. My brother tells me that happens to some women after they have a kid, but Ed knows how to fix that. A taste of this," he said grabbing himself, "and you won't wanna go nowhere." He tore at her clothes, she pushed him away. He slapped, then punched her. Emma stumbled to the floor.

"Ed, don't do this. Please, just let us go."

"Sure, you can go," he sneered, "But we're gonna have one last fuck for old times' sake. You can get out of this marriage the same way you got in."

Emma crawled toward the hall trying to get up and away. *If I can make it to Philmore's room I'll lock us in until he calms down.* Ed grabbed Emma's ankle and pulled her back into the middle of the living room. He punched her in the face, threw her on her back, and pinned her to the floor, sitting on her. With one hand he held her hands over her head and with the other he unfastened his pants. Emma was no match for Ed's six-foot, two hundred pound frame. He tore at her clothes until he reached her underwear. Ripping her panties off he forced himself into her, tearing at her until she screamed.

"That's what I want to hear," he laughed. "A little appreciation."

Neither of them noticed Philmore come into the living room. When Ed looked up, Philmore had taken Ed's gun off of the sideboard. Ed jumped up, attempting to pull his pants up while he tried to speak calmly to Philmore. "Give me the gun, son."

Philmore raised the gun, pointing it at Ed.

"You're hurting Mummy," the boy said as he pulled the trigger, putting a bullet in Ed's chest, "Bang, bang, you're dead."

⁓ 23 ⁓

March 1970

(I)

"**M**OMMY."

"Junior? What time is it? What's the matter, are you alright?" Mina was barely awake and her husband Charlie, who slept like the dead, hadn't even stirred when the phone rang in the middle of the night.

"Mom, Miss Emma, she's been arrested, for murder."

Mina sat straight up in bed, she was wide awake now. "My Emma?"

"I came in for my shift and I saw her in the holding cell down here at the precinct. They say she killed her husband, that she confessed. She's beat up pretty bad too."

"I'm on my way. Tell her your Daddy and me—we're on our way," Mina said as she tried to rouse Charlie. "Where's her boy, where's Philmore?"

"The police left him with a neighbor."

"Well at least he didn't see his mother in jail. Tell Emma we're on our way."

"I told her I was gonna call you. She told me to make you promise that you wouldn't call Mr. Withers."

"Well, son, that's a promise I ain't gonna be able to make. I don't know who else to call."

(II)

Arthur Goldman, the lawyer Lance Withers sent to the police station, sat with Emma in the interrogation room.

"Emma, you need to tell them what really happened."

"Where's my son?" Emma asked.

"Your friend, Mina, went to get him. He's going to stay with her until we get this sorted out. Is that okay?"

"That's good. He loves Mina and Charlie."

"You're lucky Detective Jones is so respected on the force. He talked them out of sending the boy to protective services."

"That's good. He's with Mina and Charlie, they're family."

"Emma, tell me what happened."

"I told the police a hundred times. He grabbed me, slapped me around. I grabbed the gun and shot him. That's how it happened."

"The neighbor's statement says it's not. She heard you screaming and when she went to your door, it was open and your husband was assaulting you on the floor. She said he stood up to talk to the boy and then she heard the gun go off. You were still curled up on the floor."

Emma looked away from the lawyer.

"Yes, Emma, there was a witness. We know the boy shot his father. The ballistic report will confirm it."

"I don't care what anyone says. I told the police what happened. I did it. They are not going to take my boy."

"Emma, your son was protecting his mother. He's three and a half years old. No one is going to take your son. Just give the police a truthful statement of what happened so we can get you out of here."

"I can't go home."

"You don't have to, Mr. Withers is here, he's waiting outside in the car. I won't let him come in. The press is here. If they see him it will be a mad house."

"Tell him to go away. This is none of his business. I told Mina and Charlie not to call him."

"They didn't listen. He wants to take you to 580 Park to recover. Is that okay?"

"I've got to go get my son."

"He's fine, remember? He's with Mina and Charlie, you said they're family. You don't want him to see you like this, do you, Emma?" Her eye was nearly swollen closed, her face bruised and her clothes were stained with Ed's blood.

"When can I see my boy?"

"In few days. Mina will bring him to the house. In the meantime you can rest and heal while the press finds someone else to pick on."

"I don't want him to see me like this."

"We won't let the boy see you until you're healed."

"No, Mr. Withers. I don't want him to see me like this."

"We can go out the back and I'll take you in my car. There's a doctor waiting at his house. He'll take care of you and I'll ask Mr. Withers to wait until you're ready to see him. Is that okay?"

Emma nodded "I just want to go home," she said through her tears. "Tell him thank you for letting me go home."

"Now, Emma, tell me what really happened?"

(III)

Lance watched Emma sitting in the garden wrapped in a shawl on the first day that promised spring. Her eyes were closed, her face tilted toward the sun. She still had a small bandage and some bruising from her ordeal a week ago but to him she looked as beautiful as ever. She'd asked to speak with him before Mina brought Philmore to her.

"How are you feeling?" Lance asked as he approached her. She looked up at him, shading her eyes from the sun, she smiled and patted the bench for him to sit down next to her. Looking straight ahead she said, "This is not how I wanted to come back here."

"I know. I'm just glad you wanted to come back. Will you stay?"

"I can't," she said immediately. "But I want you to know how grateful I am for all of your help, for letting me stay here long enough to recover. But now I have to put my life back together. My son doesn't remember the shooting but one day he will. We're both going to need help to deal with this. Hiding here will just delay the inevitable."

"What are you going to do now, Emma? Where are you going to go? You can't go back to your old life. I'm not suggesting you hide here. Just stay here, start new."

"I can't stay here, with you."

"I know that," Lance said, wishing it weren't true. "Come back to your position here. We've got an opening coming up. You were the best Major Domo this place ever had," he said brightening.

Emma looked over at Lance and smiled. "So Mina tells me." They sat side by side in silence for a few minutes.

"We aren't, we can't ever be who we once were," she said. "My son is my life now, my whole life. He is more important to me than anyone or anything."

"I understand."

Emma, looking out over the garden, nodded just as the limo pulled into the grounds. As the gate closed behind the car, Emma jumped up and ran toward it. When the car stopped, she pulled the door open, Philmore bounded out and Emma scooped him up in her arms,

"Mummy, where were you? I missed you."

Mina got out of the car and walked toward the house meeting Lance Withers.

"Thank you," he said, "I never thanked you for calling me that night."

"Thank you for taking the call," Mina said.

"I talked to her about taking her old job again."

"What did she say?"

"She didn't say yes, but she didn't say no."

"Well, then there's hope," Mina said. The two of them watched the mother and child reunion for a few seconds.

"He looks just like Emma," Lance said. "He's big for three."

"He turns four in August. You should go meet him," Mina said.

"I don't want to interfere."

"I don't think she'll mind," Mina said.

Lance walked toward Emma and Philmore for an awkward introduction to the child the woman he loved had with another man. *If I hadn't been such a fool this could have been my every day*, Lance thought.

"Philmore George, say hello to Mr. Withers," Emma said.

"Hello, young man," Lance said, tentatively touching the boy's soft locks.

"This is *my* son," Emma said, wrapping her arm protectively around the boy. Lance got down on one knee, face-to-face with the boy.

"Hi."

"Hello," the boy responded, "My name is Philmore, what's your name?"

"My name is Lance."

"Mr. Withers," Emma corrected.

"Mr. Withers," Lance echoed. "I'm pleased to meet you, Philmore." He saw the best of Emma and only Emma in his little face. There was no trace of Ed McKenna, at least from what he could remember the one time he'd seen the man and from the pictures that had been in the newspapers.

"What do you say?" Emma prompted Philmore.

"Pleased to meet you too," the boy said, then buried his face in his mother's skirts.

She's not my wife and he is not my son, Lance thought, *but they're here and that may just have to be enough.* He would shelter them just like he had when Emma first came to 580 Park Avenue. If he'd had the courage he could have changed his future and hers. He had one brief chance to be free from all of his family's lies and deception and he hadn't taken it; he probably never would.

Lance took the child's small hand in his. "Welcome to my house, Philmore," he said. He looked up at Emma and said, "Welcome home."

Epilogue

Richmond, Virginia—September 1970

LANCE HENRY WITHERS SAT ON the small bench inside the fenced Whitaker family plot in Evergreen Cemetery where his father and mother were buried side by side. He was surprised to find that Del was also buried in the same family plot. Her gravestone said she died September 9, 1931, just a few months after the family left Richmond. *That's why my letter to her was returned*, he thought. *She never knew I read my father's journals and that I understand why he did what he did.* He had wanted her to know he was working on forgiving and in that letter he had finally told Del how much she meant to him. *I never got to tell her how much I loved her*, he thought but hoped somehow she knew. He quickly wiped away the tear that formed in the corner of his eye.

He would never know that Del asked to be interred with the note he'd left for her tucked in the pocket of her burial dress.

"Miss Holder bought this here plot for Mr. Whitaker's family," the old caretaker told Lance. "I was just a grave digger when they buried Mr. Whitaker. That white woman who put him in the ground said she didn't care if they never found the grave again. But Miss Holder made it right, paid for the plot, the double headstone too—for him and his wife, everything. Like she knew someone would want to find him one day. Did you know the family?" the man asked.

"We're related but I haven't been to Richmond in a long time," Lance said.

"Heard the couple had a son but I ain't never seen him. He musta been the one wanted to extend the plot for more graves and set up the perpetual care fund," the caretaker said. "Picked out a family headstone and everything." He pulled out the paperwork he brought with him to help Lance locate the graves. "No, no, I'm mistaken. Letter here says Mrs. C. Bennett bought the additional grave space. Haven't heard a word about the additional family members but that perpetual care fund she set up keeps it real nice back here. If I remember correctly," he said, scratching his beard, "it was a Mrs. Bennett buried Mr. Whitaker without a stone. Woman that cold is hard to forget. Musta had a change of heart, never can tell about folks," he said, shaking his head.

"May I see the letter?" Lance asked.

"I don't see no harm in it, just make sure you bring it back with you to the office. Well, I'll leave you in peace. I'll be in the office if you need anything," the old man said, disappearing back down the path toward the office.

Lance looked at the history buried in this plot and thought. *We were the Whitakers. The secrets, lies and deception end with me. Our provenance is complete.* He looked down at the letter the caretaker had given him. It was Charlotte's distinctive cursive alright, he would know it anywhere.

"Charlotte, you continue to surprise, even from the grave," Lance said shaking his head. She never said anything to him about wanting to be buried here. Is that why she finally told him she'd buried *Maman* here with Daddy? Who were the other grave sites for? He read further down the letter the caretaker left with him.

> *I'm including a check for the cost of adding two more grave sites and eventually headstones to the Whitaker family plot. One for my grandson and the other for his son.*

Lance stared at the letter, it was written in August, 1966. *What was Charlotte thinking? She knew I had no children.*

The End

Acknowledgements

A writer never works alone.

I took life lessons from many experiences in creating this book — good and bad, profound and mundane — they are all valuable contributions to this writer and her story. I also offer my sincere appreciation for all of the people that have helped me learn the craft to write this story. For their unwavering support, a very special thank you to my *Six Great Books* writing group: Janet Hall Werner, Kelly Hand, Kristin Battista-Frazee, David Bonck and especially Molly Mahoney Matthews, who read *Provenance* more times than anyone. Thank you to the Writers Center in Bethesda, Maryland where I met all of the *Six Great Books* writers as well as my writing teacher and developmental editor and champion, Barbara Esstman – thank you for your honest advice. I am grateful to my first reader and friend, Janice Carter, and Mandy Campbell Moore, my beta reader, who eventually became my editor and is now my friend. Thank you one and all for sharing your time, support, expertise and encouragement with me; you helped me turn mere words into a book.

I must also thank my family, for within their hearts and minds my provenance exists. Thank you to my mother, Corien Davis Drew, who taught me how to dream; and my father, Kenneth Richard Drew, who showed me what it takes to make dreams come true. To my daughters, Elizabeth and Jacquelyn, and my sisters Ana, Carol and Paula, and all of the strong and wonderful women and men in our family; each awesome, inspiring and unique in their very special way.

Donna Drew Sawyer
July 2015

Photo: Dwight Carter

Donna Drew Sawyer advanced the creativity of others as a Madison Avenue advertising executive, public relations manager for Sesame Street and as a senior administrator for several arts organizations including the Chrysler Museum of Art and the Smithsonian's Hirshhorn Museum and Sculpture Garden. Writing to attract audiences for others led her to start writing for an audience of her own. Born and raised in New York City, she now lives with her family near Washington, DC. *PROVENANCE* is her first novel.

DonnaDrewSawyer.com

JUL - - 2016

CPSIA information can be obtained at www.ICGtesting.com
Printed in the USA
BVOW08s2042200915

418741BV00003B/6/P